PRAISE FOR *The Mountain And The Wall*

"Alisa Ganieva has aimed to write in clear-eye
a region that has been racked by violence fuel
and an Islamic insurgency."
—CELIA WREN, *The Washington Post*

"A brilliant book."
—ANTHONY MARRA, author of *A Constellation of Vital Phenomena*

"Ganieva weaves a lovely and intricate tapestry for her reader of the various factors that might influence Caucasian identity—in no way disconnected from those that allow the borrowed fundamentalism to fill the power vacuum in the novel."
—LINDSAY SEMEL, *Asymptote*

"[*The Mountain and the Wall*] reminds us why reading world literature can be so compelling... It is a mass disaster novel as viewed through the eyes of young adults who mostly just want the freedom to dance, listen to music, and engage in courtship behavior, however clumsy."
—ROB VOLLMAR, *World Literature Today (Editor's Pick)*

"The land, seen in its beauty and the depths of the past, is the beating heart of Ganieva's novel. The Mountain and the Wall asks us to love and understand Dagestan, and the ask is compelling."
—PT SMITH, *Full Stop*

"Vivid, timely, gripping, and really quite magical, [*The Mountain and the Wall*] cements Ganieva's position as one of the most exciting young voices in Russian fiction."
—Staff Pick, Foyles Bookstore in London

"At its heart, Ganieva's compelling story is a universal one of a young man trying to make sense of this crazy world, while making money, sustaining friendships, protecting his family, and falling in love."
—JOSH COOK, Porter Square Books

"Complex in a nineteenth-century, great-multi-plot-Russian-novel way; [*The Mountain and the Wall* is] compelling in its topical exploration of Islamic fundamentalism and annexation by or expulsion from the Russia Federation, depending on that nation's shifting whims."
—GENEVIEVE ARLIE, *M—Dash*

"A refreshing and witty voice."
—MORITZ SCHEPER, *Die Zeit*

ALSO AVAILABLE IN ENGLISH BY ALISA GANIEVA

The Mountain and the Wall
translated by Carol Apollonio

BRIDE AND GROOM

—

Alisa Ganieva

TRANSLATED FROM THE RUSSIAN
BY CAROL APOLLONIO

DEEP VELLUM PUBLISHING
DALLAS, TEXAS

Deep Vellum Publishing
3000 Commerce St., Dallas, Texas 75226
deepvellum.org · @deepvellum

Deep Vellum Publishing is a 501c3
nonprofit literary arts organization founded in 2013.

The Russian Original edition was published under the title "Жених и невеста"
by AST, Moscow

ISBN: 978-1-941920-59-6 (paperback) • 978-1-941920-60-2 (ebook)
Library of Congress Control Number: 2017938735

—

Издание осуществлено при участии Программы поддержки переводов русской литературы TRANSCRIPT Фонда Михаила Прохорова.

—

The publication of this book was made possible with the support
of the Mikhail Prokhorov Foundation's Transcript program
to support the translation of Russian literature.

Cover design & typesetting by Anna Zylicz • annazylicz.com
Text set in Bembo, a typeface modeled on typefaces cut by
Francesco Griffo for Aldo Manuzio's printing of *De Aetna* in 1495 in Venice.
Distributed by Consortium Book Sales & Distribution.
Printed in the United States of America on acid-free paper.

Table of Contents

—

I. A DRINK WITH A STRANGER

Completely soaked, the three of us dashed into a half-empty train car and plopped down onto a tattered bench. Artur couldn't stop laughing:

"You're out of your minds! A mandatory political meeting in the twenty-first century!"

Rain drummed on the train-car windows. We were on our way to a dacha to see some of Marina's bohemian friends. Marina was my co-worker in a Moscow city courthouse, where we spent our days in the basement, binding and copying documents. The salary was pathetic. Our fingers throbbed, and caustic ink stained our palms. But for whatever reason we viewed this pointless torment as some kind of major step up the ladder of success.

Marina's friend Artur enjoyed listening to our tales of toil in the halls of justice. He was already acting cocky, though he didn't seem to have started drinking yet. He probed us for details, guffawed, and slapped his thighs in delight.

"No way! You're kidding me!"

"Really, Arturchik, I'm not making it up," flirted Marina, playing along. "Starting this week, we have to show up to work half an hour early for the departmental briefing so the whole team can discuss the latest news. We need to build solidarity against the enemy."

"What enemy?"

"'A treacherous foe who bares his rotten maw,'" Marina recited, "'and dreams of breaking our bonds.'"

"You mean our spiritual bonds?"

"Duh, Arturchik."

The train doors squealed open and admitted a disheveled-looking man in rubber boots with an accordion. He was playing a plaintive song with a vaguely familiar melody. I was about to lean over and ask Marina if she knew what it was, but, ashamed of my ignorance, I gave up on the idea and just wriggled my foot.

"So, have you been in Moscow long, Patya?" Arturchik asked, raising his voice over the sounds of the accordion.

"A year!" I shouted into his ear, leaning across Marina. "My older brother suggested that I come and work in Moscow for a while."

There was no need to go into the details—that I'd been invited for just a year, and now the year was over, and at this point it was looking as though I'd have to go back home to my town, an outlying suburb near the city.

The melody, its title still a mystery, floated down the aisle and wafted into the next car; the city outside the windows rushed past, bouncing and splashing in the June rain, unwilling to release us. It was chilly for summertime, and Marina was bundled up in her sweater. For some reason she had undertaken to share gratuitous details about me with Artur:

"Bear in mind, Patya is not going to drink any of your Sambuca. She doesn't drink. That's how it is in her country... Islam. Right, Patya?"

Marina just couldn't get it through her head that I'm not a foreigner and that I personally do not observe any such prohibition. But I decided to let her go on.

"And don't even think of hitting on her," continued Marina, "it'll drive away all her Dagestani suitors."

"You have a lot of suitors?" Artur squirmed in delight.

"Not a single one!" I objected.

Marina was thinking of a few losers I'd gone out with. One guy had stumbled across me in a social network group and had started bombarding me with quotes from pop psychology and self-help books. He'd made himself out to be a seasoned intellectual. When I learned that the know-it-all was from near my hometown, I felt a spark of interest and agreed to meet him.

What a mistake that had been! My beau turned out to be a tall lughead with nasty little eyes. The moment I saw him, I wanted to turn and run, but he spotted me from a distance and waved a rolled-up copy of *Money* magazine in my direction. Obviously he'd recognized me from my photo.

He started in right in. "What's your trade?"

"I don't have one. I'm not in business," I parried.

We had already taken a few steps down the street before he reacted:

"As Gilbert Chesterton put it, 'Unless a man is in part a humorist, he is only in part a man.'"

It was kind of funny that he was talking in quotes. Must spend days on end memorizing them from some thick anthology.

"Do you read *Money*?" I nodded toward the magazine. Just to have something to say.

"No, I make it." He emitted an edifying smirk, reveling in his little joke.

Then, undermining the image he'd created of himself, he stopped in front of a cheap fast-food joint, packed to the gills with people.

"My treat!"

There ensued a painful forty minutes in line at the cash register, followed by more agony at a shared table with a gang of teenage skateboarders. Lughead continued to smother me with aphorisms, scan me periodically with his baby blues, and scrape his paper coffee cup against the sugar grains scattered on the tabletop. He wanted me to know about all the girls back home who were supposedly so desperate to marry him that they came up with all kinds of lies, claiming that he wouldn't stop calling them. The girls' parents would get upset and rush over to complain to his family, along the lines of: "Your lover boy has driven our daughter completely nuts with all those calls, so now let him do the right thing and make it official." But Lughead here, he wasn't born yesterday, you won't catch him that easily. True, he would let down his guard now and then and give the girls grounds for hope, but, as Winston Churchill supposedly said, a fool is a man who has never made a mistake.

At the end of the meal he made a regal gesture and, with an air of solicitous condescension, announced an excursion to the shopping center where I would help him pick out a new pair of pants. The idea was, I was being initiated into some kind of sacramental rite. I sprang up, mumbling that I would not be joining him, and that anyway I had to rush off to a meeting at work. Though what was the chance of that? I took off without looking back. He called later, texted me a few times: "How do you like me?" and then, before I could answer, "You're a strange one. Downright creepy," and then, "How's business?" until he finally fizzled out.

I'd barely managed to recover from this stupid episode when my brother—a.k.a. housemate—summoned me. He announced that his boss in the chemical plant where he works, who's from our hometown, wanted to introduce me to his grandson or nephew or somebody. It was a little weird, but of course I had no objection.

A car came to pick me up at the courthouse after work. There was a chauffeur, and my brother's boss settled into the back seat next to me. He was a sprightly older man who looked sixty or so, but in fact was over eighty. He looked me up and down with his crafty eyes, interrogated me about my job, and then launched into an inspired chronicle of his own career, punctuated by occasional giggles. You would have thought that what he managed was not a mere department in a chemical plant, but an enchanted forest brimming with unicorns.

He took me to a restaurant, where he treated me to delicacies fit for a queen (tongue gratin, creamed veal with cognac, sturgeon in pita, that sort of thing). Halfway through, the old man decided to bare his soul:

"In my whole entire eighty-three years, I have never been in love."

Now that was interesting.

"Not once? But you have a wife, grandchildren, even!"

"So?" He gave a roguish wink. "The only reason I got married was because when my mama wanted to get me to start a family, she began to remove her head scarf. Of course you understand what a disgrace it is for one of us mountain people if his mother bares her head in his presence." I wasn't completely following, but he went on: "I gave in. Got married. And boy did I put my wife through hell! Couldn't give up the ladies! I used to really get around, even before her."

Then he graced me with a tale from his youth, when he'd flown fighters in some international conflict between the Arabs and the Jews. The Soviets supposedly had no official role in the operation, and had mobilized pilots from the national republics of the USSR in an effort to conceal their involvement. The idea was that the pilots would communicate by two-way radio in their native languages, which would give foreign intelligence agents the impression that they were Arabs.

"But how did you understand one another?" It was so lame, I

couldn't believe it. "None of the other pilots would have understood when you spoke Lak, for example. And if everyone was talking Russian, then what was the point of the whole thing anyway?"

But the old man didn't hear me; he was down memory lane. Back on the military base there had been this girl Masha who'd worked in the cafeteria, a classic Russian beauty. Masha had a fiancé, some local guy, but all it took was a single waltz with this geezer of mine, who at the time was quite a dashing young pilot, and she completely forgot her beau. She followed him around, trying every way she could to intoxicate him with her beauty, but he would not give in.

"Just before my tour was up, the last night, Masha came to me and laid herself down—now I can talk about it calmly—she laid herself down on my bed, completely naked, and begged me to take her innocence. But for me that was a sacred principle: I never despoiled virgins. When she realized that this was the last time she would see me, she wept and all but went down on her knees, begging me to give her this gift to remember me by. The next morning I sent her forth from my room with her innocence intact.

"But that was so hurtful!" I cried. "To reject someone like that is a terrible insult."

"Actually, she said so herself, later."

"What, you saw her again?"

"Twenty-seven years later in the Moscow metro. I'm in one of the metro cars, and this overweight stranger is sitting opposite me, a woman beaten down by life. She sits there staring at me, crying. Tears just pouring down her cheeks. The train stops and she gets up. It's my stop too. We start off in the same direction, one behind the other. We get on the escalator, she's one step up, I'm down one, right behind her. And she turns and embraces me without a word. And we rode like that all the way to the top.

"So that was Masha?"

"It was. Compared to me she'd changed a lot. We went into a coffee shop and talked and talked. She told me that when she'd started dating her future husband, he had hated me—until he discovered on their wedding night that she was a virgin. He'd been sure, like everyone else, that I'd slept with her. So after that he respected me for preserving his bride's honor. He had only good things to say about me. But Masha's life did not go too well. She never experienced love or joy—all she did was work, work, work, morning to night, managing the household. Her husband drank. And if only the poor girl had had that one night, if I'd given in that time, who knows, maybe she would have had a happier life."

While I sat there listening to the old man and eating, it occurred to me that he was obviously exaggerating. Just showing off. Which is pretty strange, considering his role of grandfather and matchmaker. Speaking of which, where was this grandson or nephew of his? But no one showed up.

"How old are you?" asked the man, out of the blue.

"Twenty-five."

"Sorry to hear that. What a shame." His face changed, and he looked down at his plate. "I wanted to introduce you to my grandson, but you're older than he is."

I experienced a sharp pang of indignation, maybe at the tactless old man, or maybe at my brother, who'd neglected to clarify this detail in advance.

"Anyway, my grandson has been living with his girlfriend for a long time. That bothers me, so I decided to take action. But unfortunately you are a whole two years older than he is. A little long in the tooth for a bride."

When I told my brother about it the next day, he started in on me himself:

"He's absolutely right! Before you know it, no one will even take a second look at you!"

"Stop talking like your mama." Lyusya had to get in her two cents' worth.

Lyusya is my brother's wife. She's Russian, which drives my parents nuts. They had stalled and delayed before the wedding, and didn't sent out invitations until the last minute, on the chance that their son might bail. Mama feels that nothing good can come from a woman who is not one of us. That her beloved son will be abandoned, deceived, eviscerated, and drained of his lifeblood.

To top it off, Lyusya couldn't get pregnant. She and my brother went to all kinds of doctors, who insisted that both spouses were perfectly fine, but still, Lyusya remained barren. Papa's mother, my Granny, who had called from back home to ask about it, concluded that the Lord above needed to be appeased somehow, that if she went to a sheik and got a *sabab*, then maybe he would deign... My brother just laughed.

The train braked at our destination, a station with one lone platform by a damp little forest. It had stopped raining. We descended onto a footpath and tried to figure out which way to go next. Under a tree nearby, a man of fifty or so stood scrutinizing us. Except for a green raincoat, there was nothing particularly memorable about him. Marina spotted him and called out:

"Excuse me, can you tell us how to get to the dacha cooperative?"

"The dachas? Sure," he answered good-naturedly, wading over to us through the tall wet grass. "Go straight down this path, then turn left when you get to the turnstile, before the fence turn again, this time to the right. Got it?"

"Straight, left, right," Artur rattled it off.

"Want to buy some wine? My own recipe, I make it myself."

An old net bag appeared out of nowhere, and the man extracted from it a large bottle with a homemade label showing the letter X, the rest indecipherable.

"No. Thank you, of course, but we don't accept wine from strangers," snapped Marina.

"Why not?" Artur objected. Let's buy it, I'll pay."

"It's not about the money," frowned Marina, but the man in the green raincoat was already smiling and handing Artur the bottle.

We walked the rest of the way in silence, withdrawn into ourselves as after a quarrel. When we reached the dacha, we saw several people in felt hats smoking on the porch. Most had piercings in their lips. Artur stayed outside with them and Marina and I walked up some creaking steps onto a wooden veranda where a big kitchen table stood, laden with shot glasses. There was an old stove and a small refrigerator, and the floor was strewn with bast mats of indeterminate origin and purpose. Small groups of guests sat or lay on the mats, chattering enthusiastically without paying us the slightest attention. I was already scoping out which group to join when a hulking red-haired guy flew up to Marina, hoisted her high into the air, and shouted:

"Power Saw is here!"

That was weird. What was up with the nickname? I was about to ask, but Marina had already started introducing me around as her friend.

"She's a Chechen!" howled Artur, bursting in.

"I am not a Chechen," I ventured to clarify.

"Circassian, then?" speculated an effete, rail-thin brunet in a shapeless knit sweater.

"Yuri, prominent public figure," the redhead introduced him.

Yuri declaimed:

"Yonder where the Terek flows,
I saw a Circassian girl,
Her eyes pierced my heart..."

"At least you're close," I waved my hand. "I'm from around there."

"I served in the army in the Caucasus, was even wounded," Yuri declared pretentiously.

We had somehow gotten separated from Marina and the redhead, and had settled down on a bast mat like the other guests.

"It was in the nineties... You won't believe it, I was a Russian officer, but I sympathized with the natives, their love of freedom."

"You must be mixing up the nineteen-nineties with the nineteenth century," I laughed. What a bullshitter.

That hit the mark. The brunet raised a glass of cranberry liqueur to his red lips and shot me a glance out of the corner of his eye.

"You're sitting there giggling, but right here and now you have the opportunity to convey the hopes and dreams of the Caucasian people to the Russian elite," he murmured. By "elite" he meant himself, clearly.

"Such grand statements. The hopes and dreams of the Caucasian people? They're no different from what everyone else wants. A functioning system."

"Of laws?"

"Among other things. Of course, everyone has their own idea of what an ideal law is."

"You know, there's something aristocratic about you..." He took my hand and kissed it impulsively. "Imagine what big news it would be if we got married."

"Why 'big news?'"

"A prominent public figure and a Chechen."

"Dagestani."

"Even worse! Though I suspect you're a virgin..."

His directness made me laugh. The interrogation continued.

"So do they keep you under guard, monitor you? A gynecological exam every month?"

What?! I could have said something, but checked myself; it was safer just to play along.

"Yes, they do monitor me."

"Do your brothers keep you on a tight leash?"

"Very tight." Let him believe it—though my brother had let me go out with Marina tonight, no questions asked.

Yuri sighed and leaned back. I glanced around. It was a young crowd, but mismatched. A couple of half-grown boys in light linen jackets sat on the kitchen table, flapping their feet back and forth and toasting each other with cans of energy drink. Artur sat next to them gesticulating, with a bottle pressed between his thighs—the same one that he had bought from the guy at the station. Marina sat apart with the redheaded hulk and a motionless doll-faced, chestnut-haired girl in an old-fashioned flared skirt. People darted in and out of the kitchen. One guy, a man with a bald spot and a sparse ponytail, made his way toward us, maneuvering around plates of snacks that had been set out on the floor.

"Yuri, Yuri," he whispered, sinking to his knees and seizing skinny Yuri by the shoulders with both hands, "can you believe it? Kichin is here."

"And?" Yuri smacked his lips.

"He's completely without scruples. Every literate Internet user dreams of beating him up, the swine. A complete sell-out and ass-kisser. Goes around everywhere waving banners. He denounced me to the authorities, told them about my dual citizenship. I would have declared it formally in any case, but he beat me to it." The ponytailed guy rattled on.

"He doesn't scare me!" Yuri chopped the air with his hand.

"He doesn't scare me either, he's basically a quiet guy, he'll just curl up in a corner and sit there with a glass of vodka. But he's got an entourage, ultra-leftists, and they're completely out of control."

Right on cue, a bunch of newcomers appeared on the veranda: a pallid, slightly cross-eyed youth with disheveled brown hair and two sedate-looking fellows in denim jackets and bright T-shirts printed with a hammer-and-sickle design.

"They look pretty safe to me," I noted.

"Excuse me?" the ponytailed guy addressed me.

"Patya."

"A fine specimen, an Amazon from the mountains," interjected the imaginative Yuri, kissing my hand again.

Artur appeared on my other side with a full glass.

"Patya, why aren't you partaking? What did I buy all this wine for? It's really good."

I took the glass. The bottle made the rounds. I saw that Marina also poured some for herself. Outside the windows, twilight was setting in.

At this point the girl in the flared skirt suddenly came to life, strode out to the middle of the veranda, and proposed loudly:

"Let's call up some spirits! It's so much fun, you'll see!"

"Isn't it dangerous?" Yuri hesitated.

"Come on, let's do it!" shouted one of the leftist guys in a bass voice.

Other voices, the leftists, maybe, or the redheaded hulk, were already proposing to summon the spirit of Stalin. The guys in linen jackets had produced a big piece of paper and were writing some letters on it. The girl who had instigated the whole thing, and one of the guests who'd been smoking on the porch, prowled the veranda in quest of an old bowl to use in the séance.

"This is so stupid," the guy with the ponytail complained. "Let Kichin conjure up his own Stalin!"

"Come on, it could be interesting." Yuri wiggled his brows. He had already progressed from cranberry liqueur to Artur's wine.

Marina took charge. "We need to sit in a circle and join hands." She caught my eyes, winked and beckoned, and I went over to her.

"It's about to begin," she whispered into my ear. "They'll ask about Russia's destiny, about who will be in power and whether there will be a revolution, and then they'll move on to the meaning of life. They'll get into a big argument and start screaming and yelling."

"What's the point?"

"Just for laughs, why else? By the way, why haven't you said something to the host?"

"Who's the host?"

Marina pointed to a tanned, slightly horse-faced young man who was sitting on a mat and observing the proceedings. I don't know how

I could have missed him, especially since we were already acquainted. His name was Rinat. He was a Bashkir, or maybe a Tatar, and once he'd given me and Marina a ride home from work. At the time, I had thought that he might be interested in her. Seemed like a decent enough guy.

"I'll go say hello," I said, with some relief. I had no desire to go back to Yuri.

"If the spirit reveals itself, I will confess to it," Artur snickered as I walked past.

"Wouldn't be a bad idea in your case. Not here though, but in church," said the guy the ponytailed man had called Kichin. "I'm not about to be a part of this Satanic stuff."

"So go and rat on everyone who is a part of it!" the man with the ponytail shouted, groping around in the refrigerator. It wasn't clear how he'd been able to hear anything from over there, and why he kept changing his mind about the enterprise: now anti-, now suddenly pro-.

Kichin said nothing.

"That's right, don't answer." Yuri walked over toward him, bending his sharp knees like Pinocchio. "No need to fan the flames, it just plays into the hands of Russia's enemies."

"Whose side are you on, Yuri?" growled the ponytailed guy, slamming the refrigerator door.

"Easy, easy!" Marina was taking it seriously. "You can ruin everything! Spirits are touchy, they are easily offended."

Rinat stood up and greeted me. He got straight to the point:

"I knew you'd come. Let's go somewhere quiet."

We left the veranda, entered a narrow hallway and walked past a bathroom with no door—just hinges on the frame—and a steel gas water heater with protruding pipes. Rinat started up a stairway without looking back. I followed.

At the top, we found ourselves in a dark little room with ancient, mildewed wallpaper. A cold woodstove stood forlornly against one wall, faced by a faded blue sofa of 1970s vintage.

We sat down on the sofa and stared wordlessly at the stove. Rinat was holding a glass of Artur's wine.

He finally spoke. "Why do they say *in vino veritas*?"

"Because it's bitter?"

"Because when you drink, you can be seen in your true light," Rinat answered quietly.

"I don't know about that… "

Shouts came from below:

"It moved! It moved!"

"You, now," continued Rinat, still gazing at the stove, "I know you inside and out."

"Because of the wine?"

"No, because of a dream. I had a dream. But first we need to raise a toast."

He looked at me, and his equine face was completely open and vulnerable, with its blue-gray irises glimmering in the gray evening light. We clinked our glasses together. Then he took my glass, leaned over and set both glasses down deliberately on the floor, straightened up again, took me in his arms and began just as deliberately to ease me backwards onto the sofa. A chilling, numb terror crawled over my skin, but my head was completely empty. I sank back and lay staring up at the ceiling. Rinat pressed down on me from above and lay there, also motionless except for his calm, deep breathing. It was as though he was asleep. It occurred to me that someone could come up the stairs, see us, and start a rumor, but the fear subsided. A strange feeling of cosmic calm came over me. From afar, I felt the shallow trembling of my body.

"I couldn't do anything just now," Rinat said suddenly.

"Do what?"

"Anything with you. It's always like that when I feel something. If my feelings are not involved, then no problem."

"What made you decide," I asked, in a languid voice that I myself didn't recognize, "that something needed to be done with me?"

"I'm telling you, I had a dream. I dreamed that I was at home in my village, in the Volga region. I go outside, it's just after sunrise, and I see a big nest in one of the trees. And a demon cub is peering out of the nest. Its top half is like a little girl, but underneath it has a goat's body. When it sees me, this half-girl, half-animal climbs out of the nest, springs down from the tree, and slithers downward into the earth like a snake. So I pick up a stick from the ground and start poking it into the hole that the creature had made. I need to get it to come out. Then the girl-demon creeps up out of another hole and says: 'Hit the fence with the stick three times, and your wish will come true.' So I took the stick, hit the fence with it three times, and wished for you to come to the dacha today. And my wish came true."

I felt uneasy, but didn't move and just lay there under Rinat, looking out the dirty window at the rain rustling the leaves in the darkness that had descended on us.

"When I hit the fence, the neighbor's front door opened, and the neighbor came out onto her porch and started looking around, trying to figure out where the noise had come from. She didn't see me, though I was standing right there. And at that moment I understood beyond the shadow of a doubt that it was not a dream, that I really was in my village. I think that if I'd called my neighbor later and asked if she'd heard any knocking at dawn that morning and had come out onto the porch she would have said yes."

"Why didn't you make a different wish?" I heard myself ask the question. My voice was surprisingly confident.

"I don't know. Most likely your mountain spirits overpowered my river ones."

My head spun. Against my will, I felt myself beginning to believe the bizarre things he was saying. Below, the red-haired guy's bass cut through the din of indistinguishable voices.

"If you believe all this mysticism, why aren't you down there with the rest of them?" I asked.

"Because they are just communing with their own fears, and that's of no interest to me."

"But you invited all of them over…"

"Just so that you would come. That's the only reason."

The dread that had come over my invisibly trembling legs finally found its way to my consciousness. I started to extract myself from under Rinat. He made no attempt to restrain me. But instead of going down to join the others, I retrieved my glass from the floor and sat up. Rinat watched from the other corner of the sofa.

"Do you like Yuri?" he asked suddenly.

"No. I mean yes, he's nice, but he's so full of himself. He makes himself out to be some kind of god.

"Is there something wrong with that?"

"Well, yes, pride is considered to be a sin."

"Might Yuri simply have drunk some wine and come to know the truth?"

Now I knew for sure that Rinat was crazy, so I didn't try to argue.

"Unlike us, he doesn't try to distinguish himself from God. We all ought to strive for that," he explained.

"Meaning?"

"You know the fable about the poet who began to cry out in ecstasy, 'I am God! I am God!' His students decided that the poet had been possessed by Satan, and attacked him with their knives. But instead of wounding their teacher, they ended up stabbing themselves."

"Why?"

"Because the poet had lost his individuality. He became one with God and turned into a mirror. The knives intended for him turned back upon the students themselves."

"Would you also like to lose your individuality?" I asked.

"I cannot, although I am trying with all my might."

He also reached for his glass and took a sip. Then he scrutinized me and muttered:

"Hair…"

"What?"

"Your hair is covering your face. Get rid of it, get rid of the hair!" His mumbling grew louder and louder and then he was shouting.

Terrified, I sprang up from the sofa, shaking the short locks back from my forehead.

"Free yourself of it. Hair is multitude. Multitude hides the face of the One."

"Come on, Rinat." I was offended. "That's just stark raving mad."

I fled down the stairs. My heart pounded in my chest. I sensed that Rinat was coming after me and feared that he would try to murder me.

Downstairs, I groped for the door to the veranda, but it refused to yield. A wave of sheer panic came over me.

"Open up! Open up!" I wailed, desperately jiggling the rusty door handle.

"It's Patya." I heard Marina's voice.

"Don't believe it, don't let it in!" shouted one of the men, probably Artur. "It's just pretending to be Patya, it's not her!"

"Yes, the spirit is trying to trick us," the others chimed in.

"Please," I begged, "Don't go crazy on me, I'm scared!"

"Right, guys, it's not Patya, she wouldn't have yelled like that. That's not like her." Marina's voice again.

All of them, I knew, were clustered around the door, gripping onto the handle on the other side, and my yanking on it was only spurring them on.

"Patya," Rinat called from behind. My heart plunged to my heels. I pressed my back to the wall and buried my face in my hands. But Rinat did not touch me. I heard him walk past and clap his palm against the door several times. The people on the other side groaned and howled.

"They're scared, all of them," he said quietly.

I composed myself and lowered my palms. Rinat's equine face was suspended motionless in the air opposite me. It was hard to distinguish its features in the darkness, but from the faint tobacco smell I surmised that he was holding an unlit cigarette between his lips.

"It's not knocking anymore," remarked a voice from the other side.

"No, there's someone there," said another.

"All right, guys, let's not let things get out of hand," came Yuri's voice.

"There's a door on the other side. Let's go around through the garden," whispered Rinat.

"Let's," I agreed, and entrusted my hand to him. He would not let me stumble.

My terror had faded away, leaving a feeling of light amusement. And we walked down the hallway into the evening rain.

2. A LIST OF BRIDES

The train traced a line through the hot, humid steppe. Insects stuck to the windows of the economy class car, and sleeplessness tormented the passengers. Just after dawn, a new stop was announced. Women and children dragged bags stuffed with junk down the aisle and jostled one another at the exit doors. A tall traveler with duffle bag slung over his shoulder occupied the newly vacated place next to Marat. His proud face and long black curls looked familiar.

Marat immediately recalled his nickname from high school, Rusik-the-Nail. It was somehow connected with a shoemaker, though he couldn't recall all the details. When they were twelve or so, they used to taunt an old man who had a shoe-repair booth right on the main street, the long, broad tract onto which people's gates opened out, which was grandly known as the Avenue. When it rained, the Avenue swelled up and became a muddy ditch, and the residents would slosh along in galoshes and on stilts.

For some reason the boys saw the shoemaker, who presided there in his booth like a sentry, as something like the personification of evil, a detested fiend who deserved the most ruthless punishment. They used to climb up onto the booth from behind, two or three at a time, and seek out a familiar crack in the roof. Giggling wildly, they would insert the nozzle of a plastic pitcher that they'd stolen from a public toilet, and pour water down onto the villain's head. Some of the miscreants preferred to bombard the old man with scraps of paper they'd set on fire, shoving them through the same unfortunate crack. The shoemaker would rush out brandishing his hammer. Cursing and jabbering in his dialect, he would jump up and down, attempting futilely to grab the delinquents by their heels.

It was great fun, especially when the boys would make a run for it. One of them would mouth off at the old man to distract him, while the others would spring down from the roof and take to their heels, sputtering and choking with laughter. The infuriated victim could never get a good enough look at them to identify them later, though one time he did manage to grab hold of Rusik's hat; he tucked it tightly under his arm and, waving his fist with a big cobbler's nail sticking out of it, howled bloody murder:

"I nail bash you noggin!"

Rusik begged him for his hat, but the shoemaker just kept on yelling:

"Nail, noggin! Nail, noggin!"

Marat couldn't recall what happened next, but the nickname took root once and for all, just like a real nail.

"Rusik, *salam*!" He thwacked the little table with his palm.

Rusik turned, and the somber wrinkle on his forehead gently dissipated. Exclamations and handshakes ensued. It turned out that he was teaching at the Kizlyar branch of the university; he had just finished exams, and was headed home. Marat immediately forgot which subject Rusik was teaching—something having to do with economics. He was eager to hear the latest news from home.

"So Rusik, tell me, did they manage to lock Khalilbek up? Is he serving time?"

"Sure is! Right outside town, in our own prison!"

"Are you kidding me? No way!"

"We can't believe it either. No one can. Everyone's afraid, they're expecting him to be released at any moment. People are sending collective letters of support, just in case."

Yes, Khalilbek was omnipotent, omnipresent, and more. He had no official position, but somehow controlled the entire real estate market in our hometown and in the big city, as well as all the government officials of every rank and role. He was everywhere at once, in every imaginable office; he authored and published books on public improvements and on the secrets of worldwide success, ruled over bureaucrats, hobnobbed—so it was said—with bandits, looked after sick children and babies in hospitals he endowed, and turned the heads of pop singers and entertainers. The dark rumors that swirled around him only added to his stature and vigor. Without Khalilbek's approval no one would take a step in the district, buy land, or organize a conference. He had a finger in every pie and knew the details of the most minor matters; at the same time, he was behind all major shifts in power, missing persons cases, and fateful decisions.

At one time Marat's father had known Khalilbek personally, but an unpleasant incident—accident, actually—had put an end to their association. Marat had had a neighbor, Adik. He was a timid kid whom the neighborhood boys bullied and abused constantly, swearing at him and calling his mother a whore. Adik lived with his grandfather. No one knew who his father was, and his mother, fleeing gossip, had roamed Russia far and wide before finally returning home, mortally ill. Adik was by then already close to graduation. He was terribly ashamed of his mother, but by all indications had forgiven her. When she died from tuberculosis shortly after her return, he was beside himself with grief.

When Adik was little, the neighborhood boys used to beat him up constantly. As his neighbor, Marat occasionally found himself called upon to protect him from the blows. Which meant that Adik followed him around like a shadow, for his own protection. Marat's parents also took Adik in, welcomed him into their home, and fed and cared for him.

Adik's grandfather, who had raised him, died just before his mother. Word was, he had built the very prison where Khalilbek was currently serving time. He had been an architect and a passionate scholar of Arabic culture who kept rare medieval manuscripts, not only Ajam texts, but other, more esoteric documents, a thousand years old, written on locally produced paper in the ancient alphabet of Caucasian Albania. For this dubious attraction to the pre-revolutionary past he had paid with his position in the construction administration and had been exiled from the city to our town. The manuscripts were confiscated and turned over to the Soviet archives, and subsequently were either destroyed or mislaid.

Marat had only a faint memory of Adik's grandfather; he recalled his suspenders, and once had caught a glimpse of an orthopedic corset under his shirt, a memento from the Battle of Stalingrad. The former architect was reclusive, and there really wasn't anyone in the area for him to talk to. The people in town were nothing special, manual workers who had been forcibly resettled from the inaccessible mountains and who had dissolved into the swampy steppe. No cake here, just drippings from the roasting pan.

But Adik stood out vividly in Marat's memory. After graduation, the boy hadn't pursued a higher education; he started working as a carpenter in town. Early on, he married a taciturn, big-bosomed girl his age whom Marat's mother had chosen for him. Marat was constantly lending him money, and Adik would mumble in his timid, quiet voice that he would pay him back, but of course he never did.

Then Marat moved to Moscow and took a job as an associate in a law office. Occasionally, on trips back home, he would help Adik protect himself from various people in town who had set sights on his little house and were trying to smoke him out of there any way they could.

Things reached the breaking point one summer when, on one of his trips home from Moscow, Marat discovered that Adik—who, though he'd started a family, was still quite young—had mysteriously come into an impressive amount of money. Adik claimed that he had opened up a music kiosk in the city, but this story was beyond pathetic, especially since the money had been enough for a black Lada Priora with the kind of license plate everyone craved, but could not afford. Adik tooled idly around the Avenue in the car, as though to spite all those boys who had tormented and teased him during his childhood. He met Marat in a neatly pressed shirt and led him into the kitchen, where with great ceremony he produced a wad of rubles from a tin can labeled, in red, RICE.

"Paid back with interest!"

Marat refused to take it at first, but Adik took offense and nearly lost his temper, so he gave in. Adik had undertaken a completely unnecessary and hasty construction project in his yard. He claimed that he was building a guesthouse, though he and his wife never had anyone over. They led a quiet, secretive life; even their small children—who were very close in age—never seemed to cry. But then Khalilbek showed up in town, where he had a mansion, vacant and locked up, just around the corner from Marat's house. No one knew what had provoked him to get behind the wheel and speed out here alone late one night without his driver and bodyguards. Or how it happened that Adik had ended up under his wheels at that godforsaken hour.

Of course, everything had been hushed up. Marat's father had tried to figure out what happened, but he was no match for Khalilbek. Adik was laid to rest, and that was that.

After the funeral, though, something unexpected came to light. Someone whispered to Marat that Adik had been, in fact, his half-brother—that the man who knocked up this wanton, tubercular woman was his own father. Stranger still, his mother not only knew about it, but even defended his father. She said that you could understand Aselder; he dreamed of children, but she had been unable to give him any after Marat. She had loved Adik as though he were her own child, and after his death, she couldn't stop talking about him, mourned him, and cried over him almost every day. She wanted to take in the children, but Adik's wife had vanished with them immediately after the forty-day mourning period. They had gone away to the *kutan*.

Generally speaking, Marat's family had personal accounts to settle with Khalilbek. Rusik couldn't follow all the nuances. After questioning Marat about Moscow and the law office, his morose mood returned. Scratching his stubbly chin, he stared out the window at the vast wastelands flying past.

Suddenly, he snorted: "To hell with this Khalilbek guy. I have something else to worry about. Our local muttonheads. You know that I live 'across the tracks,' and over there they have... it's like an oppositional mosque. They're on me every day, like, 'Why aren't you with us?' But I don't go to the other mosque either, the one on the Avenue. I work all day, every day, either at class in Kizlyar, or in the city at the committee. I ride my bike there, and that sets them off too. 'Why do you go by bike? Why don't you wear a suit?' And at home it's on and on about 'When are you going to get married? When are you going to get married?' Not to mention, of course, they want me to marry one of *our* girls, to keep it in our nationality. And word just got out around town that that I go to tango lessons. Ooooh, everywhere I go people whisper and point..."

"So move away already!"

"Easy for you to say. You think they'll let me out of their clutches that easily? The only son, little sisters...my parents have dug in their heels."

"Stop whining, then."

Marat smirked. The guy was known for his eccentricities. He held the locals in contempt, didn't go to the mosque, conducted romances with divorced artsy types in the city, and had a fancy way of talking, with no local accent, like a proper Russian. He would get caught up in various obsessions, like collecting old maps, or numismatics, or winter swims in the sea, as though to set himself apart and to provoke everyone around him. But he would quickly abandon each new fad and lock himself in at home, where he'd mope around for days. Neither his biking to work in the city (thirty kilometers, one way, on a dirt road) nor the tango lessons surprised Marat. He questioned him about the matchmaking:

"So, have they found you a bride?"

"They're constantly dredging up some new girl and forcing her on me," Rusik grimaced, "like at the zoo."

"I'm actually on my way to getting married too."

"You, married? Who's the lucky girl?"

"Don't know yet. I have to come up with someone pretty soon. The date's been set, the banquet hall reserved. The only thing missing is the bride." Marat briefed Rusik hastily, rolling yesterday's bread crumbs into little balls on the table.

People passed up and down the aisle with towels and toothbrushes, corn puffs and cell phones, laughing and calling out to one another, and clattering tea glasses in their metalwork holders.

"Are you shitting me?" blurted Rusik.

"Ask my folks. Every summer when I come, it's a huge battle, and I barely escape. This time they went ahead and reserved a banquet hall. If I don't find someone to marry, the money goes down the tubes. The hall is nothing fancy, and it's off the beaten track, the best ones get snapped up a year in advance. But it will hold a thousand guests. My father even sold a car to get cash for the deposit. I'm also trying to save up. See? Here I am in economy class." Marat gave a nervous laugh.

"I wouldn't have expected it of you, Marat! How did you let yourself get roped into that?"

"Actually I'm not opposed. Let them get me married. I've had enough of living on my own."

Rusik stared dumbfounded at his friend for several seconds, then flicked his hair, frowned, and climbed up onto the upper bunk. Marat got up and stretched, then picked up the tea glasses and took them, clinking in their holders, to the hot water urn—the "Titan," as the conductors called it. The heat in the car was oppressive. Fat tradeswomen roamed the aisles with huge checkered plastic luggage bags, hawking leopard-print chiffon scarfs to the female passengers. The customers fingered the cloth and consulted one another, rustling their money.

"*Vatsok*, time for tea?" shouted Marat's fellow-traveler from overhead, flashing his yellow heels on his way down.

"Brilliant deduction, bro," laughed Marat.

When Marat came back with the tea, Rusik sat up and leaned his elbows on the table. They stirred in the sugar.

"What's all this trouble in town between the mosques? Some kind of brawl?" Marat scratched himself lazily and settled down on his bunk.

"Brawls, you mean. You know how it is there. There was one mosque, and they selected an imam."

"And?"

"And then some misunderstandings arose between the *tukhum* that built the mosque and the new imam. Supposedly over the question of free will, but no one knows the real reason."

"I don't get it."

"Look. The people of that *tukhum* believe that only Allah performs all actions, even those that human beings would seem to be responsible for. In other words, everything is predestined from above and none of us have any free will."

"The imam disagreed?"

"The imam taught that Allah learns about human actions only after they are completed. And there was something else, too, about the created nature of the Qur'an. Something like, the meaning is eternal, but the words that express it are created and not eternal."

"So that's what they fought over?"

Rusik snorted:

"At first the imam's opponents made a point of shunning the mosque, and they started intimidating people, saying that the imam was a Wahhabi. That happened several years ago, and it's not such a big deal any more, but at the time it was like being convicted and sentenced. Though if you get into the actual theology of it, he's not a Wahhabi at all, rather something like a Qadariyah. Or, what do they call it, a Mutazilite. It doesn't really matter. Anyway, they brought together athletes from the whole district, including some world champions and even an Olympic gold medalist. They called in the riot police and incited a knockdown, drag-out fight right inside the mosque, according to the victims."

"I heard about that, but why the riot police?"

"To trap the guys and get them on their official records. Of course they removed the imam. Then his adherents quit the mosque and started their own, a new one, 'across the tracks.' Rumor has it the money came from Khalilbek. Later, though, they forced out the imam."

"From the new mosque too?"

"Yeah, when push came to shove, the mosque across the tracks really had become Wahhabi. He didn't see eye-to-eye with the congregation."

"So what was the last fight about? Was there a reason for it?"

"Just internal squabbles. A guy from the mosque on the Avenue got into a spat with someone from 'across the tracks.' That's where the whole thing started—right in front of me, after the evening prayer. I had had an argument with my father, he'd been nagging me about getting married, and I'd gone out for a walk. I'm standing there and people are pouring out of the mosque."

"'Across the tracks?'"

"Yeah. Meanwhile, a mob gathered on the other side of the tracks, it had to be five hundred people. Right, I think, things are going to get ugly now. I'm standing there watching, and someone yells '*Allahu Akhbar*,' and they rush at each other from both sides and start throwing stones. Shooting their guns in the air, shouting... I run over along with some other onlookers to try to calm things down, to separate them. Right then a dozen or so cops drive up in Ural military trucks. My neighbor said later that the cops were in on it, in cahoots with the guys from the Avenue. But I'm sick and tired of it all. More than you know!"

"Rusik, take it easy, they won't touch you."

"What do you mean, they won't? Last week my neighbor, the same one, comes running over and he's freaking out, like, 'Mirzik's been kidnapped! They kidnapped him! He called in the evening on his way home, he said was going to pick up some bread, and would be home in ten minutes—and that's the last we heard from him!'"

"Oh, I know Mirzik!"

"Everyone knows him! Bearded guy, has two wives. So anyway, Mirzik goes missing, and sure enough, the usual story: the traffic police try to stop a suspicious-looking car entering the city, the driver opens fire, and they return fire and kill him. Turns out it was Mirzik."

"Are you kidding me?"

"My neighbor goes on and on about how it's not true, it was a set-up. That's what they always say, but who's to know what really happened? Anyway, so now they want to make him into some kind of saint. He goes, 'Write an article about Mirzik, that's something you can do.' I try to explain: 'I've never written an article in my life, I'm just a college teacher.' But they just lost it. Blah, blah, blah, what a fine man he was. And, oh, I've got to put something in about the strawberry cake."

"What's with the cake?"

"Well, my neighbor's wife, she's about to have a baby. And she starts craving strawberry cake, so she writes about it in some social media group she's in. And Mirzik's wife reads about it and tells Mirzik. They're out in the car on their way somewhere. And supposedly Mirzik pulls a U-ey right then and there, and heads straight to the bakery to get her just what she wants."

"An angel, not a man."

"That's not the word for it. Now they're after me because I refused to write the article. There's other stuff, too, it's built up. My tango lessons..."

Marat brushed him off:

"Just cave, Rusik, do what they say!" he joked.

"The only thing that saved me was that I had ghost-written dissertations for Khalilbek's people to sign. They all knew about it and didn't lay a hand on me—they were afraid of Khalilbek. But now he's in prison..."

Outside the window, they passed a canal lined with weeping willows and piles of garbage. Cows chewed their cud in silhouette.

"We're almost there," noted Marat.

The brick station building came in sight, the train braked, and before long the two of them were walking along the platform. The foothills traced dark contours in the distance. The brick buildings of the town, which had sprouted up around the station fifty years ago, expanded out in a brown grid into the steppe, which hummed with the chirring of insects. Drought had left the dirt on the roads caked and crumbly.

At the turn, Rusik shifted his duffle bag onto his left shoulder, pressed Marat's hand, and, frowning either from the sun or as an expression of his inborn despondency, shook his forelock and headed off across the bridge over the tracks. Underneath, the train was already clanking and chugging, picking up speed as it continued on toward the city.

The oppressive heat had driven everyone inside. Marat arrived home without running into anyone. His parents met him with the customary restraint, but it was clear they were happy to see him.

"How was the train, Marat? Was it dirty? Did they give you towels?"

His mother jumped right in.

"What's going on with that case you're working on? I heard it's a big deal," his father started in from the other side, grunting and wiping his rough face with both hands. "Something about human rights, some woman was murdered? They're suspecting guys from here. Do they know who was behind it?"

Marat soaped his hands at the basin and gave disjointed answers. His mind was on the dinner table, where there awaited a steaming platter of pea-flour *khinkal* and bowls of bouillon and sour cream with crushed garlic.

"Wait, first tell me about Khalilbek, Father. What happened? How did they get him?" Marat smiled, settling down on a stool and grabbing a fork. "Rusik said something to me on the train, but I couldn't make sense of it."

"Rusik who? The ballet dancer?" His mother broke in, adjusting the hairpins in her unraveling bun.

"What ballet dancer, Mama? Are you making fun of him?"

"No one's making fun of anyone!" his mother snapped. "That's what people are saying. He wanders around town like a plucked firebird, a featherless rooster, but thinks he's better than everyone else. Pride is a grave sin, Marat."

"Don't start." Marat winced.

"Khalilbek also thought that he'd managed to get onto such a high branch that no one could reach him, but the hawks swooped down and grabbed him from there. Even Khalilbek!"

"Enough already with your hawks," his father broke in. "Better not mention his name where anyone can hear you. There's enough trouble without that."

"I'm not afraid, Aselder! You're the one who was afraid! He killed your son, and now here you are cringing with your tail tucked between your legs like a cowardly wolf facing a hunter."

"Stop it, hear me?"

"And remember the vouchers? Twenty years ago. Who kept you from selling those vouchers?"

"Stock certificates, you mean."

"What difference does it make! It was Khalilbek! He insisted that you keep them, he just wouldn't let up, and you listened to him. Trusted him. Meanwhile, the Magomedovs sold theirs and used the money to buy property in the city. And we're still living out here in the middle of nowhere like peasants on a collective farm!"

"Give it a rest, you're driving me crazy! Enough about the stocks."

"And the casino! Who came up with the idea of opening a gambling den in town, who ruined our kids with lottery scams and slot machines? Khalilbek, that's who!"

"Mama," Marat looked up from his bowl. "He was out there wreaking some serious havoc and you're on and on about slot machines, kindergarten stuff. It's over, calm down. He's in prison now."

"Is it really over, though?" Marat's father shook his head. "He's been arrested three times. It's downright ridiculous. The first time, a search, you name it, everyone all worked up, thinking something big is going to happen, journalists licking their chops. Then that same evening Khalilbek sends out a statement that no one's laid a hand on him, he's free, and everything's just fine. And not a word from the police. Two weeks later, the same story!"

"What the…"

"I swear! It took three tries before they finally locked him up for real, when no one believed it would happen."

"That's just fine with me," his mother jabbered again. "May he rot in there with his damned holster strap. And Adik...such a bright boy!"

"And what's that story about the house?" Marat asked, with sudden interest.

"Adik's?" His father raised his eyebrows. "His wife went and sold it to some guy from the police. He went over there himself, talked fancy, waved some documents around."

"The hussy has no shame, who does she think she is?" His mother flared up again. "I found her on a dairy farm in the back of beyond—one of my distant cousins. I think, a good working girl, just right for Adik, she'll set him on his feet. Boy, was I wrong! Not only does she take the kids and everything, leaving no trace, but she also goes and sells the house on the sly. Not one thing for us! Every last bit of it, straight into her pocket!"

"What did you expect? Anyway, why count other people's money?" groaned Marat's father.

"I have every right. Who raised the boy from childhood, clothed and fed him? Who? That woman? By the time she came, everything was waiting for her on a silver platter. Nowadays all the young people are like that. The moment she gets a husband, it's *bam*, fork over the apartment, the house, the car. And her in-laws slaving away right next door."

"That's it, she's off to the races now," mumbled Marat's father under his breath. He reached down and picked up a newspaper.

"Adik's car, the house, that cop bought it all."

"That 'cop' of yours is actually a colonel," interjected Marat's father, without looking up.

"Colonel...general, whatever. Who needs someone like that for a neighbor? Every morning I wake up from bad dreams. I think, what if someone slips a bomb under his car, it could blow us up too. I mean, we're right next door."

"He's careful, though. Every morning he comes out and checks under the car," said Marat's father from behind his newspaper, in the same tone as before.

"Sure he does! He ought to be spending less time at weddings!" Marat's mother wasn't about to give up. "And breaking noses. Torturing people in those cellars of theirs."

"What are you talking about, Mama?" Marat was startled. He'd been away long enough, had forgotten his mother's obsessions.

"About how this colonel, or general, whatever he is, came back drunk from his boss's wedding…"

"From the city," Marat's father added.

"Right, from the city, where we, unfortunately, do not live, and instead are baking out here in this cowshed in the scorching sun without so much as an awning over our head. Anyway, he comes back from the wedding and starts in on Mukhtar's son. You know, the one who's got ischemia, and who hasn't painted his fence for two whole years. He ought to be ashamed of himself. What's his wife thinking? She just looks the other way…"

"Mama…"

"So he starts harassing Mukhtar's son. Like: 'I'm from the Sixth Department. Anti-Extremism. And who the hell do you think you are?' He had his buddies with him, from over there. Now Mukhtar's son, Alishka, he knows his rights, he backs off immediately and asks him to show his police ID. Not to mention, he's reeking of cognac, you can smell it all down the street. So the colonel hauls off and slugs him in the nose and breaks it in three places. And the other guys join in, beat him to a pulp: one stomps on his stomach, another straddles his chest. A total nightmare! And they poke the cop's ID in his face, like, 'Ha ha, take a good look, feast your eyes.' But Alishka still managed to kick one of them right into the ditch."

"Come on, like you saw the whole thing?" Father gave up on the newspaper. "You're making it up!"

"Mukhtar told me. They maimed his son, and on top of it, now they're filing suit against him for assaulting an officer of the law."

"Of course you know that poor victim of a son goes to the mosque 'across the tracks.' Who knows what they're teaching them over there. The police don't just go up to someone randomly like that..."

"Ha ha ha, very funny," Marat's mother burst out laughing. "Just don't try that on your son, he's a lawyer in Moscow—sees stuff way worse than this every day of the week."

"Mama, it's true I have seen a thing or two, but you're jumping to conclusions. You do it here at home, too, as long as I can remember. You'll stash away some important thing, or cash, somewhere, and then when you can't find it, you start to blame everyone. Making up all kinds of scenarios—who filched it, when, and how."

"Spot on," his father cackled again.

"Fine, so that's why you've come all this way, just to pick on your mother. Go ahead, both of you, gang up on me." Marat's mother stopped clattering the dishes and stood still next to the sink. "Don't think you're going to just sit around while you're here. You know that we've reserved the banquet hall for the thirteenth and paid for it."

"Just what we need right now..."

"It's exactly what we need. Or you'll never get married, not until you're way over the hill. Like old Iskhak, who lost his mind and started going to sleep every night in a grave instead of a bed. And he would read his own *yasin* for himself.

"You could at least give the boy some peace and quiet. He's been rattling in the train for two days," Marat's father took his side.

"You're not doing him any favors, Aselder. Where would you be without me?" Then, suddenly catching herself, she dashed over to the stove. "Enough. Marat, have some tea. I brewed it with thyme. I'll run and get the list. You have some too, Aselder."

Mother clanged a couple of heavy teaspoons down on the table, which was covered with Japanese oilcloth, brought over two hot glasses of tea, holding them by the brims so as not to burn her fingers, then rushed off, again adjusting the hairpins in her unruly, time-grayed hair as she went.

"Whew," sighed Marat, smiling.

His father didn't notice the smile. He was silently tugging at his earlobe, lost in thought.

"What's on your mind, father?"

"Me?" He snapped out of his reverie and moved over to the table. "I think you need to keep away from this ballet-dancer guy Rusik."

"What do you mean?"

"His family says that he doesn't even look at women. He doesn't go to the gym. Instead of martial arts he does ballroom dancing, quadrilles, that kind of stuff."

"Tango..."

"Tango-mango. And all winter long he went out to swim in the sea, like some invalid. With flippers, no less."

"Father, come on, who've you been listening to? Rusik is a

completely normal guy."

"Plus he lives near the mosque 'across the tracks.'"

"He has no connection with religion whatsoever. He could give a rat's ass about all that."

"That's a problem in and of itself. And these mosques too...Did you hear about what happened yesterday?"

"There's something every day around here."

"In a nutshell, the religious authorities sent their own imam 'across the tracks,' to replace the one they had chosen back when they founded it. Meaning, someone from the city. And this newly appointed imam cruises up in a Lada Priora with a whole entourage, a parade of cars, athletes, machine guns. There was almost another brawl."

"But what do the religious bureaucrats think they're doing? They're just making it worse."

"Before, most likely, Khalilbek prevented anything serious from happening. He had taken the new mosque under his protection, given money. Now they figure that with Khalilbek in prison, they can just put their own guy in there. But the people rallied around their imam, they adore him. They wouldn't stand for him to be replaced."

"Are they all Wahhabis in that mosque? Along with this beloved imam of theirs?"

"How am I supposed to know, Marat? Does anyone know who is who these days? But I think it was a bad move for the muftiate to try to force new imams in there and get rid of the old ones who'd been elected. Not to mention, Khalilbek could still be released."

"So you're chicken, are you?" Marat couldn't resist saying. He drank the last of his tea.

"*Le*, what, you think that since you're a big Moscow lawyer you can talk back to your own father?" his father flared up.

"Hold on, I'm sorry, I was just…"

"'Just' what? My chairman at the Institute says the same thing. I'm 'chicken'? You should see the others! No one dares to utter a peep against Khalilbek. Except your fool of a mother. They're laying low, waiting to see who's going to come out on top."

They heard steps, and Marat's mother came back to the veranda with a pen and a piece of paper covered with handwriting.

"I'm off," his father declared, and stood up.

"Where to?" asked Marat's mother loudly.

"To Shakhmirza's."

"All right, but don't eat anything over there. Or Shakhmirza's wife will think that I'm starving you to death and that you have to run over there for your Dargin *chudu*."

"Enough of your jabbering, hear me? Better sit down and go through that list of yours," Marat's father barked in his usual way and went out onto the porch to put on his shoes.

"All right, now, look," began Marat's mother. She got her glasses out of her housedress pocket and smoothed out the piece of paper with its list of vetted brides. "First on the list: Bariatka's daughter."

"You've picked a fine one to start with. She can't put two words together," protested Marat.

"What, you need her to go up onstage and give speeches? Very funny, Marat. The main thing is for her to have a conscience, and not be someone who only cares about grabbing stuff for herself. Like this one klepto bride that Zarema told me about…"

"Mama…"

"She's from Zarema's village. Turns out, first she accepts a proposal from some guy, then after he gives her a pile of gold, she takes off with it to a different village and marries someone else. Now her family can't show their face in public. They're trying to raise money to compensate the first bridegroom."

"Now that's just ridiculous. Zarema obviously dreamed the whole thing up, she's certainly capable of it. Who cares about the gold anyway?"

"What do you mean, who cares? I've already put away a hundred thousand for your bride. And I've scoped out a store in the city. I'll go there with her, let her choose whatever she wants for that amount. It'll give me a chance to check out her taste. If she goes for big shiny tchotchkes that you can see from three kilometers away, we'll beat a quick retreat. Why take up with some gypsy fool?"

"Anyway, with Bariatka's daughter, it's obvious at a single glance that she's a fool."

"What, you've talked with her?"

"I saw her web page. She's constantly posting selfies. And other pictures—kittens, children reading the Qur'an. And her status: 'I'm the hottest girl alive from Region Zero Five.' And she's a member of 'Beautiful Dagestani Muslim Babes'... Cross her off!"

Mother sighed in bewilderment, bit her lip, held her pen briefly above the line with the Muslim Babe, then drew a line through her name.

"Next?" yawned Marat.

"What are you yawning for?" Mother gave him a sideways look. "One conversation with Sabrina, and you'll never yawn again—that's how smart she is."

"Now what? Who's this Sabrina of yours?"

"Oh, she's a clever one! Like a professor! From the Shakhov family.

Her father's a military officer, mother's a cardiologist, her grandfather was a theater director. The girl is made of pure gold. Honors grad, medical school."

"Do you have a photo?" asked Marat, half-joking, half-serious.

His mother was obviously armed and ready. She reached into her pocket and drew out a photograph. A thin-lipped, thick-browed beauty looked haughtily out at him.

"Where did you get the photo?" Marat was surprised.

"I asked Firuza from the Avenue."

"And how did Firuza get her hands on it?"

"Firuza's late husband was Shakhov's brother. And her son Shakh, your classmate from law school, is Sabrina's cousin."

"So she's Shakh's cousin. Do they live in the city?"

"Right downtown. We'll go see them tomorrow. Their uncle died six months ago from a heart attack, so there's a good reason to stop by. We'll express our condolences, and the two of you can have a look at each other."

"All right, then, we'll give it a try. Who else do you have on the list?"

"Luiza's niece. Luiza talks so much about her. She was in a dance troupe as a child and now she's studying economics. I saw her at a wedding—she's as thin as a reed! And she recognized me and ran over to give me a hug and a kiss, though the last time I saw her she was just a little girl. Now that's what I call good breeding. We'll go to the Abdullaevs' engagement party, you can have a good look at her there."

"Just give me her name, I'll do an Internet search and find out whether she's fish or fowl."

"I'll show her to you in the flesh! To hell with that Internet of yours!"

"All right, who else do you have up your sleeve?"

"There's one from Aselder's office..."

"From Father's Institute?"

"Yes, they have a young specialist there, a political activist, works there as a secretary. I didn't want to put her on the list until I had a chance to see her in person. I went specially to Aselder's office and had a look: a sharp girl, alert, professional. She'll go far. Runs a little cosmetics business on the side, right there in the office."

"Well, Mother...not much to choose from there..."

"What do you mean, 'not much'? Do you have any idea how many I had to sift through? I looked far and wide. I wanted Muishka's daughter, but her neighbors didn't have a single good thing to say about her. Then I thought of the Kurbanovs, but it turns out they're really tight with Khalilbek. That's an immediate veto." She fretted. "All these years you couldn't come up with even one girl, and now you have the nerve to criticize me! Anyway, here, you know this next one: Zaira."

"Cross her off immediately."

"What do you mean, 'Cross her off?' She's one of us, from right here in town, a sensible girl."

"She wears a headscarf."

"Not a hijab though! I myself can't stand the ones who cover up, but what's wrong with a scarf? It's cute."

"And she prays. Don't make me even think about it."

"So, did Rusik turn you against girls who pray? Your father prays, doesn't he? And, *inshallah*, he'll go on the hajj."

"Mama!"

"All right, all right, I'll cross her off."

"Khadizha!" A woman's voice was hard in the yard. "Are you home?"

Marat's mother started, tucked the paper and Sabrina's photo into her pocket, and called back brightly:

"Is it you, Zarema? I'm here, come on in."

Marat got up and headed off to the bathroom before the guest came in.

3. POOR SINNER

I flew home from Moscow, and before I even crossed the threshold my mother started in on me:

"Patya, you completely let yourself go in Moscow. Why did I send you to your brother? So he could fix your cat brain! And instead you've gone off the deep end. Must be Lyusya's influence."

As it turned out, my brother had told Mama about my night at the dacha. Now, that whole night, from beginning to end, seemed strange and improbable, out of another world. I couldn't believe that I had actually lain on an old sofa like a mummy next to a man who was basically a stranger to me, listening to demented nonsense about knives and poets. And that wasn't the half of it. Thin peacock Yuri had slipped away with the girl in the fancy skirt, who turned out to be a successful designer, and who, as she put it, was making straight for the heart of life. She was so overcome with passion that by the morning after the revelry at the dacha she had installed herself firmly in Yuri's Moscow apartment and had set to work scrubbing his filthy bachelor floors with her bare hands. Marina couldn't restrain her laughter as she recounted this juicy bit of gossip.

Incidentally, she herself had gotten involved in a scandal. She'd squabbled with the half-baked boys in jackets, calling them slackers and an abscess on the body of the motherland. Orthodox believer Kichin had supported her and at one point had insulted their masculinity. The balding guy with the rattail who had spent the whole evening upholding freedom and humanistic values had hurled himself at Kichin, calling him a piece of shit and a heathen. A full-scale brawl ensued, complete with the smashing of goblets. Artur had crawled under the kitchen table and sobbed like a madman, for some reason that remains unclear. Basically, the dacha visit left a mass of disturbing thoughts in my mind. Back home, it was dusty and hot. I'd barely managed to change my clothes from the trip before I was put to work. I had to go out into the sunlit yard and beat the dust out of the pillows, and clean the carpets with reeking kerosene. Mama always loaded me up with housework when I came back from somewhere, making up for lost time.

As usual, Papa was fiddling with the milk separator in silence. All-powerful Khalilbek, for whom he had worked as a mechanic, was now locked up in a prison located on the outskirts of town, where it stood intimidating the local kids. Papa couldn't bring himself to accept it. He had always been proud that Khalilbek trusted him and would even engage him in conversation now and then. When Khalilbek had run over that fool Adik in his jeep, Papa had testified as a witness, since he had occasionally repaired the ill-fated vehicle and knew it well. The defendant was speedily exonerated, and Papa had received a bonus.

Having kerosened the carpets, I sat on the sofa beside my sleeping Granny and listened to the ticking of the clock. Papa had disappeared somewhere. Mama had holed up in the bedroom with a stack of tattered mystery novels. The women in the neighborhood thought she was lazy. She rarely tore herself away from her unpretentious reading matter, complained constantly of headaches, and started a conversation with Papa only when forced by necessity.

At one point Mama had been instilled with the conviction that she was of good breeding: her great-grandfather had been the region's first surveyor; her father had been in charge of a printing office; and all her distant relatives had been hacked to pieces in famous battles. The names of these ancestors were extolled in folk songs, where they assaulted the ears like the squealing and scraping of metal being crushed. As she herself said, she had not wanted to marry Papa, and was even embarrassed about him. When she was particularly upset, and Papa was out of earshot, Mama would blurt with inexpressible bitterness the phrase "sheepherder's spawn!" and her pale lips would form a tight, disgusted line. Papa was hurt by this condescension of hers, based on some fabricated sense of superiority, and he felt bad when his wife was ashamed to invite her former girlfriends over to visit, but he forgave her, out of generosity or possibly inertia.

Now Mama had a new set of adversities to complain about: the harpy Lyusya who had stolen her beloved son, and my prolonged unmarried state. I suspected that when she decided to send me to Moscow, Mama had been hoping for a miracle. My unwanted presence would drive barren Lyusya away, and I would finally find a worthy husband in the big city. But her plan failed on both fronts, and she fell into a state of melancholy. Her only succor was a damp gauze poultice on her forehead and her pile of tattered, damp-paged mystery novels.

Granny lay sleeping with a white scarf placed over her eyes and a string of amber beads clutched in her right hand. My papa was her son. To this day she kept his old pacifier in a heavy trunk in the back room; it looked like a little top hat, pink like pig's skin, with a rounded top. The same trunk held a pile of mildewed fabrics, sprinkled with laurel leaves, which had once been precious, but now were of no use to anyone. Granny assured me that this was my dowry.

She had not reached decrepit old age, but the world in which she dwelt had absolutely nothing in common with ours. In her world people still lived in mountaintop castles with flat roofs, divided up the fields and the harvest strictly according to ancient rules, and sent their sons to the villages of conquered neighbors to feast at their expense; after murders they demanded a vow of purging from forty men and exacted fines measured in units of grain, copper kettles, bulls, and sheep. These reminiscences descended into some infinite depth of the ages, and it was impossible to believe that she had ever personally been a part of that strange life.

Granny was originally from a mountainside village, which was a part of an alliance made up of twenty-five villages that had lived from ancient times according to a single code of law. A river flowed and gurgled in the valley below the mountain, and Granny's stories often featured a great bridge that had been built there by the locals. All of the men in the alliance had to guard the bridge in turns. Granny's uncle once refused his turn at this important duty, and he had had to pay for his stubbornness with a shawl. Judging from Granny's upraised eyebrows when she told the tale, shawls had been immensely valuable at the time.

Setting fire to the bridge was an infinitely more egregious crime. The arsonist would be exiled from the community, and there were no limits to what could be done with the outcast and his property. At one point there had been a miller in the community who had decided on his own initiative to move away with his entire family—this had happened more recently, during the Soviet period. Based on the local laws, the mill and all the associated property belonged to the mountainside community, and the man left with nothing.

In Granny's stories, there were town criers who clambered up to the top of the minarets and announced the times of the planting and the harvest, and whoever dared to go out on his own into the field and sow or harvest before the proper time would be punished. Even something as minor as a bunch of grapes plucked prematurely would elicit punishment, and villagers who had been unable to restrain themselves were subjected to cruel mockery and strict fines. One time, a special patrol had come across some grape pits in Granny's neighbors' yard a few days before the collective harvest, a time which was usually accompanied by jokes, revelry, and charity gifts of fruit to the poor, *mutalims*, newcomers, and other people who did not themselves keep a vineyard. For their violation of the ban, the neighbors had a cow confiscated, and the chief grape-eating culprit had his face smeared with tar and was paraded around the village on a donkey.

"Why so strict? Why not let you go out into your own fields whenever you wanted to?" I would pester Granny with questions.

"What would that have been like?" she would exclaim in her native language. "If the villagers ignored the orders of the people in charge, then the whole union would have fallen apart."

My favorite story was about fornicators. A murderer would be forgiven only when he had caught the culprits alone together, in the act. But when the enraged avenger caught and killed only the man or only the woman separately, he had to pay a fine of thirty cows to the heirs of the fallen victims, his finest bull to the villagers, and a payment to the entire alliance. All of this was enforced within a term of three days from the moment of the crime.

Granny admittedly reluctantly that once in her girlhood she had spotted a pair of adulterers in one of the village's meadows and had promptly informed the guilty woman's husband. The husband rushed out to the scene and caught the lovers in the act, and killed them both on the spot. He suffered no legal consequences. Within a couple of years he had taken on a new better half, Granny herself, who by then had entered adolescence.

I managed to shake out of her, bit by bit, everything that her old-woman's memory had retained from the events of her wedding week. Granny's father and brothers disappeared on the day of the wedding, and didn't come back until the very end of the celebrations, as though they sensed the awkwardness and inappropriateness of the occasion. The entertainment included, in addition to musicians and singers, a jester in a goat's mask, tightrope dancers and mummers, and people dressed in various costumes. The jester did all kinds of things! He put on women's clothes and poked out his belly so he looked pregnant, and then he made gestures imitating the bridegroom and made jokes at the guests' expense.

Following custom, on the eve of the wedding Granny went to spend the night at her guardian's house, and the groom went to the house of his best man, who had been chosen for this purpose long ago, at the groom's birth. On the morning of the wedding day, the couple was led in a procession with a *zurna* and tambourine from the homes of their hosts to the groom's parents' home. The best man walked with a long cane, the village youths carried the groom on their shoulders, and Granny herself marched proudly, draped in silver pendants, with a fine scarf veiling her face, with grains of wheat, flour, and white rice raining down on her from the sloped rooftops.

At the threshold, immediately after the newlyweds' dance, the mountainside villagers began dancing the Lezginka. Inside the groom's home, the bride was led to a special chamber, where she was seated on a sack of flour. She spent the whole day sitting there until evening, when it was time to go back to her guardian's house. The groom dined with his groomsmen in a different room, gathering in front of a broad tray laden with nine delicacies prescribed by ritual and a board arrayed with fruits. The tray, according to Granny, was called the "groom's ear," and I pictured it as a kind of round antenna, raised skyward in a prayer for prosperity.

After noon, Granny's wedding, which had already been celebrated in four households—those of the groom, the bride (with none of her menfolk present), and two temporary guardians—migrated to yet another abode. One of the guests had managed to kidnap the groom from right under the nose of his suite, which had let down its guard. They were fined for their negligence, and the wedding moved on to the home of the triumphant kidnapper, who was declared to be the groom's brother. The revelry went on for six days. On the third day Granny showed her face; on the fourth, she went to the spring for water with a silver pitcher, in that same procession, which stopped periodically along the way to dance.

Another time, she told me that there had been a sixth house, a secret one, designated for the freshly minted couple's nocturnal rendezvous. The bride's guardian took her to this secret house, which belonged to one of Granny's relatives, leading her along arched alleyways under the cover of darkness, hiding from torch-waving young men who were prowling the streets in quest of the newlyweds. The best man led the groom to the house in a similarly covert way.

"And in fact they did sleuth us out," said Granny with a sly smile. "They let a rooster in through the window, tossed kittens down the stovepipe, threw stones; they dismantled the roof in their attempts follow the progress of our struggle."

"What do you mean, struggle?"

"It's required by tradition. I cursed your grandfather with the most outrageous insults; the walls shook, but it didn't slow him down. We broke furniture, and shattered ten or twelve clay mugs."

"What for?"

"What do you mean, what for? To convince the evil spirits that we did not get along, so that they would leave us in peace. And anyway, any decent bride will put up a strong resistance. There was even a special stick hidden away in a corner for me to give him a good thrashing. He lashed out, bellowed at the top of his voice that he was in love with someone else, and that he had been forced to marry me. But I gave as good as I got, I yelled that my life with him would be pure hell. The young people sitting on the porch listened and roared with laughter."

"How could you say those things?"

"What, you think we were fighting for real? Of course not! That was how it was done. On the other side of the mountain, the next village over, newlyweds spent the entire wedding week trying to strangle each other and pouring buckets of water over each other. They say it was hilarious, a scream. Whereas in our village you'd whack each other two or three times with a stick, raise a ruckus in the room, and that would be it."

I had a sudden thought—what would it have been like to live in that long-lost time? I wouldn't have put up with any of it; I wouldn't have sat on the flour sack, I wouldn't have brought the pitcher of water... I was already slumping down on the sofa next to Granny, about to follow her and her big white scarf into a daydream, when my mother emerged from her bedroom, grimacing and massaging her forehead with her big fingers, and in a voice too sweet to be innocent, ordered me to put on my pleated dress.

I was being sent forth to meet the children of Magomed, who used to live in our village, and had made his fortune in some shenanigans involving vouchers, and was subsequently shot for it in the years of trouble that followed.

His widow, who had stayed in touch with my mother by phone even after she moved to the city, cherished the dream of bringing me together with her daughter, and especially with her son, a veterinarian. At least that's what I deduced from what my mother said.

"Such a decent, fine young man," she chanted her usual mantras, leading me into the room and digging around in the wardrobe. "A veterinarian…"

The solid-colored pleated dress emerged into the light. It looked terrible on me, and its multitude of agonizingly fine folds brought on a feeling of profound gloom, but Mama had had it made specially by a seamstress she knew, and was mortally insulted when I had showed no interest in her gift. This time I didn't put up a fight and meekly agreed to the dress, and the stupid meeting, anything, just to get to the city. I'd been away long enough that our tedious town infested with cows oppressed my eyes and ears.

On the way to the transit van I ran into a former classmate of mine, Aida. She was standing at her gate wearing a scarf tied like a turban and a bright yellow velour housecoat and holding a metal basin.

"*Vai*, Patya! Welcome! How's everything in Moscow?" she laughed, nearly dropping her basin. "Where are you headed?"

I told her that I was on my way to the city.

"Not engaged yet?"

Of course. What else was there to ask about? Aida already had three kids.

A few years of married life had added some pounds on her, filled her out, and pasted an eternal, contented smile on her face.

"Listen," she lowered her voice into a whisper, "When you get back, be sure to come see me; Amishka's fiancé broke up with her. We need to go try and comfort her."

"What do you mean?" I gasped.

After this news, my upcoming encounter with the veterinarian stuck in my throat like a bone. I could hardly wait to come back and learn all the details of Amishka's misfortune. The whole way to the city I fumed about Mama's enterprise, about Magomedov's children, about my stupid dress.

The Magomedov siblings were waiting for me in the city center, in a new coffee shop. Outside on the street, cars squealed their brakes as they rounded the corners, kicking up dust, honking and blaring loud music. The women selling kvas shouted back and forth with the van drivers, people argued with each other under the coffee shop canopies, workers were up on the rooftops doing some kind of repair work, loiterers clustered in groups on the sidewalks, scrutinizing passersby, and girls, dressed to the nines, teetered by on spike heels.

A wedding salon on every block. European designer boutiques, shops for Islamic wedding fashions, crinolines, trains, smoky-colored shawls, fur boas, exclusive collections... Posters advertising "Matchmaking Halls for Rent," covers of the latest issues of countless wedding magazines on display: advice from a former *tamada,* confessions of newlywed movie stars, advertisements of new beauty salons offering special procedures for brides, silk threads, revitalization, intimate laser depilation. Weddings, weddings, weddings. As though there was nothing else to do. I walked briskly a couple of blocks and ducked into the cool air of a coffee shop.

Magomedov's daughter turned out to be a pleasant-looking, plump chatterbox. Over tea and macaroons she told me all about her tastes, her joys and hobbies. She chirped on and on about her gouache paintings, her crochet hook that had broken the day before, her favorite books, and about her cat, who had caught some horrible disease and lost all its fur. Magomedov's son, the veterinarian, sat glued to his chair the entire time without contributing so much as an interjection. He even kept his silence during the saga of the bald cat, though it would seem to have merited some reaction. He looked quite beyond his youth and, to be completely honest, ugly. His nose looked like an eggplant, and dangled right to his upper lip, and his hands were red and peeling from some unsightly skin disease. The whole time we were talking, he fiddled with his napkin and tore it into pieces. By the end of the conversation the entire tabletop was littered with tiny flakes of paper.

The veterinarian's silence didn't faze his sister in the slightest. You'd think that he didn't exist at all, that at any moment he and his eggplant nose would dissolve into thin air. When he went out for a smoke, the plump girl lowered her eyelids and mumbled under her nose, as though to herself:

"He's nervous. It means he likes you..."

"But he's obviously bored!" I objected loudly.

"What are you talking about?" the plump girl was alarmed. "He's just modest. Not some blowhard from off the street. A working man, wants to start a family. I should have married someone like my brother, but was blind. Couldn't think straight for love."

"I didn't know you were married." Now this was interesting.

"Was," said the plump girl. "I left him. If my papa had been alive when I married that crook, he wouldn't have allowed me to fall into the trap. So let me give you a piece of advice, Patishka: don't fall for some guy with a handsome face."

Her forehead furrowed from the strain. I regretted taking the conversation out into the deep steppe, but Magomedov's daughter went on:

"I dragged him around on my back for three years. Mornings in the store, evenings I'd knit things to order. The one blessing is that we didn't have children. But he spent all his time in the *halal* café jabbering about the *Hadiths*. I nagged him to go out and look for work, but he just snarled at me, like, I can't do *haram* work, I'm like, he goes, studying. But really, what kind of studying is that—cramming religious brochures from morning to night? That's supposed to be work, sitting around arguing about the Prophet's *Sunna*? And all those guys who sat with him in that café blabbing, every last one of them was a real meathead. So one day I go: "*Le*, Yusup, what about how a man is supposed to take care of his wife, and if he doesn't, she has the right to declare a divorce, is there something in your books about that? So he starts screaming and yelling. Fat this, fat that, can you picture it? He goes, dozens of beautiful girls are dreaming of him, but he turns them down, just so as not to veer from the straight and narrow. He goes, like, I don't appreciate him."

"How could he? What does he mean, fat?" Admittedly it was a little hypocritical, but it just slipped out.

No matter how handsome her slacker husband was, it would have been hard to forgive something like that. True, Magomedov's daughter's had plump hands, and her face was round, soft, and oily like a pancake. But there was something doughy, warm, and comfy about her.

"So now he's welcome to spend all the time he wants with scrawny girls, no one will stand in his way. Let him hang on their chicken necks; mine is too pretty and healthy for him. Enough, I've had it, I've done my time dealing with two..."

She would have gone on and on, but the taciturn, long-nosed veterinarian, whose entire body sagged southward, came back to the table after having his smoke, and started in on the napkin again with his red hands. I had a brief fantasy of tipping him over with my hand, toppling him like a chess piece.

It was time to make my escape. I explained that I had to visit some relatives. The veterinarian summoned the waiter and requested the check. His voice sounded dim, as though he'd crawled into a tarred barrel and was broadcasting from inside. Magomedov's daughter suggested we stop in the ladies' room before leaving.

Once in there, she cupped her palms comically around her mouth and whispered into my ear:

"Don't think that just because my brother isn't a talker he won't be able to stand up for you and himself. He's not some run-of-the-mill twerp. Why hang around Moscow courtrooms grubbing for a meager pittance? Come back here, my brother will set you up in his veterinary clinic; they need someone there to deal with the paperwork. You can go to work together, and you can keep an eye on him. Don't get hung up on his looks, OK?"

"We'll see," I murmured, "You can't judge anything at first glance."

"You'll can see him again, spend some time together," Magomedov's daughter pressed on, waved her puffy hands in the air.

I couldn't help myself and blurted out:

"Spend some time together?"

She took offense: "Have it your way." She shrugged and ducked into one of the booths.

In short, a failure. I'd figured it would be.

By the time I got to the van stop, and from there back to the settlement, and knocked at Aida's door, it was already getting dark.

"Just a minute—let me get the baby to sleep," she said, seating me in front of a plate of pilaf.

I sat there eating the pilaf, waiting for her to tuck her third boy into a wooden cradle; she attached a couple of straps to the smooth crossbar, installed a wooden pipe into a special hole between the baby's swaddled-together legs, then inserted her son's little appendage into the pipe so that the urine would flow straight into a pot placed on the floor under the cradle.

The baby frowned, twitched his lips and emitted a muffled bleat. Aida rocked the cradle with her foot, and, signaling me to wait just a little longer, crooned the refrain of the classic lullaby, "*Laillia'a-il-lala-a-a Muhammad-rasulula-a-a-a.*" Five or six iterations of this simple song lulled the baby to sleep. I rinsed my plate, and we set off for Amishka's.

She really was a sight for sore eyes: thin and disheveled, with puffy blue eyelids and no makeup.

"Ami-i-shka," Aida embraced her. "Why are you still upset! You're only eighteen. Look at Patya here. She's turning twenty-six, and isn't even engaged yet."

I nodded. Sure, why shouldn't Amishka take comfort at the sight of an old maid? But she just sobbed bitterly, doubled over and sank to the floor.

"*Ama-a-an,*" moaned Aida.

"How did it happen?" I went straight to the point.

Amishka's fiancé had been a fellow student in the university, in the city. They had met casually in the modern way, gone to the movies, had written each other sappy love notes. He'd gone so far as to introduce her to his parents and extended family, and had shown his face here in our out-of-the-way settlement. I was struck that Amishka's parents had allowed it.

"How did it happen?" blubbered Amishka, lifting her tear-stained face and trembling chin. "The fairy tale came to an end. We dated for a whole year, and now he's got his diploma and decided to propose to some distant cousin of his."

"What about your engagement?"

"We didn't go through that."

"What do you mean, didn't go through that? He visited your family! And his parents knew about you."

"So what? They didn't give their word, we didn't put on rings, didn't pack our suitcases!" howled Amishka.

It was as bad as it could get. I couldn't come up with anything to say and just gazed in silence at the back of Amishka's woeful head.

Meanwhile Aida brought the sufferer a glass of water.

"Enough, time to get over it. To hell with him! Or mama will figure it out. Where is she? At Aunt Zarema's?"

"Yes," sobbed Amishka. Her teeth knocked against the cold rim of the glass. "She knows everything. She says no one will marry me now."

"What do you mean? Leilashka's first fiancé broke with her because she didn't want to take the veil. Didn't matter; someone else came along. And now she's married with two children."

"But she had gone through a formal engagement. And there's

nothing that bad about the veil!"

"What is 'that bad' then?"

"Karim said that I was dishonorable. Told his whole family."

"What did you do to deserve that?" Aida clutched at her head.

"I used to go to his house when no one was home and clean up. One time his aunt caught me there with a broom. She was surprised that there was no one else there. She asked whether my parents knew about it. I told her that Karim had asked me to come over and tidy up. And his aunt says, 'it's not your job to clean up at Karim's; he's nothing to you yet…'"

"She's right," Aida interrupted. "What made you go to his place? It was the aunt that ruined everything."

"No, that's not it; he broke it off himself. He's the one, the two-timing…" cried Amishka.

"Excuse me," I interjected cautiously, "no question he's in the wrong, the worst of the worst, but come on: were you really alone with him in his apartment, wearing a smock and sweeping up, and we're supposed to believe he never even tried to touch you?"

Amishka was silent, wiped her damp face with the hem of her skirt.

Aida joined in. "Maybe you gave him some reason?"

"He said that we would get married in any case," said Amishka without looking at us. "That it made no sense for him to betray me, given that our parents knew about us. That we had an open and honest relationship. That he had never dated anyone so long. He talked about love. He said that they'd tried to get him to marry his cousin twice removed, but he refused, said we were fated to marry. He even let me smoke the hookah. Said that it was milk."

"But…"

"But it turned out to be vodka."

Crushed by what she had said, Amishka got up and limped out of the room. Apparently she'd sat too long on her foot while she was down on the floor, and it had gone to sleep.

"What an idiot!" sighed Aida, her eyes bugging out. "What an idiot!"

My voyeuristic curiosity gave way to an aching compassion. Amishka, whose family had spoiled her from childhood for her blue eyes, pitch-black hair, elegant nose, and graceful walk, had never put on airs, never gossiped or gone behind people's backs. That's why I liked her. Any naïve, pretty girl in her place would have yielded to romantic temptation. This big-city Romeo, Kerim, had come out to the settlement and played everyone for a fool, for a whole year, with his showing off. He would have five hundred fifty-five scarlet roses delivered to Amishka, or would send her a note that he had ordered a song to be dedicated to her on the local TV station. No wonder she lost her head.

I followed the devastated girl into a dark room where she lay face down on the large bed.

"What are we going to do?" I asked uncertainly, in a trembling voice.

Aida strode over to us, tapping her heels hollowly on the floor, and issued a command: "Don't you dare try to keep it secret. If you meet a guy, *inshallah*, tell him the truth."

"I'm not going to meet anyone else," Amishka buried her face into the pillow, and burst out sobbing again.

"What do you mean, won't meet anyone?" thundered Aida—though I'm sure she didn't believe it herself. First of all, you could still get Karim back. Threaten him, pin him to the wall."

"No way! He'll tell everyone!"

"He's going to do that anyway." I couldn't stop myself. "He's already proclaimed it to the rooftops that you've lost your honor."

Aida jabbed me with her elbow, sat down next to Amishka and stroked her on the back:

"Don't be upset, Amishka, it won't help. There are all kinds of guys out there. There are even some here in the settlement who could care less whether you're a virgin or not..."

"You're lying!" Amishka blurted out amid her tears.

"Lying? Take Rusik, who lives across the tracks, the one who takes tango lessons."

"Boo-hoo-hoo!" Amishka just kept bawling.

"Look at her, 'boo-hoo!' Though in this case you're right; they say that Rusik doesn't believe in Allah. But there are others, modern, cool guys. But the main thing is, don't try to keep it a secret."

"Why?" Amishka looked up from the pillow.

"Well, first of all, Karim might go see your new fiancé and blab everything. Or show a tape. Did he take any videos?"

"I don't know." Amishka burst into tears again.

"Well, let's say he didn't take any pictures and won't tell anyone. But then doctors might let it slip."

"What do you mean, doctors?"

"Just listen... One of our relatives in the city found a fiancée for her son. Everything's fine, everyone is happy; a month goes by, and she runs into a gynecologist friend of hers. The friend congratulates her and starts questioning her about the girl, where they found her, what her name is. And it turns out that this fiancée was one of her clients, she'd come in for a hymenoplasty. So this relative goes ballistic, rushes home, grabs the fiancée by the hair and throws her out the door. And she was pregnant, though our relatives refused to recognize the baby because they didn't know whose it was."

"Did her parents take her back?" I asked.

"Of course not! She had to go to Rostov, or to Astrakhan, to start a whole new life."

Amishka lay forlorn and crushed. She'd been her family's favorite; it was hard to imagine her driven out of her comfortable life, without friends or anyone who cared.

"There are some girls," she said quietly, and haltingly, stopping to swallow the lump in her throat, "like that prostitute Angela. They run around, ride in guys' cars with practically nothing on, spend all their time in night clubs, and then, as though nothing happened, they put on a veil and become someone's second or third wife."

"Don't judge veiled women based on Angela's example," Aida frowned.

"That's not the point. It's just that even the worst of them can get lucky. But me, I fell in love, made a mistake. Trusted him…"

I also remembered Angela; she was daughter of a divorced woman who worked as a janitor in the local prison. She was the talk of the town; rumor had it that Khalilbek himself had seduced Angela back in her youth. After that, she passed from one man to another, evidently feeling no shame for her behavior. I had seen her cruising down the muddy Avenue in the back seat of a car full of carousing young men, howling with laughter, or coming back from the city on the main road, for some reason on foot, in a short skirt, smiling alluringly at all the guys she passed, under a chorus of catcalls.

"What, did Angela take the veil?" I couldn't help asking.

"She did," blubbered Amishka. "And some big shot crook took her as his second wife, he comes out to visit her sometimes."

"Impossible!" My thoughts were all jumbled up. "Maybe you should take the veil too?"

"Patya!" Aida was angry. "*Astauperulla*, what are you talking about? If Amishka covers, it's not because that slut Angela did it."

I heard a shrieking sound, and shuddered. Amishka was laughing hysterically, snorting and beating her hands and feet on the bed. She was trying to say something, but we couldn't understand a word. Aida ran out again and brought some water.

The poor girl calmed down for a second, but then burst into tears again.

"What are you blubbering about? Stop howling and tell us. I have to get back to the baby," Aida chided her.

Amishka buried her face in the pillow again, "It's just that I think I'll have to be part of a hard sell, forced on men as a bonus. Or, like Sidratka, remember her?"

"What Sidratka?"

"What, you don't remember her? They lived at the station. Her elder sister was gorgeous, but Sidratka was cross-eyed, scrawny and hideous to look at. Though basically a nice person."

"And?"

"And so these matchmakers come from Khasaviurt, they're after the elder sister—the pretty one. But on the day of the wedding the bride's mother switched her out for Sidratka, because no one would have taken her otherwise. She was under the bridal veil, and so they didn't notice anything."

"So then what? Did they send her back?"

"No, they left her in Khasaviurt. The mother-in-law taunted her for five years, until she gave her a grandson. She was a kind person, and ultimately they got used to her, came to love her. And now supposedly her husband treats her like a queen."

"So you see," I smiled, "a happy ending."

"And in general," Aida turned serious, "some people have real problems, Allah forbid. Compared with them yours isn't worth shedding a single tear over."

"Easy for you to say, Aida. And meanwhile my life is ruined."

"Stop it, Amishka; remember Zaripat?"

Of course I thought of Zaripat. In the past, she had been a singer, well known in the settlement, and not least for her unrestrained behavior. Zaripat had been known to stay out late in the city, in a restaurant, and to leave in a car with an admirer, but she had a real talent and people appreciated it. A few years ago, this singer had married an observant Muslim man who wouldn't let her sing, perform, or even listen to music. She gave up wearing low-necked dresses and wore only shapeless garments, and started having children, one after another. And became completely domesticated.

"Haven't you heard?" Aida interjected. "Zaripat was diagnosed with cancer and now she's in the hospital, at death's door."

"What about her husband?"

"He's in prison now; after you left he was arrested for extremism."

"Oh, right, my mother told me about it."

"So anyway, he's in prison now, and she's on her deathbed. Think of the children, *ama-a-an*. But that's not all. Can you imagine what she did? Just a couple of days ago...the whole settlement is talking about it."

"How could she do anything?"

"She invited her brother to come see her; he's a musician too, he performs in the city, you know him."

"Of course I do."

"Her husband had forbidden Zaripat to have any contact with him. So anyway, the brother comes to see her in the hospital, and she whispers to him, 'I know I'm dying, grant me one last wish.'"

"What was the wish?"

"She wanted to sing! So her brother brings instruments and recording equipment to the hospital room, and sets everything up right there, and sure enough, Zaripat starts to sing! I don't have the recording, but Maga played it for me. I'll Bluetooth you the file. Patya-a-a, if you only could hear her sing! Better than when she was healthy! It's hard to believe she's at death's door. It's like Allah sent strength to her lungs, I'm telling you!"

The door slammed. Amishka's mama was home.

"I'll pretend I'm asleep," said our friend anxiously, wiping the salty moisture from her face and turning to face the wall, "or mama will know I've been crying again."

We comforted her one last time and left her to lie there motionless. Aida and I lingered at the gate, sighing and clucking. We sighed over Zaripat's sudden illumination.

We tried without success to remember ugly Sidratka. It's possible that Amishka had thought her up or had mixed her up with someone else.

"Well, Allah grant everything works out okay for her, she's such a fool." Aida sent up yet another prayer to Allah. "You too, Patya, come on, get married. I'm raising my third child already, and here you are... You won't find anyone in Moscow, they wasted a whole year sending you there. So, tell me: which of our local guys might appeal to you?"

"I don't know," I murmured. "This guy Timur is writing me, he says he's from here, but I don't remember him."

"Timur who?" Aida perked up.

"He's an activist. He's in some kind of political group or association."

"A-a-a," Aida nodded her turban. "I know him. He's quite the speaker, gets all fired up. There's going to be a meeting in the club in a couple of days. That's it, Patulya; get yourself dressed up and go to the meeting, absolutely. Not in that dress, though. Find something pretty, how about your blue one with the sparkles? And if the baby goes to sleep, I'll stop in too, to have a look at you and him."

She winked. I already regretted saying anything. Now she'd start jabbering, would tell everyone in the neighborhood about it. And this Timur could very well turn out to be some windbag. But I decided to go to the meeting anyway, even without Aida's pep talk. If for nothing more than to have something to do.

We said goodbye, and when I got home my mother met me with predictable excitement:

"Where were you? Did you go to Aida's? Magomedov's wife already called me and told me that you made a real impression on her kids, and that her son really likes you!"

"Mama, he didn't say a word the whole time," I brushed her aside.

"Again! Picky, picky. Nothing but a prince will do!" Mama was mad. "Soon even the old men won't look at you! And in three or four years you'll be barren, like Lyusya!"

"What's that all about?"

But Mama just waved her hand melodramatically in the air and disappeared into the back room. Where the yellow-paged mystery novels awaited her. I took a few moments to think, then went to find Papa or Granny. They were hiding somewhere, like snails, within the plaster-spackled walls of the house.

4. OUT VISITING

The Shakhovs lived in a whitewashed six-story apartment building on the central city square, nestled behind a disorderly clutter of shacks and garages. Under a pitted acacia tree, whose branches occasionally dropped little pods rattling with seeds onto the ground, children in bright-colored T-shirts were playing Nine Stones. They had chalked a square on the asphalt, had divided it into parts—as for Tic-Tac-Toe—and were raucously erecting a little tower out of pebbles in the center square. As he walked past the cluster of little players squatting on their haunches, Marat tried to recall the rules, but he could only remember shreds: Rusik-the-Nail is standing by the rubble of a toppled tower aiming a ball at Marat, and Marat is hastily trying to set out the stones in each sector before his opponent can "tag" him.

Marat and his mother proceeded up a set of neat, gently rising steps through the entryway. Some of the doors had old-fashioned labels nailed to them: PROF. OMAROV G.G., ENGINEER ISAEV M.A.... Marat's mother, who had put on a long, openwork shawl for the somber occasion—they were calling on the Shakhovs, as they had agreed, to convey their condolences upon the death of their uncle—followed him up the stairs, clutching onto the railings and voicing a never-ending litany of instructions:

"Remember, the girl's name is Sabrina, don't get it mixed up."

The door opened and Shakhov's wife, a withered woman with short hair, appeared. She assessed Marat quickly with her sharp eyes and nodded a greeting, then kissed his mother, who was whispering words of sympathy, and indicated a couple pairs of slippers for them to put on. The walls of the small entryway were lined with wooden shelves, laden with medical reference books; above them hung some black-and-white photographs. From one of them a large bearded man wearing a hat and a natty suit with a boutonniere frowned suspiciously out at Marat. This was Shakhov's late father, a musical theater director, folk song collector, Don Juan, and great carnivore.

He had gone on numerous expeditions in quest of unknown melodies, traveling far and wide with phonograph cylinders, audio recording devices, sheaves of notebooks, and bundles of dried mountain sausage. Every day, rumor had it, Shakhov Senior would eat an entire ram's head, and after a successful premiere he would also down a hefty serving of boiled tripe, which they would prepare for him in a special kitchenette installed in the theater for that purpose. Shakhov Junior vehemently denied these tall tales and claimed that throughout his life his father had suffered from gastritis and that there was no way he could have digested that many rams' heads, even if he had wanted to.

"And plus, how could we have gotten hold of so many sheep? We didn't have that kind of money anyway!"

It was hard to say whether he was telling the truth. Shakhov had worked at one time in the military industry and had retired with medals for some top-secret heroism; all he could do was talk about the former privileges he'd had and lost. The moment he sat down with Marat at the sparsely set table, he started in complaining about the workers at the torpedo factory who had dismantled and sold everything down to the last bolt.

"Asses! Embezzlers!" he wailed, rolling his eyes. "Traitors to the motherland!"

"You're just asking for trouble, talking like that!" His dried-up wife shrugged wearily as she trudged back and forth from threshold to table.

Marat's mother would go along with anything. She added fuel to the fire:

"You're so right, they're just plain criminals! That's what I tell Aselder all the time. He really wanted to come to see you, but there's some kind of bedlam going on in the Institute over that damned Khalilbek."

"Khalilbek? So you think he's guilty too?"

"Absolutely, completely guilty of everything. You don't think so?" Marat's mother was getting worked up.

"What about you?" Shakhov addressed Marat.

"No, I don't. The case is too complicated, and the prosecution has its facts wrong. It's mostly rumors, malicious gossip."

"You're so right, let me shake your hand!" Shakhov squeezed Marat's palm tightly. "Don't let those women convict the man prematurely!"

"Where's Sabrinochka?" Marat's mother changed the subject.

"She's here, Khadizha," Shakhov's wife responded from the kitchen. "She's in her room studying. Probably didn't hear you come in. Sabrina! Sabrina!"

"Enough! Stop calling her," muttered Shakhov. "She's not a princess, she ought to understand that we have guests."

The living room also had an array of dark photographs on the walls. Again the theater director, this time in jodhpurs and riding boots, with a silver belt around his ample waist. He stood proudly against a background of seven or eight smiling, tambourine-bearing chorus girls in bright-colored, floor-length scarves.

Next to that one hung a portrait of Shakhov's deceased uncle, captured in his younger years astride a muscular black mare.

He was a passionate equestrian, an expert on Akhal-Tekes—tall, hardy, long-legged horses with no manes. At the time of the photo, his career had just started to take off, but then everything came crashing down because of one careless phrase.

Shakhov's uncle had been twenty; he was with some friends from the stud farms who were descendants of herdsmen from the Atly-Boyun Pass. They had taken the horses to the seashore for a therapeutic dip in the surf. While some guys held the horses, others swam naked, laughing and roughhousing. Uncle nodded downward at his male pride, leered, and blurted out:

"Stands there erect like Stalin on the tribune!"

The joke cost Uncle Shakhov ten years in the camps. Construction of the Igarka-Salekhard Railway, frostbite, exhaustion…But he stubbornly returned to life and made it to advanced old age, until, covered with wrinkles, childless, and rail thin—you could count his ribs—he finally died in his sleep from a heart attack. Next to his stout elder brother, the theater director, he had looked like a candle-wick.

Long-browed Sabrina entered the room reluctantly, with an air of forced civility. Shakhov's wife was serving turkey with mashed potatoes and fresh vegetables. Everyone sat around the table, and Shakhov resumed his rant:

"I arrive at the plant, and everything is in a state of neglect. No one there to meet me and show me around. I used to kick open the director's door with my knee. I had a company car, a Volga with a special banner. Whenever the chauffeur would be stopped for speeding, they'd see my officer's stripes and immediately salute me, 'Oh, excuse me sir, have a good trip.' So what do I care about our local nobodies if I've got generals in Moscow bowing down to me? You, Marat, sit up there in your offices and have no idea who is who. By the way, what's the latest on that big case—the murder of the human rights activist? She must have been poking her nose in the wrong places and gotten into some deep shit. Tell me, is the suspect guilty?"

"No."

"Well you're a lawyer, you have to say that. But tell me straight."

"It's really complicated. There are a lot of details. All I can say is that it's going to be tough for the defense, because the masterminds are way up high."

"Well with us it's always like that, shift the blame onto someone else. Let the higher-ups take the rap, right? That's your logic. Same thing with Khalilbek. They've tried to pin everything they can on him. By the way, he and I were practically friends. Him, me, Ivan Petrovich Borisov…A couple of years ago the three of us got in a motorboat and took off full speed out into the open sea to take a look at the eighth shop."

Marat recalled the eighth shop of the defense plant: decrepit with age, it towered over the sea three kilometers from the shore, where it stood atop a gigantic reinforced concrete box filled with water, looking just like a great stone duck. In the shop's heyday, they used to test the torpedoes by releasing them from the shop's bowels into the depths of the Caspian. And during storms the workers would come up to the surface in freight elevators and take shelter in rooms on the upper level.

Indeed, from a distance the monster facility's watch tower, which now served as a perch for raucous cormorants, looked a lot like a duck's beak poking up out of the water. When he was a boy and had seen it from the shore, Marat had imagined that the duck was about to bend over and peck at the horizon, right at the point where the sea met the sky. The shop had been abandoned after World War II, but Shakhov claimed that until very recently you could still see polished parquet floors, and even the remnants of furniture, in the facility's cafeteria and the library.

Marat's mother tried to engage Shakhov's wife and Sabrina in conversation. Sabrina sat stiffly, with a grim expression on her face. To judge from the shreds of conversation that Marat was able to catch, they were talking about Uncle Shakhov's memorial banquet. Marat's mother prattled:

"Well, what are guests usually given when they come to pay their respects? Sugar and towels, right? Three kilograms each of sugar and towels. But when you're grieving, when there's a tragedy, of course it can be hard to find them for a good price. So I bought some for myself in advance."

"How could you, Khadizha!"

"What's wrong with it? No one knows when we're going to die. Here today, gone tomorrow. And Aselder is hopeless when it comes to managing things, he'd buy the wrong gifts, he wouldn't know how to make arrangements, and he'd bring shame down upon the whole family. He had a son on the side; why bother trying to hide it? Everyone knows. He was a good boy, Adik, lived next door to us. He was walking one night down the road, and along comes our superman Khalilbek in a jeep. Ran over him, killed him."

"That's horrible, horrible!" moaned Shakhov's wife.

"Killed him. And a cop got his house. Adik's wife secretly sold it to a particularly pushy one, on the sly. And then off she goes, before you could blink an eye, to the mountain pasturelands. With both kids. Aselder wasn't paying attention, and he missed his chance to prevent it. anyway, I bought a couple of sacks of men's socks just in case, to have them to give guests at my funeral. Towels, too, sets of three. You know: one for your face, one for your hands, and the third for you know where."

Mother glanced briefly down at her belly. Sabrina blushed and turned away in disgust.

"What, you think you had a claim on the boy's house?" Shakhov's wife asked primly.

"What are you talking about? That colonel from the Sixth Department started renovating it immediately. We've already forgotten about it."

Shakhov, who was enumerating his awards and honors to Marat as he ate, overheard this last sentence and perked up.

"Hey, was that the same colonel from your town who climbed in through the window to that woman who was a terrorist?"

"What are you talking about, Papa? She was just a woman in a niqab," Sabrina corrected him.

"There's no such thing as 'just' a girl in a niqab around here." Shakhov struck the table with his fist. "They are all future terrorists. Especially that one. A black widow. She's already had two husbands killed in the woods."

"Wait, the colonel climbed in the window to see a black widow? But why?" Marat looked up from his plate.

"Well, we don't know for sure whether he did or not. It's just something people are blabbing about."

"He did, Papa, you know he did," Sabrina interjected. "He hauled her out to be interrogated, She was in there with her children and girlfriends...He dragged her out, took her to the police department, and there…"

Sabrina broke off.

"Raped her," Shakhov's wife finished the sentence.

"Oi, oi, oi," Shakhov whirled around on his chair. "So now we have human rights activists getting in on the act. Anyway, it has yet to be proven whether he raped her or not. And even if he did, maybe she led him on, to create a scandal. These widows of the forest militants are worse than streetwalkers, they'll throw themselves at anyone and everyone."

"Papa!" Sabrina frowned.

"What? Everyone is moaning and groaning about police brutality. Meanwhile, our boys in the police are dying heroic deaths to protect us from these criminals in niqabs. It's all an act. The bearded guys are only pretending to be peaceful Muslims, pure as the driven snow, but look at them! All they can do is loiter around the mosques and complain about the government: '*Taghut, taghut, taghut…*'"

"What if there's good reason for it?" Sabrina was still upset.

"They can always dream up some reason. Like they're being kidnapped. Or beaten up. Attacked with grenades. Tortured without cause—with no basis whatsoever, just for observing Sharia law. Don't make me laugh, please."

"You're a lawyer, right?" Suddenly, Sabrina addressed Marat. "So why are you sitting up there in Moscow making money on those high-profile cases, instead of defending the violated rights of your fellow Muslims in your own home town?"

"Muslims?"

"The police here beat up people who go to oppositional mosques. It's happening everywhere in the district. But it's especially bad in your suburb."

"The mosque 'across the tracks' is Wahhabi," Marat parried weakly; the attack had come out of nowhere.

"What do you mean, Wahhabi? That's just a word in the news. It's obvious you live in Moscow. They're not Wahhabis, they're truth-seekers. The real bandits are in the government offices. Do you think a single one of them is going to end up in prison? I hope they keep this Khalilbek locked up forever!"

"Sabrina," Shakhov's wife tried to calm her daughter down.

"By the way, Khalilbek was helping those truth-seekers of yours. He even gave them money for their mosque," Marat added, with a note of sarcasm.

"He was playing both sides, yours and ours, he's a real double-dealer." Sabrina was unfazed.

"What are you on about, you pip-squeak?" Shakhov suddenly tuned in to the conversation.

"Well, youngsters often go astray," jabbered Marat's mother, obviously trying to clear the air. "I totally agree about Khalilbek, he's a sly one. He set up a lottery scam in town, can you imagine? And he wouldn't let Aselder, who was his associate at one point, sell some really valuable stocks. Others made a killing, and here we are living on nothing."

"Mama!" Marat flared up. "Khalilbek is accused of serial murders, of large-scale corruption, and you're on and on about stocks and casinos!"

Shakhov sprang up from his chair and started pacing back and forth.

"We raised our daughter, gave her everything she needed, and she sits right here in this room and declares that these idiots in niqabs are right, and her father, who has thirty medals on his chest—real, legitimate ones, by the way—is wrong!"

"Don't get worked up, sit down, let's have some tea and pie." Shakhov's wife was the voice of calm.

"Don't interrupt!" sputtered Shakhov. "Just tell me, Sabrina, what is the point? Who is going to put an end to all this?"

"Justice will triumph, I should hope," answered Sabrina, with dignity.

"No, Khalilbek will dot the 'i'! He always used to tell me, "It all comes down to a point, comrade Shakhov, that single point where it all ends."

"Bullshit," Sabrina muttered under her breath.

"There you have it!" Shakhov pointed his finger triumphantly at his daughter. "Feast your eyes, Marat. Her father is talking sense, and she just sits there muttering to herself! And she has turned down every single suitor who comes her way!"

"Oh, I'm sure a beautiful girl like her has no end of suitors," interjected Marat's mother.

"She'll soon be too old and they'll stop coming. And then she can put on her niqab and go off into the forest to her friends, where she'll find a husband in no time. Or two or three!" Shakhov was in a fury.

"*Astauperulla*," Marat's mother said, alarmed.

"What are you saying?" Shakhov's wife flipped her short mane and went out to the kitchen to get the pie. Marat's mother stood up, smoothed her skirt with her thick palms, and followed her.

Marat got up as though to stretch his legs, and strolled along the wall, inspecting the framed award certificates.

"Are they yours, from school?" he asked Sabrina.

She didn't answer.

"You're being spoken to," Shakhov said to his daughter.

"Can't you tell they're mine?" Sabrina hissed, without looking at anyone. "I've taken them down from the wall a hundred times, and Mama just hangs them up again. What is she after? Next thing you know, she'll post my term papers up there for people to gawk at."

"Just look at her, Marat!" Shakhov turned beet red. "Can you believe what she's saying? *Yo*, your mother is proud of you, that's why she put them up on the walls. We got you into the top school, hired tutors, helped with university, and set you up with an internship. Could I even have dreamed of such a life? I worked from the age of twelve!"

"You've used that on me enough, Papa!"

"Before my father got his job in the theater, we lived in the middle of nowhere, in a village. In the morning, I worked on the collective farm, in the afternoon at school, and at night in the garden and my workshop. My uncle was in prison, times were hard, and my father wasn't accepted into the Party."

"Enough already! I've heard it all a thousand times!"

"Your mother spoiled you rotten!"

"Why are you criticizing her again?" snapped Shakhov's wife, bringing in the pie. Marat's mother minced in after her, bearing a tray with teacups.

"Here's why," Shakhov went on in a rage. "Your daughter isn't serving tea to our guests. There she sits, talking back to her father. Khadizha, sit down. Let Sabrina serve the tea."

"Oh, it's no trouble, goodness. I'll do it!" clucked Marat's mother. "Sabrinochka's time will come for serving and table-setting. When she gets married she'll be the one putting on feasts."

"Don't make me laugh! Her husband will throw her out of the house the day after the wedding!"

"What are you saying?" Shakhov's wife finally lost her patience. "Shaming your own daughter in front of guests! Retirement has completely pickled your brain!"

Marat was desperate to leave; he could hardly hold himself back.

"What a delicious pie! What's the filling—apricots and nuts? Did Sabrina make it?" Marat's mother oohed and aahed over the desert, digging in.

"I can't cook," Sabrina declared insolently. "Mama went and bought it at the bakery."

An awkward pause set in; everyone squeaked their chairs and clinked their teaspoons. The pie was indeed fresh and delicious, just as good as homemade.

"My mother used to make pies," Shakhov began, but there came the sound of the front door closing in the entryway, and Shakh's voice was heard. Shakh was Shakhov's nephew and Marat's childhood friend from town.

"Why do you leave your door open?" asked Shakh gaily, approaching the table and shaking the men's hands. "No, no! I won't eat anything, I'll just sit and have some tea with you."

Shakhov's wife scowled in Sabrina's direction, and Sabrina went to get another glass.

"So you and Shakh are colleagues?" Shakhov nodded to Marat.

"Yes, we were in school together," Marat confirmed.

Rowdy Shakh, with his broad shoulders and rippling muscles, had always seemed too boisterous for Marat. When he was a student, he'd been a mover and shaker who had managed to study, earn money on the side, spend his evenings at discotheques, go to youth festivals, ruin girls' reputations, win amateur boxing matches, and drag everyone around him into his endless escapades. He was like a wind-up toy, never slowing down.

"What's the latest news about Khalilbek?" Shakhov turned the conversation back on track.

"Everyone's asking about it," Shakh took up the theme. "But no one can understand a thing. Not even the investigators."

"Who's doing the investigation, the locals?"

"No, people from Rostov. Anyway, at this point Khalilbek has only been officially charged with one crime: the murder of the investigator. And even that's pretty flimsy."

"I knew it," Shakhov said, with relief. "They can't take him with their bare hands!"

"The problem is, there's a long chain of intermediaries. Khalilbek supposedly handed the investigator job over to this guy he knew, Akula the Shark, and Akula gave it to someone else, who then passed it on, and this went on for eight rounds. And the eighth guy roped in his cousin once removed. They caught and interrogated the cousin, but now they have to comb through all the intermediaries and work back up the chain. By the time they get back to Khalilbek, the whole case will probably have collapsed."

"Wow, just imagine..."

Sabrina brought in the cup with trembling hands. She set it down in front of Shakh, proudly raised her elegant chin and announced:

"Pleasure to see you all. Unfortunately, I have to study. Goodbye."

"What do you mean, 'goodbye?' When the guests leave, that's when you say your 'goodbye!'" snapped Shakhov.

"Of course, Sabrinochka, you go study, dear. Let me give you a kiss."

Marat's mother kissed Sabrina, who turned and sailed forth.

Shakh cast a sly glance at Marat.

"You'll have to excuse her. She has a very tough schedule. She is up late practically every night with cardiology," Shakhov's wife said.

"So she's in cardiology, just like you!" Marat's mother exclaimed.

"Yes, my wife is a renowned cardiologist. She's even treated Khalil-bek—though she missed her own husband's heart attack," seethed Shakhov.

"You never had a heart attack," his wife retorted coldly.

"What do you mean? I was at death's door!"

"He doesn't get enough attention," commented Shakhov's wife under her breath.

Before long, Marat and his mother were putting their shoes on in the entryway. The openwork shawl had come undone and its ends grazed the hardwood floor. As they saw their guests out, Shakhov kept up his monologue and his wife maintained a dignified silence. Shakh volunteered to drop Marat's mother off at the department store and to take Marat home. After Marat's mother got out and they pulled away from the store, the two friends were finally alone. Shakh burst out laughing:

"What made you think, Marat, that my cousin would be right for you? She's a real dragon. Don't you remember that time she came out to see me?"

Marat did remember. Sabrina had come just once. They were about nine years old. The girls had a tea party for their dolls in Shakh's shed, making sand cutlets and soup out of water and soggy bread crumbs. Little Sabrina spent the whole time whining and complaining. Nothing satisfied her. She needed to switch the dolls, she refused to be the guest, and insisted on being the hostess. Then the boys raided the party like a plague of locusts, knocking the neatly groomed and dressed dolls from their chairs, tipping the table over, sending the refreshments flying, and made off with the soup, the only thing that was edible. Marat seemed to recall that Rusik-the-Nail had been with them. Shakh assured him that he hadn't been:

"You're mixing him up with Abdullaev."

"Really? Maybe so. How's Abdullaev these days?"

"He's got his engagement party in a few days. You're going, too. Aunt Khadizha said so."

"Oh yes, I remember. Yes, I am."

"He's so gullible, I could make him believe anything, all kinds of weird stories that I'd heard in court. Though who knows, maybe they were true. Anything can happen."

"For example?"

"Filthy stuff, you wouldn't like it."

"I expect nothing less from you, Shakh."

"All right, then, here's one. My colleagues told me about a security guard who raped a woman, a janitor in a village school. Or rather, she said that he had raped her, but the guard claimed that she consented."

"That's the second time today this topic has come up," Marat smirked.

"Anyway, this janitor stands by her story. Says she screamed and tried to get away. They decide to check it out. The teachers would have heard her if she really had made a fuss. They conducted an experiment..." Shakh chortled.

"What's so funny?"

"Picture this: They set up everything the way it was on that day, and had them act the whole thing out. And the defendant up and raped her again."

"What the...?"

"I kid you not! They fired the prosecutor for it."

"Are all your fables below the belt?"

"*Le*, don't play naïve. There was one more story. This one supposedly took place in the city, in the police detective's office. Also a rape."

"Shakh!"

"Who does a better job of entertaining you than I do, Marat? So anyway, this one involves a carrot. It was material evidence, and was on a shelf in the investigator's office. This co-worker comes in, and he's hungry."

"Don't tell me he..."

"Eats the carrot!"

Shakh brayed again. They drove past construction sites, canopied kiosks, and highway patrol posts, barricaded on all sides with sandbags. Drowsy soldiers holding automatic weapons peered out from behind the sandbags.

"So who is Abdullaev going to marry?" Marat leaned back in his seat.

"A regular girl. I myself helped investigate, checked up on her past. Everything nice and clean. Though Abdullaev has gotten himself in some deep shit. There's a girl on the side, and she's about to have a baby."

"What?!"

"He's a jackass. When we were in graduate school, he kept wanting to copy me, envying my success with the ladies. And he would spend his entire stipend on this one prostitute once a month, because that was the only way he could get laid." Shakh again bared his strong white teeth.

"I knew about that," Marat said. "I used to get on his case about it."

"Know what else he used to do?" Shakh was on a roll. "He'd buy some Viagra in the drug store, gulp it down. Then he'd go to the sauna, to the prostitute. The point was, he could plow her several times in a row and save money that way."

Marat couldn't stop himself, and joined his friend's laughter. Abdullaev really was an idiot.

"What about the girl he got pregnant? Did he buy her off?"

"It's the prostitute, duh! And she's threatened to come to the matchmaking ceremony with her brothers and ruin everything."

"Does the bride know about it?"

"Not yet, but she will soon." Shakh smacked his lips and fell silent. Then he added: "And what's up with you—have you decided to join my family?"

"It's my mother's idea. But it sure doesn't seem like I made a good impression on your cousin."

"Come on, level with me. It's you—you don't want to marry a dragon!" Shakh took his hand off the wheel and clapped Marat on the knee.

They drove on toward the suburb. There wasn't much traffic, and, judging from the undulating steppe grass and the dust devils up ahead, the wind had picked up. Soon the friends passed a gray, two-story barracks, which used to house the public baths. One time long ago, when they were kids, they had piled some bricks up against the bathhouse walls, forming a rickety tower, and had clambered up to the top. Teetering on tiptoe, they had peered in though the tall, steamed-up window of the women's bath.

It was Shakh, of course, who had come up with the plan. He came running to his friends with his eyes bugging out, and blabbed that he'd seen their math teacher naked, covered with lather. The teacher was a wheezy, big-breasted widow who pronounced her "g's soft, like an "h," in the southern way. Everyone wanted to have a look.

They cast lots. Marat's turn came last. He waited until the others, giggling quietly into their sleeves, had satisfied their curiosity. Though it was highly dubious that they had actually been able to see anything through the fogged-up windowpane. Most likely they'd just pretended, to impress one another.

Marat was unable to verify this in person, though, since Rusik, who had already positioned himself with his left eye up against the glass, to the tune of suppressed snickers and queries from his co-conspirators from below, suddenly lost his balance. The clumsily piled-up bricks gave way in all directions, and the luckless peeping Tom clattered to the ground.

"Who's out there?" the guard hollered. Abdullaev hissed, "*Atas! atas!*" and the boys took off running, abandoning Rusik, who was flailing around in the brick pile. Marat later tried to convince himself that if he'd known Rusik couldn't get up he never would have run off after the others. But his conscience refused to believe it and nagged at him: "Traitor! Traitor!"

As it turned out, Rusik had broken his foot in the fall. The guard who caught him at the scene of the crime told his parents and the school director what had happened. Rusik was locked up at home with his ankle in a cast and nothing but books for company, and was forbidden to show his face outside. They said that his father had flogged him on his bare back with a rubber hose. Still, at the first sign of weakness from his keepers, Rusik hobbled out on crutches to join his friends in soccer and "hunters and ducks," and never uttered a word of reproach.

"Listen," Shakh suddenly recalled. "There's something going on tomorrow—a gathering at the club."

"What club?"

"Ours, the one in town, in the auditorium. They're even going to have a concert—in honor of Khalilbek."

"His supporters?"

"Anyone who wants to get on his good side, just in case. The people think that Khalilbek is going to be released, and they need to show their loyalty. Shall we go have a look?"

"Sure!" Marat agreed.

Shakh dropped Marat off at his house and they parted in good spirits. Shakh rushed off in his Audi to prepare some appeals, and Marat checked his computer to see if there was any news from his Moscow colleagues about their big case.

In the evening, Marat's parents were home. His father sat amid a pile of manuscripts, and his mother stood on the veranda venting about their visit to the Shakhovs.

"Sloppy, lazy, stuck-up, just sponging off her father and mother, no use to anyone. That's what she is, that scrawny Shakhov girl! What good is a diploma if she can't serve tea?"

"I get it, Khadizha, I get it," Marat's father said, without looking at his wife.

"And did you hear her defending those veiled women! Did you, Marat?! Before you know it, she'll take the veil, and the Shakhovs won't be able to do a thing about it. They've let her slip through their fingers. Dust on their shelves an inch thick! I checked with my finger."

"Didn't you have anything better to do?"

"Quiet, Aselder, you weren't there! You would have been horrified too! And her mama, her mama..."

"What?"

"Makes herself out to be the Minister of Health. So what if she treated Khalilbek's heart? I bet she pocketed at least a grand from him."

"If you don't know something, then don't say it, Khadizha. Why aren't you saying anything, Marat?" His father looked up from his scrawled pages.

"What can I say?" Marat gave an indifferent grin. "You're the one who kept praising this Sabrina, Mama. So now just cross her off the list."

"You're glad, aren't you?" She was alarmed.

"What do you mean, 'glad'? But I'm getting the feeling that there's not going to be anyone for me come August 13."

"Oh, we'll find someone, you can be sure of that!" his mother said confidently. "We'll go to the Abdullaevs' engagement party, you can have a look around there."

Marat got up, went out onto the porch and strode onto the street, clattering the gate shut behind him. The wind blew a little cloud of sand into his face. The air was dry and stuffy, crickets sang, and dogs called out hoarsely to one another.

A man came walking down the empty, dark street, greeted Marat quietly—"*Salam alaikum*"—shook his hand and continued on his way. Marat passed the house where Adik had lived—it was deserted and silent. Obviously the police colonel wasn't home, the one who had taken possession of the house, who had beaten Mukhtar's son Alishka, and who had crept in the window of the *Salafi* woman in the niqab.

Marat suddenly recalled that no one had mentioned whether this malevolent officer of the law had a family. Most likely he did, but they probably lived somewhere in the city.

The street stretched on monotonously, lined on both sides by gated fences until it dead-ended into a scrap heap, with the broad steppe behind it. Elevated gas pipelines ran to the suburbs, and beyond them the wetlands stretched on with their tangles of wild sedge. The red lights of the prison towers flickered in the distance. There, within its walls, Khalilbek languished, and the janitor, wanton Angela's mother, swished her mop along its tiled floors.

Marat continued down the deserted street toward the prison, his mind a chaos of thoughts—Sabrina's petulant little nose, Shakhov's anger, and all the work that awaited him in Moscow. His leave was short, and his mother's fantastical enterprise was careening toward its inevitable failure. He was sure that no bride would be found, and that the banquet hall that had been reserved for the thirteenth would, on the thirteenth, be empty. He felt sorry for his parents, and at the same time found the whole thing hilarious. He kept walking through the sleeping town, coughing, or, maybe, laughing.

5. A CONCERT TO REMEMBER

Next morning, after cleaning the house, I put on my blue dress with the sparkles, the one Aida had suggested, and sat staring in dumb despair at my double in the mirror. My hair had grown down to my protruding collarbones; thick and disorderly, it poked out every which way like a windblown haystack, making my face look broad and flat. I could have rushed over to the neighbor's and mooched her curling iron, but Timur was already waiting outside the school where we'd agreed to meet. On the phone he'd tried to get me to let him pick me up at my house. That was a little scary, and I made excuses. Timur pressured me:

"I need to know where you live, you know, so I can meet your father."

"Why?" I winced.

"What do you mean, why? To ask for your hand in marriage."

I shuddered; maybe it wasn't a joke. Ultimately we had settled on the school, which was closed for summer vacation. Meanwhile, something had to be done about my hair. I resorted to a trick I'd learned back in high school, when the junior and senior girls used to let their hair down and set it without their family knowing.

I plugged an ordinary clothes iron into the wall socket, knelt down, and spread my mane on the ironing board. Then I placed the hot iron on top of it and started tugging the hair out from underneath. Good thing no one caught me at this ridiculous operation. After five minutes of this, my curls straightened out and fell neatly, as though I'd just been at the beauty parlor.

I hurried to the school on high heels that sank into the ground. Timur greeted me at the gate: "You look nice."

Oh no-o-o-o... He looked completely different from what I had pictured from his photos. Timur's hair was blond and coarse, and stuck up like a hedgehog's; his mouth had no lips to speak of, and above his wrinkled, sun-darkened brow his temples showed telltale signs of male pattern baldness. He was built low to the ground like a wrestler and his biceps swelled under the sleeves of his jacket—which he wore in spite of the heat—like thick sausages with the filling about to burst out of their skins. We started walking along the fence, and next to him I felt ungainly and as skinny as a beanpole. The wind gusted, billowing the hem of my dress, and out of the corner of my eye I noticed Timur periodically sneaking glances at my exposed knees.

All my former expectations and hopes congealed into a hard lump, which leapt up inside me, squealing: "Make a run for it! Run, now!"

But I couldn't give him the slip so soon, and just fumed at myself for agreeing to go out in town with this burly stranger, right under the noses of my friends and family. Along the way, I tried to come up with a plausible story in case someone noticed the two of us out here by ourselves—looking like a couple—and would torment me with nasty conjectures. For his part, Timur didn't seem the least bit concerned, quite the opposite—he was downright cocky and fully in control; he treated me as though I were his girlfriend, not a mere acquaintance. He asked about my parents and grandmother, told me about his family—his sister was a college student, his parents were building a two-story house near the mosque—and veered off into blatant self-promotion:

"So I inspire the youth, like, to public service, you know. I organized, like, a cell. We meet and everything, we discuss the region's pathways for spiritual and financial development, and, like, in the energy sector."

Back when we were communicating on the Internet, he had written to me about his zeal for public service and activism; oddly enough, that's what had appealed to me. And his face on those fuzzy cell-phone photos had looked smarter, somehow, like that of a man of significance and promise. I had envisioned an encounter with a "thinking reed," a visionary, transformative hero. But in real life Timur turned out to be a run-of-the-mill loudmouth, spewing vapid clichés. With unsightly, overdeveloped biceps, to boot.

We turned onto the Avenue, where a fair number of people were out walking. Everyone was headed for the club, to the free concert in support of Khalilbek. I was relieved to be able to blend in with the crowd, but we still attracted glances from passers-by, both men and women. I had a kind of weird presentiment that at any minute they would all open their mouths at once and jeer, in chorus:

Timur and Patya, sitting in a tree
K-I-S-S-I-N-G…

With an air of proprietary self-satisfaction, Timur led me along like some goat he'd bought at the bazaar, at a speed that was beyond my abilities to match. Along the way he shook hands with men he knew, and nodded importantly to local matrons in colorful kerchiefs, whose ample, shapeless garments billowed in the wind.

"Timur, you're probably going to be busy. Let's just get together at the concert," I finally proposed.

"What, like, have you've forgotten?" he was taken aback. "We're going to the meeting first. I already told our activists that I would, like, bring a girl from here who has experience working in the Moscow courts and everything."

"I don't know a thing. All I do is bind papers."

"What are you talking about, Patya! What, like, I can't introduce you to my colleagues? I mean, you're like one of the family!" Timur smiled.

How? How could I be like one of the family when I had never even seen him before? It was true, we had communicated online for five months; though meager, irregular, and intermittent, it was still a correspondence. The locals would interpret it as a pledge of true affection, love and fidelity... How could I have made such a mistake? Why had I led him on?

The questions whirled around in my head, stupefying me. I ascended the steps of the club in a daze, like a sleepwalker.

"Don't be nervous," Timur soothed me, misinterpreting my agitation. "You won't have to, like, make a speech or anything. Just sit and listen, maybe ask a few questions."

The office featured a solemn array of official-looking flags on tripod poles. A dozen or so muscular young men in business suits sat around a round lacquered table. When Timur entered the room they all rose like schoolboys greeting their teacher. Everyone shook hands. Then Timur brought me a cup of tea on a gilded saucer, with two lumps of cane sugar. The moment I started stirring my tea, he took out his phone and snapped a picture of me from above, from an unflattering angle.

"To mark the occasion," he explained. "I'll show my family."

I cringed and said nothing. A girl of about thirty in a business skirt clicked into the room on high heels and turned on a Dictaphone.

"All right, then, like," began Timur, rising from his seat and pressing the pads of his fingers together. "Today we gather on the night of the concert, like, dedicated to a worthy son of our Motherland, Khalilbek. But, you know, our agenda includes not only the fate of this toiler, scholar, and citizen who cares so deeply for his people, but also, you know, the upcoming youth camp forum. Kids come to this camp, like, from all the towns and villages of the region. It's so important for our government, you know, to take on itself the spiritual and patriotic education of the youth..."

Everyone listened solemnly, focusing intently on Timur's lipless mouth. The girl even jotted down some hasty notes.

"There are going to be seminars for sharing experience and panel discussions to encourage dialogue, and they'll set up dance floors and courts for sports competitions."

"Is there going to be wrestling?" someone asked.

"Of course!" Timur exclaimed. "But the most important thing is the spirit of unity, like, coming together. Because what do our authorities need to do their job successfully? The youth. So let us provide this support in a spirit of friendship! We have already made some very important contributions: we've given out St. George ribbons to inspire patriotism among the population, and gathered humanitarian aid for refugees from the imperialist countries. I'm, like, so glad that the guys out there unanimously supported our 'Like Chorus' project: hundreds of kids simultaneously 'liked' the tweets of our region's leaders!"

"Is there going to be another one like that?" The listeners stirred.

"Maybe. We can't talk about it today, you know, with the concert about to start. People go, like, why does our association support Khalilbek? Intriguers are like, hey, are we really going against what the higher-ups in the government are saying?"

"Right, Timur, people are on me about that, too!" nodded the girl.

"Here's what you need to tell them," Timur instructed crisply: "That our youth association is, like, constructive, and only works in cooperation with our official mentors at the higher levels. They have more wisdom and experience and everything. They protect us from, like, the temptations of extremism, drug addiction, and other social evils."

"So true!" the girl agreed.

"Anyway," my suitor strode out in front of the round table. "Like, I have personally met with some deputies, and with other, so to speak, respected *khakims* too. All of them say they, like, value what Khalilbek has done for our region's advancement. No one has even come close to claiming that his arrest was justified. It could be a conscious strategy to trick the real crooks into letting up their guard. Or like, some stupid mistake on the part of the cops."

I should have kept my mouth shut, but something made me jump in:

"All right, let's grant we don't know anything about the dastardly crimes that Khalilbek supposedly committed," I said, surprising myself with my vehemence. "But we do know the minor stuff. That he built a casino on illegal land in town…"

"When was that? A hundred years ago!" They spoke in unison, like a choir.

"Patya," Timur gaped at me, bewildered. "Your own father, like, worked for Khalilbek, how can you say something like that? Plus, they closed that casino a long time ago."

"Moved it into a basement near the mosque" giggled the girl with the notebook.

"I'm simply stating the facts."

"The facts!" Timur exclaimed, raising his index finger and silencing the group. "And you know, like, facts come from the devil himself."

The listeners rustled. "Tell us what you mean, Timur, explain it to us!" they whispered.

Timur was all fired up; he launched straight into a sermon: "Do you recall, friends, what the devil used to tempt Adam, *alaikhi salam*, and Eve? Reason! He appealed to reason. He said: 'Allah does not permit you to pluck the fruit of the tree of knowledge, because he fears losing power over you.' And the first humans did not heed his teaching. They heeded not, and they fell. The only, like, salvation from reason, which tempts us and sets us down the pathway to hell, is faith. If a man comes up to you and begins using facts, arguments, and logic to challenge your faith, and your, like, faith begins to waver, know that this man is the devil's accomplice."

Oddly enough, what he said cheered me up. If he saw me as the devil's accomplice, maybe Timor would release his grip. But no such luck. He stared deep into my eyes, wrinkled his tanned forehead, and orated on, leering at me with his lipless mouth:

"It is particularly easy, you know, for a beautiful girl to stray from the true path. We observe the vice of the West, and we stumble. Especially girls, with their weaker minds. But there is one salvation, you know, and that is to remember. To continually remember that degeneration and vice are mutations pressing in on us from outside. And our country is the only zone that remains uninfected."

"Mutations," a big husky guy on my left, rapt, repeated quietly. The girl scribbled energetically in her notebook.

"Right!" Timur cried, paying no attention to the rogue rays of sunlight playing in his bristly blond crew-cut. "Look at the debauchery going on in America and Europe. It's all mutations!"

"Without mutations, though," I interrupted, "there is no evolution."

Total silence.

"What's this about evolution?" sneered a guy with a youth camp badge on his jacket lapel and ears maimed from boxing.

The others sat respectfully, waiting for Timur to respond. He stopped pacing from corner to corner and gave a loud snort. Then he leaned on the edge of the table, opened his mouth, and, after a moment of silence began to reciting to me deliberately and wearily, as though to a particularly dimwitted pupil:

"There is no such thing as evolution. Darwin's theory, you know, proved its own invalidity. The first man, Adam, *alaikhi salam*, was created by God out of clay."

I even snickered, it was so unexpected. How could I have corresponded with this loser for a whole six months and not seen through him? Why was it only now, after we had met in person, that I realized what a moron he was?

"The dinosaurs..." I began, at a loss.

"The dinosaur bones were forged by *kafirs*," the guy with the mangled ears corrected me.

"A complete fiction, the whole thing. A plot against true believers by the sinful world," Timur chimed in.

I cast a pleading look at the girl, but she was nodding ecstatically.

"Look, it's not like we're in the mosque on the Avenue right now, and the last time I checked you were not a mullah, Timur." I had managed to get my bearings, but at that moment a plump woman in a gilt-embroidered scarf, with scarlet-painted lips, appeared at the door.

"The concert is about to begin. Timur, you are on the program. Don't let me down," she announced in a voice that came from deep in her belly, then flitted away.

"That's all for today. We'll meet again tomorrow, same time, same place," Timur said.

The girl reached over to turn off the Dictaphone, and everyone rustled and murmured. Timur came up to me and reproached me indulgently:

"What are you saying? Did your year in the big city make you forget your roots? Don't worry, we'll spend some time together, just the two of us, and get this foolishness out of your pretty little head."

"Actually, Timur, thank you," I recoiled, barely holding back my irritation. "It was interesting for me to sit in. But I have to run."

"Wait," commanded Timur. "We're going to the concert together. That's, like, what you wanted to do. You said so yourself."

I couldn't come up with a response. When we went down to the auditorium, the program had already begun. The seats were full, including benches that had been specially brought in; people were even sitting on the floor on old newspapers.

The local school director was making an announcement from the stage:

"Neighbors, recall all those times Khalilbek stepped in and saved us from disaster! People disappear—Khalilbek finds them. The water gets cut off—Khalilbek gets it turned on. People get into conflicts—Khalilbek reconciles them. Our club or the school gets shorted in the budget—Khalilbek arranges for subsidies. He's not simply a man, not simply a citizen. He's our rock, our cliff, mighty as a mountain. Nothing can break him, not even the strongest battering rams! There's no way to explain what happened, the fact that he's not here with us, but behind bars! It's impossible, it's strange, it's crazy. I refuse to believe he's guilty!"

The hall erupted in applause.

"I'm sure the time will come when we will say '*salam alaikum*' to him!" cried the director, but his voice was drowned in a frenzied ovation.

I saw Aida, recognized her by her turban. She was waving to me from the other side of the hall, with her thumb raised in the air in the Roman gesture of mercy. I was sitting on a square plastic milk-bottle crate that Timur had slid over for me. He stood regally beside me with his legs spread wide, responding occasionally to greetings from acquaintances. His entire team, including the girl with the notebook, had fanned out and taken places throughout the dimly illuminated hall.

The first song was announced, the hall filled with sound, and the audience roared. The first singer was a woman from the city. A deafening audio track kicked in, and some idiot in a track suit leapt up onto the stage from the first rows and started to dance a Lezginka around the singer. The audience howled with laughter, and Timur stuck his fingers into his mouth and gave an ecstatic whistle. This was the last straw. I began plotting my escape.

At the chorus, the singer's trills spilled over into a blood-curdling shriek. The die-hard girls in front hooted and hollered, singing along hoarsely. I scanned the hall again, looking for Aida, but her turban had vanished behind the backs of the spectators who had leapt to their feet and were dancing ecstatically, flicking their fingers in the air.

The singer had barely finished, when another woman appeared onstage. This one launched into a special song about Khalilbek. I could hardly make out the words—just:

Our Khalilbek's name
Will bring glory and fame.

Timur bent over from behind and yelled straight into my eardrum:

"I know her personally! I can introduce you!"

Oh, great. I twitched and shook my head.

After the song, some deputy was called up onto the stage. He huffed and puffed, got his words mixed up, and sprayed saliva into the microphone.

"Khalilbek is like a father to me. He is my rod and my staff. Like an elder brother. He advised me, supported me constantly. I even…my yacht…I mean, it's not a yacht…my boat…I named it in his honor after this one dodgy case. Let me tell you about it. The boat was registered to the state fishing collective. And me and Khalilbek would go out for sturgeon…I mean, not sturgeon, of course. Herring, of course, nothing more, we'd just go out and scoop up a few white bream and that would be it. So anyway, this one time we're riding the boat past the Black Stones, and Khalilbek gets out an axe and—THWACK!—brings it down right into the deck!"

The audience giggled.

"I yell: 'What the? You about frigging hacked through the bottom!'" His listeners' warm reception emboldened the deputy. "But Khalilbek just stands there, doesn't say a word."

The audience cackled and clapped, and the deputy blushed with pleasure.

"That really hurt my feelings, I swear. I figured Khalilbek had gone berserk and tried to drown me. But later I realized why he had done it, and comprehended his great wisdom. The fish collective wrote off the yacht, I mean the boat…as defective, and in the meantime I sprang into action, pulled some strings, and…"

The audience guffawed, drowning out the deputy's words. "Nice work, atta boy!" "*Saul* to you!" "What a badass!" came from all sides.

At this point I recalled that I had seen Khalilbek once with my own eyes. I'd been eight or so. At that time, Khalilbek had an empty house in our suburb, and he would occasionally order a car to pick him up from the middle of nowhere. Papa would drive out to some steppe village surrounded by abandoned oil towers, or a roadside motel with scorpions rustling within its pitted, sunbaked adobe walls. Mama got on his case for going on these expeditions; she assumed that Khalilbek was involved in criminal gang activity, and that Papa would get caught in the middle and have his head bashed in by some crook's rifle butt.

"Don't you think it's weird that he sends for you to go out to who knows where, when he has his own regular driver in the city?" She would nag.

It wasn't Papa, of course, that she was worried about. Mama was tormented with fears for her precious first-born, my brother, who at that time had not yet fallen into Lyusya's trap and was still tied to his mother's apron strings. They could kidnap him for ransom, figuring that his papa could get money from Khalilbek. They could take revenge on him for being the son of one of Khalilbek's people. There were any number of reasons—Papa's boss had plenty of enemies.

Mama wasn't worried about me. I was too much like Papa, and that irritated her. I even recall one time when, scrubbing me with a loofa in a Soviet enamel bathtub—which Granny had stashed away from ancient times—she exclaimed, almost with loathing: "You even have paws like his!'"

Anyway, one time Mama was really down in the dumps. She lay flat on her back on her damp bed (the briny soil on which our suburb had grown would sometimes become saturated with swampy water, and the air would rot and fester). She lay there motionless, staring in horror at her wrist. Just under the surface of her fine skin a blue blood vessel throbbed in time with her heartbeat, and she lay in bed observing it, rapt, day and night. She imagined that her pulse was speeding up, beating faster and faster, and that any minute the vessels would suddenly pop, and her heart would stop, and that would be it.

Infected by mama's panic, we would summon doctors. They would come, take her blood pressure and listen to her heart, then conclude, with some impatience, that it was all nerves and prescribe herbal sedatives. Mama would complain behind their backs that they were liars and quacks; she would put on her best yellow dress, the one that her favorite seamstress had made, and take to her bed. Then she would summon my brother and make him sit at her bedside, to wait for death to come. One time, frightened by her racing pulse, she even dragged her folding bed out into the bathhouse with the intention of expiring in there, to make it easier when time came to wash her corpse.

The days dragged on, but mama's death drew no nearer. People in town started to cast suspicious looks and to come up with various conjectures. When neighbors came to call, Granny complained to them that a *shaitan* demon had taken root in her daughter-in-law, and was speaking through her. My brother lost his temper, and categorically refused to spend any more time in the bathhouse listening to her bitter tirades about the happiness that had eluded her with the late Magomedov—that same guy with the veterinarian son who had repelled me with his eggplant-shaped nose. It turns out that Magomedov had once courted Mama, but they hadn't let Mama marry him, considering him an outsider. Frankly, she herself had shown no particular interest in him, but now, on the eve of her imagined demise, she saw the unrealized dream of family life with him as a paradise that had slipped through her grasp. Meanwhile, during the whole drama, Papa simply gave up bathing at home so as to avoid entering the bathhouse, where he would have to contemplate the sight of the figure in yellow, sprawled on the folding bed with its frail wrist raised to its pale nose.

On one of those days he took me with him on one of his jobs for Khalilbek. He needed to deliver a suitcase to an eatery on the shore simply called the Tavern. Khalilbek, a man of medium height, solidly built, with a round, ordinary face, was there amid a crowd of regulars. He smiled, drew me close, pinched me on the cheek and gave a sigh of admiration:

"*Vakh*, just look at that mole on her cheek, a perfect black dot!"

For some reason that stirred up the Tavern regulars. One after another, they called me over and tousled my hair with their calloused hands. Papa stood with the suitcase next to the boss, keeping his distance, and somewhat taken aback by the men's interest in me.

Once I had made the full circle I again found myself between Khalilbek's knees. He picked up a thick, green glass goblet and handed it to me, saying:

"All right then, say a toast!"

"What's in the glass?" my father was concerned.

"It's just wine—specially for children, very weak."

Khalilbek looked me up and down with his big observant eyes, and I took his green glass, cast a glance around at everyone, and gulped down the sour brown liquid all at once.

"Hey, what about the toast?" chortled the men.

"Let her grow up first, then she'll give a toast," Papa answered for me.

What happened after that has slipped from my memory, but that evening I came down with a fever. This brought Mama's confinement in the bathhouse to an end. She immediately forgot about her pulse and the palpitations, stopped gazing at the artery in her wrist, and returned to the house, where she started in immediately on Papa:

"What made you drag the child the devil-knows-where to those drunkards? Tell me, what will become of the children if I'm not around to take care of them?"

Khalilbek's wine had a strange effect on me. I got sick but felt no weakness or self-pity, and did not whine and complain. A bright sense of peace came over me, and I realized beyond the shadow of a doubt that nothing really mattered, ultimately. That I wouldn't make a peep if Mama gave my favorite dolls to Aida, as she had often threatened to do. I imagined myself floating above the world, holding on by a string to a great balloon, and though I loved my parents and Granny, and—at times—even my brother, and ice cream with caramel sauce, still, I knew that I could not take them with me. And I did not want to.

It was a strange sensation. It's possible that I filled in the blanks much later. Meanwhile, as I sat there in the concert hall lost in my memories, a government bureaucrat named Ivan Petrovich Borisov had his shining moment on the stage. He grandly listed all the awards and medals that had been bestowed upon the glorious prisoner. Then the imam of one of the feuding local mosques—apparently the traditional one, the one on the Avenue—rose to the podium, where he prayed loudly for Khalilbek's release. After that, the strains of the *nashid* sounded forth and several men in skullcaps appeared onstage to sing some traditional religious songs.

Behind my back Timur consulted with one of the organizers who had run over to where we were in the back rows.

"Hold on, Patya," he barked into my ear from behind. "They're about to call me up onstage. And after that we'll go somewhere and sit and talk. You're pretty smart, but you still have a lot to learn. And grow your hair out—it's too short."

Having unburdened himself of everything that needed saying, Timur headed toward the stage, climbing over several rows of seats that had been improvised out of boxes. I decided to take advantage of his absence and slip away. But at this point Aida appeared by my side and grabbed me by the elbow:

"*Vai*, Patya, he's so hot!"

"Who?"

"What do you mean, 'who?' Your Timur, that's who."

"Oh, he's not mine," I snapped. "And, anyway, I don't even like him."

At that moment Timur was announced. I couldn't make out his title—Youth Association Chairman, or Innovation Forum Fellow, or something. He blabbed something tedious and sickening.

"We, the youth, you know, are honored to be contemporaries of the great Khalilbek..."

"How can you not like him?" Aida hissed. "He's going to go far. He'll be a deputy someday, I guarantee it. You'll live in the city, spend every day in beauty salons, getting facials and spa treatments..."

Before she could finish her sentence, someone came up from behind, grabbed us by the shoulders, and pressed us together, laughing. We turned and there was Shakh. Shakh used to hang out with my brother, and often used to tease me, calling me a grasshopper. But Aida disliked him. Once, before her marriage, she had been head over heels in love with him. She lost her appetite, and used to hover secretly outside

Shakh's gate; she'd get all dressed up and just happen to run into him out on the street. But he just toyed with her feelings; either he wouldn't notice her at all, or else he would all of a sudden seem obsessed with her and keep her on the phone for hours, driving her into a state of euphoric delirium.

Poor Aida was suspended between heaven and hell, carrot and stick, tenderness and pain. She endured this torment for years, until finally she learned that in addition to countless lovers, some of them decent, if naïve girls, Shakh had maintained serious relationships with at least two women, and that he had absolutely no intention of marrying anyone, because he didn't believe in pure feelings as such.

Why he didn't believe in them, I had no idea, but after five long nights of weeping and moaning, Aida came to her senses and accepted a proposal from a simple man who owned a food shop, and resolved to forget Shakh, the man of her dreams, once and for all.

"How are you, Aidka? How's the husband? Kids? And you, Patyulya? Why did you come by yourself? Where's your brother and his wife?" He bombarded us with questions. Then he nodded toward a well-built, handsome young man standing nearby. "And this is Marat, in case you don't know him. Marat, this is Patya. By the way, she worked in a courthouse in Moscow, though you're already back here for good, right? And this is Aida."

Marat held his hand out to us in the European manner. His palm was soft and strong at the same time.

"Are you enjoying yourself here?" he asked, addressing either both of us, or maybe just me, but if so, using the polite form of address.

"It's so great! The singers are amazing!" Aida pressed her hands to her chest.

"Yes, it's been fun. But I'm leaving!" I added.

"Leaving? If you're headed to the Avenue, I can go with you." Marat suggested.

I agreed without the slightest hesitation.

"Of course!"

Everything inside me rejoiced, and something leapt feverishly in my chest, up and down, up and down again. I got up from the box, hoping to slip out as quickly as possible from the auditorium, together with my new acquaintance.

"We're staying!" Shakh declared, sinking onto my newly vacant seat and glancing sideways at Aida.

"No one gave you permission to sit here!" she cried.

"What, so you've gotten married, had a few kids, now you're all high and mighty? Queen Margot!" Shakh snickered.

Aida tossed out some comeback, but I couldn't make out the words. There was no chance of that, with a song blaring from onstage about a majestic eagle caught by bandits.

"Shall we go, Patya? We're friends, right?" Marat smiled. I just nodded and let myself smile back instinctively. We made our way through the crowd of people standing in the back, nodding to acquaintances as we passed; they had lost their inhibitions, and were scanning the room for girls they might potentially hook up with. If Marat hadn't been next to me, I would have never made it to the exit. How strange, we had lived our whole lives next to each other, and I didn't remember him at all.

"Patya!" A shout came from behind. I turned, stood on tiptoe; back where we'd left Aida and Shakh, I saw Timur standing stock still, glaring at me. My heart plummeted to my heels, and I began to push through the crowd of gaping listeners. Marat seemed to have noticed nothing, but he matched my pace, and we made it outside.

"Let's take a detour," I proposed, terrified that Timur would try to pursue us.

Marat agreed readily, and we started briskly down the empty street that encircled our suburb, where cows stood placidly munching the wheatgrass by the roadside. I turned off my phone, which had begun vibrating furiously, and abandoned myself fully to my conversation with Marat. We interrupted each other, asked questions, told each other about our jobs, shared what we'd heard about the conflict between the mosques and about Khalilbek, talked about the mosquito-infested steppes around the town and the snowy Moscow winters. Marat acted out for me his long search for a private apartment in Moscow—his non-Russian name had scared off all the landlords. And I told him about how my colleagues in the court, except for Marina, of course, had recently begun half-jokingly to vilify the "blackasses" when we crossed paths in the cafeteria. Then someone would without fail announce: "You know Patya is from there too," and those colleagues who had been stigmatizing our southern lands would cringe and start to justify themselves:

"Don't think that I'm some kind of fascist, they're not all like that."

Or:

"But Patya, you're different, you're like a regular Russian. No one would say you're from Blackassia, so don't take offense."

Marat laughed:

"No, in my office practically everyone has visited the Caucasus, and they have a positive attitude."

"What kind of cases do you work on?"

The most critical case they were handling was the murder of a human rights activist, a woman, which had been attracting a lot of attention in the press. Marat began to go into the details, but then we reached my house. On the other side of the gate I saw my father. He had his back turned to us and was digging around in the car's engine, but could turn around at any moment and spot us together. Marat had to leave immediately. He asked for my number. I quietly blurted it out, then flew into the yard, overwhelmed with feelings teeming inside me, feelings I didn't fully understand.

"How was the concert, Patimat?" My father looked up from the engine.

"Boring!"

"Why would they even go to all that bother! Wait until they let the man out, then go dance and sing," he muttered under his breath.

I ducked into my room, flopped down on the bed, and turned on my phone: nineteen missed calls! Before I could even come up with a strategy, Timur called again. Without thinking, I accepted the call.

"No hide nor hair of you!" he shouted into the phone. "Where did you go? Shakh told me that you split with some guy!"

"I..."

"'I' this, 'I' that... What had we agreed upon?"

"Nothing. I was in a hurry."

"She was 'in a hurry!' If you had been in such a hurry, I would have walked you home!"

"You didn't need to. Timur, thank you for everything, I had a good time. Not sure what else you want."

"Hold on, why the official tone?"

"What do you mean?"

"Talk normal!"

"I am talking normal!"

"What's with the attitude? Like, who do you think you are? Don't smart off to me!"

"I'm being polite..."

"Don't interrupt me! When are we, like, going to get together? Who was that dude with you? Where did you go? I was looking for you!"

"I am leaving for my aunt's place in the city today, I won't be able to see you any more."

"Don't you lie to me. Like, hey, what's going on? You double-crossing me?"

Everything groaned inside me: how had I managed to get myself into this mess?

"Sorry, Timur, Papa is calling! See you!" I said, and tossed the phone aside.

When it rang again, I didn't pick up. My hands were trembling.

"Patya!" My mother's voice came from the kitchen.

"I'm here!"

"Wandering the streets all day long like a tramp! Get in here, make some filling for the *chudu*!"

I slipped out of the sparkly dress, threw on a robe and headed for the kitchen. My heart ached from a strange combination of joy and terror. I wanted to flee our town that minute, to get as far away as I could from Timur. But first, there were onions to fry, and potatoes to boil in their skins and scrub and mash together with dry *tvorog* bought from a neighbor to roll into balls...

And then just wait and see.

6. A CURSE

Abdullaev Senior and his wife stood greeting their guests on the restaurant's front porch. Marat's mother kissed the hostess and plunged into the colorful crowd of familiar faces inside to exchange hugs, whispers, sighs, squeals, and gossip. Marat and his father stayed at the entrance to talk with the men about yesterday's concert for Khalilbek.

"If they allowed them to have a concert out here, that means that before you know it, they'll be having them in the city. And at that point they'll release our hero," predicted some.

"You'll see, this whole story with the arrest is just a clever move to distract people from the overall mess we're in," claimed some know-it-alls.

"They say that the real Khalilbek is free, and the guy in prison is just a lookalike they've put in there," others whispered.

People spread the utterly absurd and fantastical rumors about a double with particular conspiratorial zeal, if not full confidence in their validity.

"How did they come up with that? Who did they hear it from?" Marat's father grumbled. "What a crock!"

It turns out, Khalilbek had been seen in the city park, playing chess with the regulars who populated the benches there. And at the market, too, where he was spotted expertly weighing out figs. And in a fishing boat at the abandoned shoreline with some local teenagers, their skin burned dark from the sun and permeated with sea salt. And at the morning *khutbah* in the mosque "across the tracks."

And outside the "official" mosque on the Avenue, thoughtfully studying the leaflets being handed out there. Here, there, everywhere, even in this very restaurant, where everyone had gathered today to celebrate young Abdullaev's engagement.

The Khalilbek frenzy swelled like dough on yeast. In the banquet hall, dignified family men exchanged fantastical tales about his secret release and omnipresence, like ghost stories told to frighten children, with a mixture of half-belief and suppressed excitement.

"They'll see someone who looks a lot like him, then make something up and pass the story around, and it all escalates," Marat remarked skeptically, raising his palms to shade his eyes from the blinding luminary overhead.

"You're so right." A grim, puny-looking guy standing next to him, shifting from one foot to the other, unexpectedly confirmed his theory. "Khalilbek would never play chess."

"Why not?" His listeners were surprised.

"Didn't you know?" The puny guy raised his index finger pedantically in the air. "The *hadiths* forbid the game."

"Only the apocryphal ones, bro!" countered a hefty mustachioed guy in a fashionable shirt whom Marat knew from school. "It's not approved, but not forbidden either. The main thing is that the game not distract from serving Allah."

Several of the men laughed, including a sweaty, pudgy guy of around sixty with a split lip. The know-it-all standing next to him slapped his comrade's drenched back with the flat of his hand:

"You need to be more careful what you laugh about, Ismail, you've got a bad enough reputation already."

Marat later asked Shakh about this Ismail, who he was and what that thing was about his reputation, and Shakh explained that it had to do with the new school director, who was constantly clashing with the more rabid parishioners. He was having particular difficulty with the ones who attended the mosque "across the tracks." Ismail refused to admit girls in hijabs into class and required them to wear the prescribed white blouses and blue skirts. The parents of veiled girls were upset, brought suit, and threatened the director with reprisals. His split lip, as Shakh merrily explained, was the handiwork of Mukhtar, a local resident with a teeming brood of children.

"That same Mukhtar whose son Alishka was beaten up by our neighbor, the policeman?" Marat recalled.

"Yes, yes, the whole family is devout," Shakh nodded.

But that conversation took place later, when the two of them were sitting together at one of the tables and watching the dancers. Guests invited each other to dance by waving a wedding baton, a napkin, or a sprig of dill. At the end of the dance, the baton would be passed to someone else: batons and napkins made their way from hand to hand: boy-girl, girl-boy. Marat managed to exchange disjointed congratulatory exclamations with the groom, Abdullaev, who was in constant motion. He danced a few rounds with his young betrothed, who was dressed in a crimson dress and had her hair curled and fixed in a fancy coiffure on the back of her head. Then he moved on to her friends, ostensibly demure girls representing both his and the bride's sides. Then he rushed off to discuss something with his friends, then would again invite someone to dance, and then vanish again.

The hostess hobbled anxiously back and forth to the kitchen to make sure that no one was stealing the food, and to see whether the woman who had been hired to salvage the leftovers was cheating as she scooped the uneaten *chudu* and mutton chops into plastic containers. Back in the hall, she waddled between the guests' tables, waving her fringed scarf and inquiring after her son:

"Now where has our groom gone again? Given us the slip, has he?"

As far back as Marat could remember, she had had trouble walking. One time she had climbed up onto the roof of her house when it was under construction, to keep an eye on the workers, and had fallen and injured her leg. Shakh also kept showing up and then disappearing. The faces of former friends and classmates flashed by. People questioned Marat about his law office and his escapades in the city. They asked:

"Do you have a special someone in Moscow?"

Marat laughed off the question. Individually or in groups, people were called up to the microphone, where they expressed warm wishes, well-meaning advice, and identical, monotonous toasts. They predicted a throng of offspring to the poor bride, as many as ten or fifteen kids. In the middle of it all, Marat's mother, decked out in her finest, with elegant earrings shaped like flowers with tiny phianites—"Let everyone think that they're diamonds!"—came up to Marat from behind, arm in arm with a bleach-blond woman in a leopard-print evening wrap.

"Marat, say hello to your Aunt Luiza!"

Marat greeted the woman and even managed to recall the names of Luiza's children and husband.

"Feast your eyes." Marat's mother addressed the leopard print-clad lady, shaking her head with the braids tucked up in back. "They've turned the matchmaking into a whole wedding! Remember how things used to be? It would all be done quietly, in the family. They would bring a suitcase of gifts to the prospective bride, would give her gifts, work out the necessary details, and that would be it.

Now look! Now you rent a restaurant, and there are so many people, it's like the hajj."

The leopard-print lady nodded and clucked.

"But all right," continued Marat's mother. "The bride is such a marvelous girl. And the groom—a fine falcon, isn't he? I remember how he used to come running over to our house when he was a little boy. Adik really loved him."

It was a lie. Adik had not liked Abdullaev at all; on the contrary, he had been afraid of him, but Marat did not protest, especially since his mother's voice trembled perilously when she mentioned Adik's name.

"Hey, look, there's Luiza's niece!" She perked up and poked her chin significantly in the direction of the dancers. "What a beauty, look how she moves! So graceful! And her waist? Thinner than my finger!"

"Stop it, Khadizha," the leopard-print woman laughed, "Don't slander my niece. She's not at all thin! Or bony! She's a good eater: healthy, strong. And she has a bright personality."

"What did you hear me say, Luiza? Did I say she was bony? Muishka, the Gadzhievs' daughter, now there's a bony one, she's like the walking dead. And her hands are so delicate. What can you do with hands like that? How can you cook? I bet she can't even open the oven door. Now that niece of yours is an absolute delight. Allah grant any woman a daughter-in-law like that."

Marat watched Luiza's dancing niece without the slightest interest. His mother's effusive compliments were not inaccurate. He liked the girl's figure, though he couldn't make out her face. Her long hair, which reached down to below her waist, kept spilling onto her chest and across her cheeks, which were red with cosmetics. He recalled Patya's almost childlike, intelligent face, and felt warm inside, and, at the same time, a little sad.

"Invite her to dance, Marat, go on!" his mother whispered, as she got up and headed off to the women's tables with Aunt Luiza in tow.

Marat lazily observed the girl as she went back and sat down in her seat, in a conspicuous place next to Abdullaev's bride. On the tablecloth lay a pink rosebud that someone had left there, with petals that were already a little worse for the wear. He picked it up by the stem and made his way over to Luiza's niece.

She noticed someone coming her way, and immediately became engrossed in her late-model telephone. Deaf and blind to the world, she energetically tapped the touch screen with her manicured fingers. When Marat extended the bud to her, she put down the phone and rose slowly, looking not at Marat but at the smiling girls sitting next to her and at Abdullaev's bride, who, as you could see from up close, was still just a young girl, with a thin angular profile.

Luiza's niece turned out to be an exemplary partner. She glided gracefully across the restaurant's filed floor, tracing all kinds of loops and fancy moves in time with the brisk music. Marat sensed that she stayed with him longer than the two or three minutes considered decent. Though of course it could have been that time had slowed down.

"Do you know anything about that girl? The one I was dancing with just now?" he asked Shakh, who showed up in his former place immediately after the dance.

"I do. She's really full of herself. She likes luxury, though her family isn't all that wealthy. In short—a fool. What, do you like her?"

"My mother does." Marat smirked. "And she can dance. But her face…"

"It's obvious at one look that she's an airhead. Girls like that used to drive me wild. Now they just bore me: been there, done that."

Shakh fussed with the water bottle. "Marat, Abdullaev is a little spooked. That girl he knocked up has been calling him all day."

"And he...?"

"Doesn't pick up. But she texted him. Said he's going to be sorry."

"So she's threatening him?"

"Yes. He's already asked me whether he can get rid of her somehow through the courts. Accuse her of blackmail."

"He could, but then she would claim that she was seduced or even raped, that he got her pregnant and then abandoned her. And then they could do a paternity test..."

"There might be some other way out. But the relatives of that tramp could show up here and ruin everything. Can you imagine the disgrace?"

"What is Abdullaev doing about it?"

"He wants to cut off access to the restaurant, so as to head off her posse, which is marching this way in a righteous wrath, so to speak. Will you join us?"

"If he asks me himself. It's his private business, after all..."

"Cut it out, Marat, don't be such a Rusik-the-Nail!"

"I don't feel at all sorry for Abdullaev, he got himself into this mess. If I go with you, it's only to ensure that his fiancée's special day won't be ruined. Though she's bound to find out one way or another."

"The main thing is for her to learn about it after the wedding, not now. His parents would be devastated. They worked so hard for this!" Shakh turned serious.

"*Le, salam*," he was interrupted by a red-headed guy Marat had already greeted on the porch. He was one of five carrot-topped brothers. In town they were known as the "Red Army," and each one had his own name: Red Army Rashid, Red Army Farid, Red Army Gamid, Red Army Saigid, and, simply, Roma, the youngest one. That was actually his name: Romeo. His sentimental mother had chosen this name for her fifth son; she herself was just as orange-maned, and had enjoyed local fame in the distant past in an amateur theater in a mountain village. Her husband had forgiven her this weakness, though the locals grumbled that he should have been renamed Ramazan.

The "Red Army" soldier who had interrupted them was this very Roma. He sat down at the table and poured himself a glass of vodka, chugged it down, and chased it with a bite of salad.

"Sure you can handle it?" Marat smirked.

"Shut up," Roma's temples twitched. "You should have seen how much I drank at our Gamid's wedding..."

"But Gamid doesn't drink!" Marat was taken aback.

"You're right. Doesn't drink, doesn't dance, doesn't listen to music. Basically, instead of a wedding we had a *mavlid* for him." Shakh was there, he knows. But not all the guests were like that. Guys like to have a drink. Anyway, right in the middle of the *mavlid*, people started sneaking outside to gather in little groups in their cars and drink secretly from plastic glasses. And then they'd go back in as though nothing had happened. When Gamid found out about it, he went berserk, believe you me!"

"What did he say?" Shakh bared his teeth and popped a grape into his mouth. "I hadn't heard anything."

"Don't even ask! He didn't catch me, but he smelled cognac on Father's breath and really gave him an earful. He said that we'd ruined the whole wedding...But hey, where did our groom go with his guys?"

Roma was obviously clueless; he knew nothing about the dark cloud that hung over Abdullaev, a menacing stew of vengeful brothers and a spurned girl with a belly swollen with sin.

"What, have they gone already?" Shakh stood up and began looking around anxiously. "Why didn't they tell me?"

"*Le*, what's this all about?"

Roma didn't get his answer; the monotonous buzz of congratulatory toasts suddenly gave way to a strange rasping sound. Marat glanced at the dance floor, where he had just been dancing with Luiza's niece. An old woman with sun-blackened skin wearing a long black scarf stood at the microphone. Baring the whites of her eyes, she croaked ominously:

"I wish the bride and groom as many goats as there are stars in the sky, and as many misfortunes as hairs on those goats! May their clan rot, may their purses and their intestines leak their contents and shrivel up! May the heavens squash them flat, may their souls burn in the flames of hell, may they be wiped away there and rendered to ash! May their children remain unborn, or if they are born, may they bewail the day their accursed father took for his wife their long-suffering mother. May ulcers, the seven-year-itch, worms, seizures, pestilence, and tumors bring them low, may leprosy mar their faces, and may their limbs rot in Siberia! To the groom I wish impotence, shame across the land, and a lifetime of gout! May your mother weep over you eternally, may your father grow out his beard in mourning! May the columns and beams in your house topple to the ground, may the roof cave in on your head! May all decent people spurn you like a pestilential cur, may you be driven from hearths, wherever you go! May you be a homeless vagabond and a stranger, may you lug your belongings on your back, may you rot away behind bars! May not earth, nor sea, nor sky bear you on themselves! May the mountains hurl you from their saddles!

May you be betrayed a thousand thousands of times over! May your soul be spit into, as you spit into the heart of my innocent daughter! May you know no happiness from this black day forward!"

The curses rained down, and for some reason no one attempted to tear the microphone from her wrinkled hands. Abdullaev's fiancée sat ashen, her lips wide open in shock. Luiza's niece, in contrast, covered her mouth with her hands in horror. Abdullaev's parents stood motionless in the aisle, and the guests exchanged stupefied glances.

"Who is that? What's going on?" Roma-Romeo babbled, gaping at the woman in black.

"Must be the mother of that girl, the one he knocked up. Snuck in here with her curses. And where's that mutton-head?" Shakh, who himself had been momentarily paralyzed, managed to utter.

"Knocked up? *Le*, come on, guys, tell me what's going on!" Roma persisted.

"To your descendants, if they are to be, I wish cystitis, colitis, poliomyelitis, rhinitis, otitis, stomatitis!" the sun-blackened hag cawed on.

Abdullaev rushed into the restaurant with a bunch of friends.

"Grab the microphone!" he shrieked. "She's insane! I don't know this woman!"

"Call EMS! Call EMS!" Marat heard another shriek—this time his mother's.

"The bride's mother is feeling sick," Shakh clarified, peering over at the women's tables.

At last everyone launched into action. The men wrested the microphone out of the hag's hands, and the women began dragging her off to the side. Once caught, she put up no resistance, but when they loosened their grip, she broke away and raised her finger high into the air.

Threatening the entire gathering with her upraised finger, she stalked through the crowd and vanished through the main entrance.

"Catch her, catch her!" cried Abdullaev's mother.

Meanwhile, the *tamada* jabbered into the microphone: "The celebration continues, we resume. Pay her no mind!"

Shakh ran over to the groom and brought back an update: the pregnant girl's brothers had been caught just outside town and had been rounded up by Abdullaev's closest friends, but they either had not dared to touch the girl's mother or had not recognized her, so she'd been able to make her way into the hall unhindered.

"Don't leave, dear guests! Pay no heed to maniacs! I hereby announce a rousing Lezginka, just for you!" The *tamada* endeavored to soothe the shocked guests.

The hall filled with loud music, but no one ventured onto the dance floor. The bride had fled sobbing to the restroom, and all her bridesmaids rushed in after her, perfumed handkerchiefs at ready. Her mother had been administered heart drops and brought back to consciousness, and she and the bride's scowling, bristling father were consulting with the aghast Abdullaevs, who were yellow with shame and disbelief.

Marat's father came over and hoarsely declared, "Listen, things being the way they are... We're better off staying out of it. The bride's side is breaking off the engagement. Let's go."

"Is everyone leaving?"

"Your mother may stay, but that's up to her. There's no point in men getting mixed up in this scandal."

The music thundered on. The guests, buzzing like bees in a hive, closed in around the hosts of the ruined celebration and listened to young Abdullaev's heated explanations. His bride still cowered in the restroom.

Marat decided to leave with his father.

As they went down the porch stairs, talking under their breath with the other meekly retreating guests, Shakh rushed up to Marat. He was all in a lather:

"Are you leaving? That's fine, there's not going to be a fight anyway. Our idiots let the whole gang of them escape."

"What gang?"

"The knocked-up girl's brothers. And her mama—the filthy-mouthed old witch—she seems to have given us the slip, too."

"So the marriage is off?"

"No shit. Though who knows... Listen, I had something else to tell you. What's up with that girl Patya?"

"The one you introduced me to? Nice girl, sincere. What's up?"

"Well, she's dating that wrestler guy."

"What wrestler guy?"

"Timur, from the youth committee. He told me himself. So be on your guard."

"If they were dating, she wouldn't have given me her number."

"What, she gave you her number just like that?" Shakh gave a whistle. "Be careful with that one. Her brother made a bad marriage. Shacked up with this girl, then went and married her. Totally henpecked. Patya, too, she's friends with that fool Aida."

"Not the Aida who had the hots for you all that time?"

"That's the one. And they also have this friend Amishka. Barely out of high school, she took up with some guy, and the entire town knew about it. Some hotshot from the big city. No matchmaking, he'd just show up with some flowers, that's all."

"So what?"

"So what? He lured this Amishka to bed and then dumped her, the guys say. Hilarious! She resisted at first, but he goes, 'Come on, just let me in half-way.' Ha ha, so as not to damage anything. And then…"

"That's enough, Shakh, I'm going home. I've got work to do." Marat waved him off wearily, and began to shake hands with Shakh and the other men who were lingering nearby. His father had already gone ahead, but guests were still emerging from the restaurant. Some stopped to whisper to one another, others went around the corner, and still others got in their cars without exchanging glances with anyone and drove off.

Several girls skipped out of the kitchen exit on the side of the building. Behind them came Luiza's niece with the vapid eyes, embracing Abdullaev's tearstained bride, with her mournful, drooping curls.

When Marat got home, both his parents were already there. His mother still had her best dress on, and the phianites still sparkled in her earlobes. She paced back and forth on the veranda, swollen with emotions like an overfilled tire. His father sat over his notebook writing some report for work.

"*Vai, vai*, Marat," his mother repeated. "What's going to happen with the Abdullaevs now?"

"Why worry about it, what does it have to do with you?"

"You heard, didn't you? You heard the curses raining down on their heads? And what a day for it! You know what caused it all, don't you, Marat?"

"That's their problem."

"No, it's ours! Luiza's niece is the cousin of that poor girl, Abdullaev's fiancée."

"But the curse has nothing to do with her, don't worry about it!"

"Are you joking?' his mother stopped. "Do you think that it's easy to be related to such a family? Of course Abdullaev's fiancée, of course, has nothing to do with it, but still, it's pretty bad. She has been demeaned, shamed, and cursed in front of everyone."

"Who demeaned her?"

"Her fiancé! Don't pretend that you don't know. That hag's daughter is expecting his child. She's some student type. Turns out no one knew about it, but now it's all come out in the open. If we were to become related..."

"Related to whom? What, are you proposing to marry me off to Abdullaev's fiancée?"

"*Astauperulla*," his mother recoiled. "What mother would approach Abdullaev's fiancée now? Her entire family is now cursed. I was talking about Luiza's niece!"

"What made you think that we were going to get together?"

"What do you mean?" His mother collapsed onto the nearest chair. "You danced with her for such a long time! I thought..."

"Mama, forget about Luiza's niece, I have no use for her, got it?" Marat couldn't restrain himself.

"Why are you yelling at your mother?" His father looked up from his scribbling.

"I'm not yelling. I just don't need anyone foisted on me."

Marat made straight for his room, to his computer. He had to get in touch with his Moscow colleagues, to see what was happening with the case of the human rights activist and to go over some documents, but Shakh's warning whirled around in his head. So Patya was dating some pompous blowhard named Timur. Impossible. She was way too smart for him.

Then he had another thought: of course Shakh would badmouth Patya; he didn't want Marat to prefer anyone over his cousin—Sabrina Shakhova.

But Marat immediately rejected the thought: "No, he himself called Sabrina a dragon."

His hand reached out on its own volition for the phone, to dial Patya's number, but froze in midair: "It's only been one day, it's too early to call. She'll think that I'm desperate."

And Marat turned to the computer screen fully intent on forgetting about Patya, at least for now.

Meanwhile, Luiza's niece, having seen Abdullaev's grieving bride home and sent her off to the bathroom to clean herself up, lingered alone in the foyer. She smiled into the tall, gilt-framed mirror on the wall and tried out some poses, then rounded her supple shoulders and started quietly singing a popular song that she'd heard yesterday at the concert for Khalilbek:

You are my ray, my light,
Full of fire and might!
Tu-tu-tu, tataram...

Before the party erupted in scandal, her aunt had hinted to her that the guy with the intense eyes who had danced with her was in quest of a bride. His name was Marat. He had looked right through her! She had seen him again when she and the other girls were leaving the restaurant, and again he had given her that look. So that was it, he was in love! True love! And his mother, Khadizha...she was always so friendly, so thoughtful. Something was about to happen, for sure. Something marvelous, full of enchantment...

Luiza's niece sank into a reverie. She began planning her wedding in her mind. There would be two ceremonies, of course. The first one, "the bride's," would be just for her relatives and parents, and Marat would come with his groomsmen. The second one, "the groom's," would be the next day, and would be more extravagant. The "bride's side" could not attend this celebration; the only people there would be the bride's sisters, cousins, and closest girlfriends, and a couple of men serving as delegates representing her family.

On the first day, she would wear a golden dress, with a corset and glittering gemstones in her hair. The second day, her dress would be show-white with a silver belt, and she would wear a long veil like in that magazine... She would get a henna tattoo and have her eyelashes permed. He'd pick her up in a cabriolet. And the groom would definitely wear cufflinks. She would just die if her papa didn't hire the very best photographer and invite a dance group in leather slippers. She would make her entrance into the banquet hall, with her two-meter veil trailing behind her, and everyone would gasp! Banknotes would rain down onto her high, baroque hairdo (note to self: don't forget to make an appointment)...

The bathroom door slammed, interrupting Luiza's niece's fantasy. She assumed an expression of sympathy and prepared to resume her task of comforting the freshly washed former bride. But the girl was no longer crying, and showed no sights of distress. She just went over to the window, under which a stray cow was lowing nervously, and sighed audibly:

"All right, then. It's better this way."

"Indeed it is," Luiza's niece confirmed.

"Um-bu-u-u-u!" the innocent cow chimed in.

7. NEIGHBOR WOMEN

I laid low for several days. I imagined Timur's spies lurking behind every corner and at every crossroads. The moment I crossed the threshold, the streets would close in around me, seize me, and deliver me into the hands of my detested tormentor with the blond crew cut. He called several times a day, demanding that I meet him; he shifted to threats, and from there moved on to tender babbling and endearments. He was definitely brewing something ominous.

Aida came to visit me with her two elder sons, whose heads were flattened in the back from so much time in the cradle. She let it slip that Timur had already approached her and asked for advice on how to win me over. Aida claimed to have told him to back off. Obviously, Timur had not gotten the message.

"It's your own fault, Patya!" Aida chided, rewinding her turban from left to right. "You shouldn't have corresponded so much with him from Moscow. Why did you even agree to meet him?"

"I didn't know what he was like!"

"She 'didn't know.' Well, now you do, so it's time to reap what you sowed. Of course he figured that if you wrote to him and answered his messages, that meant you want to marry him..."

I was desperate to talk things over with Marina, but she was on vacation somewhere in Bulgaria. Would I get to see her? Would I even go back to Moscow at all? Mama had already put her foot down and said no, no Moscow for me, not for all the tea in China. In Moscow, I would completely forget how to make *khinkal*, I would go stale and shrivel up into an old maid.

"Soon you'll be twenty-six! No one will take you, even for free!" she would nag.

Papa noticed that I was holed up in my room, and offered to take me to the city:

"You have girlfriends from university there, don't you? Uma, Masha..."

How had he even remembered their names? I did have friends there, but one of them had gone to the mountains for the summer to drink spring water, wander around alpine meadows, and breathe the thin, wholesome air. Another had rushed off to serve as a volunteer organizer for that very youth forum that Timur was so worked up about. I prayed that he would be whisked away to the forum too, and I would be rid of him. But this was not to be.

When his relentless calls brought no response, Timur sent me a terrifying message:

"You will be mine, come what may!"

I pictured myself kidnapped and locked in the trunk of a car with a sack thrown over my head. It rattled me so much that I went into the front room to sit with Granny and listen to the "magpies," the neighbor women who had come over to shell a gigantic pile of pumpkin seeds. Why they would be doing that, I didn't even bother asking. My parents were out. Papa had gone to a demonstration that had been hastily organized in the city to advocate for Khalilbek's release. Mama, who cursed and condemned this enterprise, had decided at the last moment to tag along, not to the protest, of course, just to visit friends in the city. Maybe the Magomedovs.

The neighbor women sat on the sofa in their cheap cotton robes that looked like nightgowns. They hunched over a mass of seeds that had been spread on mats the floor, picking through the white pumpkin husks and spouting the most arrant nonsense to Granny in a wild mix of Russian and our native language. They were discussing amulets. The imam of the mosque on the Avenue scratched secret formulas in Arabic ligatured script on slips of paper, which he folded and whispered prayers into. Then he sewed them up in leather triangles, attached a string, and sold them off to the locals as charms to protect their children.

"My son," babbled one of the neighbor women, "was taking a final exam in school. And he had forgotten his amulet, had left it in his backpack. He's sitting there in the classroom. His telephone is under the desk. And I'm out in the schoolyard with the textbook. He texts me a question from the test, but my answer refuses to send. Then he remembers about the amulet. He explains to the teacher that he has to get it out of his backpack. He gets it out, hangs it around his neck, and—bingo!—receives my answer.

"So he passed?"

"*Vababai*! Of course he did!"

"Did you hear what happened with the Abdullaevs?" asked another of the neighbors, bugging her eyes out.

Everyone ooh-ed and aah-ed and shook their heads in their multi-colored kerchiefs.

"I was at the engagement ceremony, I heard all those curses! A simple *sabab* amulet has no power against something like that!"

We already knew that our neighbor had been present at the scandalous event. She had spread the news around the entire district practically the moment it had occurred. She had come to our house as well, rushing in all flushed and breathless. She had been wearing a gold-embroidered scarf that sparkled in the sunlight; it had not been tied crudely at the back of her head like her everyday one, but was pinned fetchingly on the sides into flower shapes. It gave the effect of a fancy formal hairdo, only with the scarf instead of hair.

"Not just anyone can undo a curse," Granny announced, with some authority.

"You're so right, so right," nodded the women.

"But what exactly happened there? Why did they crash the engagement ceremony?" one of them, a silver-toothed woman sitting to the side, asked in a nasal voice.

"*Wa*, didn't you know? He got some city girl pregnant, and it was her mother who barged in. They say that the girl is a real prostitute!"

"What a nightmare!"

"*Astauperulla*..."

"What a disgrace..."

"The Abdullaevs are related to our mullah, didn't you know that? It's no good that they have something like that going on in their family." Granny smacked her chops.

"Or maybe young Abdullaev was created to test girls' powers of resistance!" suggested the one who had helped her son cheat on the exam, without the shadow of a smile. "He makes a point of tempting them: the strong ones turn him down and preserve their honor, the weak ones give in. So it's that pregnant girl's own fault. Instead of throwing curses around, her mother should have spent more time setting her daughter on the right path."

"So true, you're so right."

The silver-toothed neighbor noticed me. "Patya, why are you sitting around at home? You should go into the city."

"Oh, don't go now," objected Granny. "There's a demonstration going on today for Khalilbek."

"Oh, of course, you're right."

"Papa went," I interjected.

A white steppe butterfly fluttered into the front room, did some flips in the air, and alit on the window, where it flattened its wings out against the pane.

"Do you know," the older of the neighbors lowered her voice and whispered conspiratorially, "what people are saying about Khalilbek..."

"People will say anything."

"Have you heard about him being a saint?"

"Who said that? Where did you hear that?"

"My husband told me, and he heard it from people in the know, that *barakat* flows out from Khalilbek's cell in prison, even into the neighboring cells. Do you remember that Wahhabi who was imprisoned for spreading extremism?"

"Zaripat's husband?"

"Yes, that's the one, that Zaripat who used to be a singer and who got cancer."

"But she died!"

"May her sins be washed away."

"She died. But Khalilbek's grace came down onto her husband, and he was miraculously amnestied and released. When he got out of prison he learned that Zaripat had sung a song before she died. And Wahabbis do not allow music, they don't recognize it."

"May their intestines be torn apart in the afterworld, the thugs," muttered Granny.

"So, anyway, he learned that his wife had sung a song and had even recorded it..."

I joined in: "I heard that it was really beautiful."

"Everyone's heard it. People sent it around. She sang like an angel, as though the illness had left her body at that moment."

"And what did he do?"

"He cursed her memory, abandoned the house, and left for Turkey, taking the kids with him."

"How could they have let him in with his criminal record?"

"It's a complicated system. The children went separately, with his sister, and he managed to finagle a way there via Ukraine, like a lot of people do. Anyway, they were already expecting him in Turkey. Everyone who was on the official surveillance list here and unable to follow the religious requirements because of police harassment has managed to get set up pretty well there. After Barishka's son was held in the Sixth Department and investigated for extremist ties for five days, he took off for Turkey. Same with the Isaevs' son. They've started up a business there, and they follow *halal* law. Once they decided to become observant Muslims, they found they couldn't live normally in Russia. They needed to go live with the people who shared their faith, so they wouldn't have to violate their laws."

"Let them go, then, devil's spawn, savage beasts that they are," Granny grumbled again.

"So Khalilbek is some kind of saint simply because his neighbor in jail got released early?" I took the conversation a couple of steps backwards.

"What do you mean, Patya? He performs all kinds of miracles, that's what people say."

"But he can't get himself released?"

"He must not want to yet." The older neighbor lady rustled the pumpkin seeds with her hand. "But there's a demonstration today, which means that they'll let him out soon. Don't you remember the kind of people they had performing at the concert? Deputies, leaders... That Borisov fellow. Famous singers. All for Khalilbek... people are saying that he's Khidr, a prophet."

"Khidr!" Granny repeated reverently.

"What do you mean, Khidr? Explain it to me!" I asked.

"How can you not know Khidr? He's a holy man, servant of God, teacher of Musa."

"Wait, I'm not following. By Musa do you mean Moses? But he lived thousands of years ago!"

"But his teacher is eternal. His name is Khidr. And he can manifest himself in any form. But mostly he's in green."

"Wait, you're telling me that Khalilbek goes around in green clothes?"

"That's not important. What is important is he's wise, very wise."

"But if Khalilbek is the magical and immortal Khidr, the wise teacher and all that, then why did he murder the investigator?" I pressed on.

"Shhhh, Patya!"

"Or Adik from our town?"

"Patimat, you're not being rational. You're judging on matters you don't understand," Granny admonished me sternly.

"People can never explain Khidr's actions when they witness them. They are bewildered, and they criticize him. Because they cannot see the essence. And then later it turns out that Khidr was right."

"How can it be right to kill someone?"

Neither Granny nor the neighbors could come up with an answer, and so they resumed their collective task, genially busying themselves over the basins of shelled seeds.

"Patya, go make some tea!" commanded the older neighbor.

I obediently went to the kitchen, turned on the electric samovar, and got out the broadleaf green tea, cloves, black peppercorns, little bags of dried marjoram and mint, sage, thyme, bay leaf, and a jar of caraway. Scald the inside of a teapot with hot water, add just a pinch or a couple of pieces of each herb, pour boiling water over the mixture, then set it on a distributor over a low flame...

Why didn't Marat call? Had that loathsome Timur driven him away? I thought about it day and night, slipping into dreams and fantasies about how we'd met so unexpectedly, imagining confessions of love and other sentimental scenes. The more naïve the pictures in my mind, the easier it was to endure the uncertainty of the present.

One of the neighbors—the one who had spread the news about Abdullaev's broken engagement—came into the kitchen and started in on me: "Well, Patya, how are things with you in general?"

"Fine, thank you."

"What's keeping you from getting married?"

"Well..."

"Look, Elmira waited until she turned twenty-eight and now she can't get pregnant."

"Not everybody can."

"No one can, if they wait too long! Look at the ecology! For some it's a problem with the ovaries, for others it's the cervix—they simply can't carry a baby to term."

I said nothing, hoping that if I didn't react, the neighbor would give up. But she persevered. She inspected Mama's kitchen utensils, the towel hooks, the glass canisters of whole grains, and the Balkhar clay figurines on the shelves. Then she sat down, crossed her legs, and stared at my shaggy head.

"Where did you get that haircut? In Moscow?"

"Yes…"

"Why did you do it? Is it the fashion?"

"I don't know. That's just the way they cut it, that's all."

"So how do you dry it? Do you use a hair-dryer or do you towel-dry it?"

"Just air dry. It dries fast."

"Of course it does," the neighbor nodded. "It's so thin—not much to speak of, is it?"

Then she got up and watched over my shoulder as I took the teapot off the distributor and got out the tea glasses.

"You brewed it with herbs, right? My mother-in-law doesn't like it that way. She gets mad if I use herbs…"

"Uh-huh."

"But sometimes I do it for my husband. There's a mixture you can make just for men, to keep them from slipping off the path and make sure they love only their wives."

"How does that work?"

"When you get married, I'll tell you. I know a lot of formulas. Even Liuda came to see me, the one whose daughter was dumped by her fiancé."

"Amishka's mama?"

"Yes. She asked for something really strong that could calm her daughter down."

"Did it work?"

"They sent her to the mountains. There's some distant relative up there who is willing to marry her. Rumors from here don't always make it all the way up there."

"What rumors?"

"You know yourself. That Amishka is not a virgin."

I sighed audibly. I was sick and tired of the neighbor's jabbering. I was ready to fly out onto the street this very minute, even if it sent me straight into Timur's clutches.

"Do you wear pants outside, too?" continued the neighbor, changing the subject.

"Not here, not yet."

"You shouldn't, not here in town. People won't understand. You should at least untuck your T-shirt over them or something."

She leaned her elbows languidly on the windowsill and gazed out the window at the bathhouse, where Mama had holed up that time:

"Hmm, what's going to happen with that poor girl now?"

I asked, "What poor girl?"

"I'm thinking of Abdullaev's bride. What mother would marry her son to her after all those curses?"

"Well, if someone is afraid, he can take her to a fortune-teller, or whoever you take people to in cases like this."

"We do have one here in town, Elmiuraz."

"So let them take her to him." I picked up the tray with the glasses of fragrant tea and a bowl of figs and carried it out into the front room.

There they were still discussing Khalilbek's miracles.

"The red commander has a dairy farm, you know," the silver-toothed neighbor was saying.

"The red commander?" I asked, distributing the tea glasses around the table.

"Patya, have you been on another planet? The red commander is the father of those red-heads: Farid, Gamid, Saigid."

"Oh, of course."

"Anyway, something was wrong over there on the farm. The cows weren't giving enough milk—there wasn't enough for sour cream, cheese, or whey. It had been that way for almost a whole year, they were in danger of losing everything. And right then Khalilbek shows up in town, holding some twig, and he's walking past the farm. He sees the commander and starts talking with him, pats the cows a little—and that's all it took. They immediately started giving milk."

"Oh, come on!"

"I swear by my tooth!"

I pictured the neighbor's calloused hands reaching into her mouth and extracting the tooth, and giggled.

"What are you laughing about, Patimat! Like a donkey in heat!" Granny silenced me.

The neighbor women abandoned their pumpkin seeds and settled down around the table. The butterfly continued to doze on the windowpane.

"Plus, Khalilbek cured Khadizha. That was a long time ago," began the one who had pestered me in the kitchen.

"Khadizha?"

"Aselder's wife. They also have a son Marat, a handsome guy who's a lawyer in Moscow. He went to law school with Shakh. You know, Firuza's son, Shakh."

My palms started to sweat. Marat! They're talking about him! I scraped my chair on the floor.

"How did he do that?"

"What do you mean, how? At that time Khalilbek had some dealings with Aselder, but then they had a falling out. Adik, the one who was run over, turned out to be his son."

"Whose son?"

"Aselder's! Illegitimate. So, anyway, Khadizha had these horrible headaches, she said it felt like she was growing a horn in her forehead. She tossed and turned, and couldn't get any sleep. She moaned with pain all day long. Then one day Khalilbek dropped in informally for *khinkal.* "What's the matter, Khadizha?" he says. He took a teaspoon, dipped it in some tea, and laid it against her forehead, like this!"

The neighbor woman took a teaspoon, dipped it in her glass of hot tea and laid it, bowl side down, on my forehead. It burned my skin and I gave a little yelp.

"That's exactly what he did to her," laughed the neighbor.

"Did her headaches really stop?" chirped everyone all together.

"It was like he removed it with his hand, like magic! Khadizha said so herself. But now she's denying it!"

"Oh, she's a temperamental one..."

Our gate squeaked, and a child's voice was heard from the yard:

"Is Patya home?"

I ran out to see who was asking for me. The brown-haired neighbor girl stood on our porch, a little disheveled, in bright blue stockings.

"Patya, someone's asking for you!"

"Who is it?"

"Aida. She says come out right now. She's outside."

"Why doesn't she come in?"

"Come out and ask her yourself."

And off she ran. I looked out the gate, but no one was there. Just the neighbor girl's cheap skirt fluttering as she ran around the corner.

"Aida!" I called, trying to get a better look. "Are you here?"

And immediately found myself face to face with Timur. He had obviously been lurking behind a post, waiting for me to come out.

"Patya!"

"What are you doing here?" I hit the gate with my fist.

"Whoa, slow down there! Quiet! Why, like, so mad? You didn't pick up the phone!"

"I didn't want to!"

"Hey, what's with the attitude?"

"I asked you to leave me alone."

"Hold on, like is that any way to do things? You wrote to me for months, since winter."

"I made you no promises. Just shot the breeze, because you're from back home."

I wanted someone to appear and save me from Timur. Take him away, seal his mouth with clay, tie him up, roll him up into a ball, and tuck him away in their pocket. But at the same time I was terrified: what if the person who showed up was Marat? He would see me with Timur, and would naturally deduce that we were a couple. No, no, I had to deal with this myself.

"Listen," Timur huffed, flexing his strong shoulders. "That's no way to do things. We need to go over this normally, to, like, explain the reasons. What's the problem? What I said about Darwin, was that it?"

"Timur, what difference does it make?"

"It makes a difference to me. We'll, like, talk, I'll lay it out, how and why, the whole scoop. But don't brush off people who are smarter than you, who know more stuff."

"Wait, so you're 'smarter people?'"

"You're a real spitfire, aren't you! Your papa home?"

"No."

"Why are you lying?"

"You can see his car's not here. What do you need my papa for?"

"I'd tell him how things are, that you and I have been together all this time."

"We aren't together any more," I was close to tears. But there was no getting through to Timur.

"What's the matter? I told you about the house, it'll, like, be built soon. If you want to live in city, we can rent something there, I work in the Youth Committee, I've got, like, tons of money."

"What do you need me for, Timur? There was that girl at your meeting, she's much better for you."

"What girl? Oh, Diana, you mean…But she's divorced, she's got a kid, a little girl."

"What makes me any better? I have no desire to grow my hair out or discuss Darwin with you. And I don't pray. That's not happening."

"I won't put pressure on you. You'll come around on your own. No one is going to force you," he flexed his sculpted biceps and glanced at his watch.

"They're about to call the *azan*, I gotta go. So cut the sass, you hear me? Act normal, and things will be normal."

Having shared this tedious aphorism, Timur gave me a playful wink. I could hear the neighbor women laughing inside, and suddenly realized that one of them could come out any minute and see me at the gate with Timur.

"That's it, I'm going back in," I snapped, terrified at the mere idea.

"Go on. I'll be coming to see your father in any case."

From the Avenue came the sound of the mullah's hoarse voice chanting the *azan*. Evidently, the mullah—the Abdullaevs' relative—had caught cold.

"It's the afternoon prayer," Timur said, with an air of importance. "I'm off to pray. And you go put on a skirt."

He nodded toward my light-colored pants, turned, and strode off, to my profound relief. I lingered at the gate, listening to the air, which was filled with the chirring of grasshoppers. Across the street, off to one side, a house stood vacant. It had belonged to the late Mashidat Zalova, our literature teacher. She had been six feet tall, an old maid, polyglot, and passionate bibliophile. Her father had traced his ancestors to khans who had been in favor with the Russian tsar; his forefathers had worn generals' epaulets. He himself had been an engineer and had designed a gigantic hydroelectric plant in one of the mountain canyons. In the nineteen-thirties someone had informed on him, and he'd been falsely accused for providing secret data to capitalist spies; he had been tortured mercilessly. They kept him awake in a basement cell and made him stand in icy water up to his knees. The unfortunate prisoner ultimately collapsed into the water and drowned, but through it all he had remained steadfast and had refused to confess and repent.

As for Mashidat Zalova, she had been assigned to our school after graduating from the Institute. As the daughter of an enemy of the people, she could not be allowed to work in city schools, but our out-of-the-way suburb was no problem. Rumor had it that she had been wooed by Adik's widowed grandfather, an architect and veteran of the Great Patriotic War. He had been persistent in his attempts but she had foresworn family life and closed herself in with her dusty tomes and folios. When I was in school, I used to go to the old woman's place to get rare books. Every book's flyleaf bore the calligraphic inscription: FROM THE LIBRARY OF M.Z. ZALOVA, along with the year and place the book was acquired. The margins teemed with exclamation marks, check marks, and commentaries: "So true!" "Sic!" "Completely unoriginal," etc. She was buried in the local cemetery near the prison.

Next to Mashidat Zalova's empty house lived a childless deaf couple—Gagarin and Supia. They communicated with each other through gestures, punctuating them with strange, non-human sounds. The neighborhood kids tormented them constantly, especially Gagarin, who was easily provoked. Sometimes I used to join in. We would scramble over the low fence into their garden, climb the stubby apple trees and grab handfuls of the sour green fruit, then flee the enraged, incoherently howling owner. Gagarin sometimes managed to whack one of us kids over the head with a wooden stick, but we were usually able to escape without any casualties. We would drive him into a frenzy by sticking out our tongues and making faces at him. And despite Gagarin's deafness, we would yell a cruel ditty at the top of our voices:

Gagarin's rocket tries to fly,
It's a ripped-up paper sack.
Shoot it up into the sky,
It somersaults and tumbles back

Falling to the ground,
Mooing as it tumbles down:

"Moo moo moo, moo, moo moo:
I don't trust any of you!"

Now Gagarin spent every day in the garden making strange-looking wooden chairs with weird, knotty backs. On Saturdays, his wife would take them to the city to sell at the bazaar. Next door to the deaf couple was a complex of lean-tos and outbuildings clustered around a cobble-stoned inner courtyard, where Mukhtar's big family dwelt. The whole family—sons, daughters-in-law, and children—zealously observed all the religious dictates. The women and the girls over the age of seven wrapped themselves completely in hijabs, concealing from view even their sharp little chins; the men attended the sermons at the unofficial mosque on the other side of the tracks. This led to periodic conflicts with the neighbors, especially with the school director, who had even been beaten up once by Mukhtar's sons. Our neighbors and Granny suspected Mukhtar and his family of all kinds of deviltry, and when they met on the street they would spit on the pavement in their wake.

"Why do they hide their chins!" the women would gripe. "Why do they wear those black rags, like they're in mourning? That's not how we do things around here."

At first Mukhtar and his whole family were treated as pariahs, but with time the number of strictly observant believers grew and grew. The conflict between the two mosques intensified, and I got tired of hearing about their endless squabbles and disputes. Khalilbek's role in all of this remained unclear. Some insisted that he gave money to the congregation "across the tracks;" others scoffed indignantly:

"Come on, how can you possibly claim Khalilbek is a *Salafi*? It's ridiculous!"

It was not surprising that both sides had gone to the city to the demonstration for Khalilbek. At any rate, not a sound could be heard from Mukhtar's yard.

I stood a while longer, thinking, then went back into the house, to the chattering neighbor women and Granny, who was always eager to hear the latest gossip. The white butterfly that had been on the windowpane was nowhere to be seen. It had fluttered away, leaving just a tiny smudge on the pane.

I resumed my place with the others and set to cleaning pumpkin seeds. Suddenly, I knew what to do: "I'll call Shakh," I thought, "and ask him to protect me from that dastardly Timur. If only out of friendship with my brother, Shakh won't refuse." The thought gave me some relief. And Marat's silence tore just slightly less at my heart.

8. FORTUNE TELLING AND A DEAD MAN

Marat's mother started in on his father at the crack of dawn. She had decided to drag Marat to Elmiuraz the fortune-teller.

"He can tell us if Marat will be married on the thirteenth or if we'll lose our reservation for the banquet hall."

"What does the banquet hall have to do with anything, Khadizha? You're an educated woman, what's this about some Elmiuraz quack?" Marat's father groaned.

"Fiddle-de-dee," his mother retorted. "You obviously don't care if your son gets married or not!"

"What I care about is for you not to make a fool of yourself, like some bird-brain. What if my friends find out? Aselder's a scholar, does research. He's planning to go on the hajj, and meanwhile his wife is running around to fortune-tellers."

"He's not a fortune-teller, he's a psychic. Marat! Get a move on!" she raged.

"Come on, Marat, aren't you ashamed? Who are you going to listen to?" his father snapped.

Marat looked at them both and laughed.

"Papa, I couldn't care less about this Elmiuraz and his hocus pocus! I'm going for Mama's sake. It'll make her feel better."

"Good boy," his mother clucked. "Hurry up, let's go before your father eats us alive with all his learning."

They started off toward the field of swamp sedge that began beyond town, stopped at the last house, Elmiuraz's, and knocked at the shiny, freshly scrubbed gate. A homely woman in a housedress came out to meet them, holding a broom. She collared a little boy who was tooling around the yard on a tricycle and delegated him to show the guests into the house. Marat and his mother followed the child into a room cluttered with furniture and children's toys.

"All right, then. Don't you worry about the fee, it's already been taken care of. I'll go now, and later you can tell me how everything went," his mother whispered to Marat, and she left, mission accomplished.

Marat began to wait, sneering internally at the whole enterprise. No one showed up to greet him. A young woman passed through the room several times with a bawling baby in her arms, paying no attention to Marat. Then the child pattered in again in his bare feet and stood in the corner, where he gaped at Marat, silently mouthing a lump of sugar. When Marat tried to strike up a conversation, the boy ran away.

Finally, Elmiuraz himself appeared. He was a feeble, narrow-chested man with unshaven cheeks and sweatpants ripped at the knees.

"*Salam alaikum*," he greeted Marat quietly, "I'll make some coffee."

Marat looked around for a Turkish coffee pot and a gas burner, but Elmiuraz unceremoniously took a jar of instant coffee off the shelf and stabbed the button of an electric tea kettle with his hairy finger. Evidently, it had just been used; the kettle immediately started gurgling, then turned itself off.

The fortune-teller spooned some instant coffee into a cracked cup, poured hot water over it, and slid the cup over to Marat.

"Go ahead and drink it. I'll be right back."

He disappeared again. Marat shrugged and obediently sipped at the scalding swill. On the other side of the wall, the baby squealed and fussed.

The homely woman came in from the yard, dumped a pile of dry, not yet ironed laundry onto an armchair, and vanished without a word. Several more minutes passed, then Elmiuraz reappeared. He shuffled in with his back hunched over, sat opposite Marat, and waited for his client to polish off the contents of the cracked cup.

Marat finally finished his coffee and triumphantly extended the empty cup to the psychic. Of course, there was no residue on the bottom and sides, just a faint discoloration. But Elmiuraz closed his eyes and overturned the cup onto the saucer.

"Um..." Marat began.

"Wait!" Elmiuraz raised his index finger into the air and, eyelids still closed, whispered a string of unintelligible incantations.

Then he took the cup in both hands, lifted it to his nose and, exhaling, "*Bismillah, Bismillah, Bismillah,*" fixed his gaze on the pale brown edge of the coffee stain. A minute or two passed. A cuckoo sprang out of the wall clock and chirped, bouncing on its spring. On the other side of the wall, the baby resumed screaming at the top of its voice.

"I see a blind figure," Elmiuraz finally uttered.

"A blind figure?"

"Yes, holding a set of scales. The goddess of justice. She stands between the present and the future. She seems to be leading you forward."

Marat immediately understood that his mother had already established a relationship with the fortune-teller. He clearly knew everything there was to know about the law office.

"Glasses... Put on dark glasses when you're going outside, to meetings, it will help ward off the evil eye."

"All right..."

"Ahead of you the road splits in two. A choice... Either you'll have a wedding very soon, with a good girl..."

"Or?"

"Or some kind of incomprehensible emptiness."

"What do you mean?"

"Only you can know the answer."

"Great. What else?"

"Be sure to take care of your health, or you'll have problems in old age."

"Aha, brilliant. What else?"

"Do not expect great wealth, though you will not sink to the bottom. The long road will bring joy. A celebration. I see two rings joined together."

"So, which is it to be, two rings or emptiness?" Marat asked, squinting, not without guile.

"Two rings, with emptiness inside. It might mean that you need to get married as soon as possible. And, also, a model of the Universe: space, the planets, Saturn..."

"Why Saturn?"

"It's the star of your own personal fate. Now..."

Elmiuraz covered his face with his palms and again mumbled some prayers. The baby's squealing ceased immediately, as though it had been chopped off. The homely woman appeared again in the room, this time with an iron, trailing its cord along the floor. Scorning the sacraments underway in the room, she clattered the ironing board open, turned her back to the fortunetelling, and started in on some wrinkled duvet covers.

"I see a number, another number... Thirteen, eight... Bottles of wine, the sea or the ocean. You are to be a stranger wandering the world, simply passing through. You are to die before your death."

"Huh?"

"*Bismillah, Bismillah, Bismillah.* You will meet a teacher. You will acquire a girl."

"A girlfriend or a wife?" Marat decided to follow along. He cast a sidelong glance at the woman and her spluttering iron.

"Both."

"Meaning, someone I haven't met yet?"

Elmiuraz thought, then spoke:

"If you haven't found anyone yet, then, *inshallah*, you will in the very near future."

"Of course, I figured that," Marat snickered.

Suddenly, a buzzing, remote-controlled toy jeep invaded the room, followed by the child that Marat had seen earlier. The woman set down her iron and yelled shrilly at the boy in a language Marat did not recognize. The child stamped his bare feet in protest. The psychic was unperturbed by the commotion around him. He just rolled his eyes and resumed his chanting.

While Elmiuraz was soaring around in the astral sphere, a clamor arose outside on the street. There came the sound of women wailing, along with the excited babbling of teenage boys in their newly acquired low voices. Elmiuraz snapped out of his trance. Hiking up his sweat pants, he rushed out to find out what was going on. The barefoot boy followed, slapping his bare heels and occasionally letting the jeep drop with a clatter onto the floor.

The homely woman shouted something after them, but then abandoned the iron on the ironing board's grating and shuffled outside herself. The wailing on the street intensified. Marat figured there was no point in staying there by himself, especially when the young mother reappeared from the inner rooms and hastened to join the crowd outside, complete with her bawling nursling.

Marat ran out too. There he beheld the Elmiuraz clan interrogating a cluster of agitated women and teenagers, whom, evidently, he had never seen before. He blurted out:

"What's going on?"

"They say that someone was killed on the Avenue. A guy from here."

"Who?"

"They said he lives 'across the tracks.'"

The young mother jiggled the baby, who had stopped sobbing and was now making little grunting noises.

"Probably the mosques going at each other again."

"This morning, at the crack of dawn, I heard voices saying, 'Something is going to happen this afternoon.'" Elmiuraz, directing this last utterance to no one in particular, scratched his stubble and looked downward, onto the dark earth, Then he raised his eyes to his client, as though anticipating an expression of awe or further cross-examination. But Marat just distractedly extended his hand to the psychic:

"I'll go and see what's going on over there. Thank you for the coffee."

"One does not say 'thank you' after a session, or what is fated will not come to pass," mumbled Elmiuraz.

But Marat had already rushed off. A shaggy band of teenagers in dusty athletic shorts trailed after him.

The Avenue was at the other end of town. A crowd of rubberneckers had gathered along the streets leading to the scene, and an ambulance maneuvered through them, occasionally having to back up. Marat immediately spotted in the crowd a couple of the "Red Army" redheads, Gamid and Roma. Spotting Marat, Roma skipped the prelude and jabbered:

"It's Rusik, Rusik-the-Nail! They just took him away. He's dead—the doctors didn't make it in time!"

"What?" Marat gasped.

He had seen Rusik literally just the other day, pedaling to the city on his bike. Rusik had been in a bad mood, had complained about the local proselytizers who had latched onto him and wouldn't leave him alone:

"They came the day before yesterday, they came yesterday, they came today... 'Look,' they say, 'do you think the people around here are real Muslims? For them it's just a word. They steal, they drink, they turn living people into idols, they hobnob with *kafirs*, and they're fixated on miracles.' They say that people have made Khalilbek into some kind of holy man. They say, 'You're not like that but you will become mired in your disbelief. Come to our mosque, just once...' Blah, blah, blah, you know as well as I do. They don't understand the meaning of the word 'no.' Won't shut up! They're bugging the shit out of me!"

Marat had invited his suffering friend to go with him to a private beach, to have a swim in the sea. They had agreed to go today, in fact, but now...

"Can you tell me what happened?" he asked the redheads.

"That Rusik of yours finally got what he had coming to him," Gamid stated grimly.

A young man in a cheap T-shirt who was eavesdropping butted in:

"Look, brother, here's the long and short of it. That devil, that Rusik asshole, goes and makes a placard saying that there's no Allah, and he's out strutting around with it on the Avenue. Our guys spot him out there. They go over to, like, scope it out. Not to make a real dent or nothing. But Rusik loses it..."

"So, then they killed him, you mean?" shouted Marat.

People started to look and gather around. Someone countered from behind, in a cracking voice:

"No one, like, offed him! It was just a stupid accident. Dude brought it on himself."

The voice belonged to Timur, the bruiser from the youth committee. Marat had spent a lot of time over the past few days thinking about this guy in connection with Patya. She hadn't answered his call. Then Marat had gone to her house, but hadn't been able to catch her there at a moment when she was outside. The vixen had taken root in his heart, had beckoned to him, and then vanished.

"What do you mean 'a stupid accident?'" Marat growled.

"Mukhtar's son Alishka goes over to ask about the placard," the guy in the T-shirt eagerly explained. "But Rusik loses it, gets up in his face. And then the shit hits the fan. They were standing over there, on that square in front of the grocery store. Abdullaev got sucked in too..."

"I saw them and went up in case I could, like, maybe break it up," Timur swaggered. "Anyway, so right outside the store there's this crazy dude with his placard, and our guys are on the other side of the square. Things were cool at first, no pushing and shoving, it was like, you know, they just sort of told him to put the placard away. But the dude starts in with 'I have the right,' shit like that. And they were kind of like, 'No way in hell.' And, then, like, it's a free for all..."

"Were they packing heat?" Marat interrupted.

Everyone started yelling at once:

"They didn't have nothing on them, man!"

"What do you mean, heat?"

"Alishka just gave him a little nudge, that's all."

"No, he didn't! It was Abdullaev," corrected Gamid. "And then the idiot slipped and slammed his head down on the concrete."

"It was his own fault, it was a total accident!" Timur concluded.

For a second it seemed to Marat that they were messing with his mind. This whole stupid thing couldn't possibly be true.

"Marat, believe me, they're not shitting you," Roma babbled. "No one offed Rusik. They're normal dudes, they just got pissed that he would do stuff like that. Rusik even got up again after he fell, ask the guys."

"He was talking, too!" people shouted in the crowd.

Roma held up three thick fingers:

"I run up to him, I go, 'How many fingers?' And Rusik grins, answers, 'Three.' And then he takes a couple of steps and *bam*! Just konks out on the concrete! We call the paramedics, but he's bit the dust."

"It was Allah struck him down, you know, you could say," Timur waved his hand in the air, "for not believing in Him."

"Hold on, I don't get it about the placard," Marat mumbled, looking around to see if there was anyone official nearby.

A short distance away, a row of policemen stood with their feet planted importantly on the pavement, automatic weapons across their bellies, surveying the scene.

He started threading his way through the crowd.

"I'm going over to ask the cops."

"You go ahead and do that, and while you're at it, ask those curs why they took Alishka," Gamid spit wrathfully onto the ground, "You're a lawyer, so do something."

Marat stopped.

"Alishka, Mukhtar's son? They arrested him?

"Yes, you got here too late."

"Well, they did the right thing if they arrested him. Abdullaev too?"

"Him too." Roma nodded. "But Shakh is trying to figure something out. They're going to call witnesses later."

Shakh was with the policemen. Marat had not noticed him behind the crowd. He was gesticulating and haranguing an imposing-looking, well-built man of fifty in civilian clothes who was holding something made of poster board, folded in half.

"Allow me to introduce you. This is Marat, also a lawyer. He's working on an important case in Moscow. And Marat, this is Colonel Gaziev. You're neighbors, by the way."

"Aha-a-a-a, you're Aselder's son?" The colonel put two and two together. He had an indeterminate mountain accent, and slightly mis-pronounced his words.

"Yes. And I knew the deceased," Marat clarified. "Is it premeditated murder?"

Shakh started: "What are you saying, Marat?" he hissed.

"Well I'm at this very moment trying to convince your colleague, that yes, it is," the colonel reported, raising his right eyebrow.

"Unpremeditated murder, of course," interrupted Shakh, who had broken into a sweat. "Article 109. All the eyewitnesses have confirmed it. Abdullaev is basically just a witness. He's got absolutely nothing to do with this."

"We'll figure everything about Abdullaev later, but the second one, Ali Mukhtarov, has been on our books for quite some time," the colonel squinted and unfolded the poster paper.

Marat realized that it was the placard.

He leaned over toward the colonel's shoulder and read, in thick red oil-painted letters, "I am an agnostic."

"Whew, Rusik-the-Nail really outdid himself," Marat blurted out.

"They're right to call it a provocation. He knew exactly what he was doing!" Shakh grinned. "If it comes to a trial, this sign will play right into the defense's hand. The victim was not in his right mind and was headed intentionally to suicide."

"Can you hear yourself? First, you say he slipped accidentally, and now, all of a sudden, it's suicide?"

"Wait..."

"We'll figure it out, it's either A or B. Excuse me, I have to go." The colonel folded the poster board and turned his back.

"People say the man's a jerk, but you can't really..." mumbled Marat, following with his eyes the movement of the shoulder blades plainly visible under the departing colonel's shirt.

"What made you take Colonel Gaziev's side?" Shakh was enraged. "Why did you start in with that stuff about premeditated murder? Have you decided to help me with my case?"

"So you're defending Rusik's murderers?"

"You have no idea what happened! You showed up out of nowhere, after everything was over—when there was no longer a body, and no suspects in sight! I can get Abdullaev out, he's basically got nothing to do with it. Of course when he saw Rusik with that moronic sign, he went up to ask about it. Wouldn't you have done the same?

Then Alishka stuck his nose in it. One thing led to another, and all of a sudden we're in the middle of a shitshow. What was Rusik thinking? He could have taken a stand on his own turf, 'across the tracks,' but no, he had to stir up trouble all the way down here on the Avenue! What is that supposed to mean, 'I'm an agnostic?' Are you following me? Neither Alishka nor Abdullaev even know what the word means. All they understood is that he's badmouthing Allah."

"Shakh, the end result is that Rusik is dead. Who's guilty?" Marat felt a strange sensation of weightlessness, and just blurted it out.

"What, so now Rusik was your BFF?" Shakh squinted.

"BFF or not, the guys who pushed him have to answer for it."

"Alishka, Mukhtar's son—let him answer for it, I don't feel sorry for him at all. The colonel has been after his whole family for being Wahhabis. Not so long ago they dragged Alishka into the Sixth Department on suspicion of extremism, and once someone goes in there, forget it, he's done for. But Abdullaev... I've already sleuthed out how much has to be given to whom to get them to let him off. The family will collect it."

"What does he face? Negligent homicide?"

"Article 109, just what I told you, though that devil of a colonel is trying to slap him with 105, so the two of you are in cahoots. The only hope is the witnesses."

"But look at the witnesses, Shakh. The half that goes to the mosque 'across the tracks' will come down hard on your Abdullaev, the other half will try to nail bearded Alishka. Either way the judge has to get his cut," Marat said venomously, rubbing his throbbing head.

"Gotta go, Abdullaev's old man is calling," Shakh barked. He took out his ringing phone and stepped away.

The crowd hadn't yet dispersed. They lingered, shifting from one foot to the other, chattering. Marat caught sight of Ismail, the school director, standing with Timur, who was practically jumping out of his skin trying to convince him of something. Marat had had enough. Hoping to slip away unnoticed, he walked past the cordoned-off concrete square in front of the store—where Rusik had been killed—and turned down a filthy alleyway. At that instant he heard a sharp whistle and stopped short. He turned and saw a woman wrapped completely in a shapeless garment, with only her oval face and hands exposed to the sun. She was laughing.

"Don't you recognize me, Marat?" she asked, a little too casually.

Then, noticing a crowd of old women hurrying toward the Avenue, she caught up to Marat and beckoned. It was Angela, the prison janitor's daughter: tramp, slut, spawn of the devil—the girl had been called every name in the book. When he was still living at home, Marat had been drawn in by the strange power of this girl who was everyone's lover; he had refused to believe the evidence before his eyes, and was terribly possessive. When he was alone with her, he had spouted the most ridiculous nonsense about his feelings. But one day the obsession passed, and it was as if it had never even happened.

Angela turned the corner, bumped a gate open with her hip, and slipped inside a courtyard, beaming back at Marat and beckoning with her pink finger. He followed her and found himself in a small room, which, to judge from the electric range, also served as her kitchen. Angela showed him to an old sofa, sat down opposite, and asked again:

"So, you didn't recognize me, Marat?"

"Not right away."

"I didn't recognize you at first either. Your shoulders are broader now," she giggled. "And me? Take a good look. I'm married."

"Congratulations, I didn't know…"

It seemed to Marat that he had plunged deep into the turbid waters of the Caspian and was trudging through a layer of thick, sandy mud at the bottom. His ears clogged up, and his body was drained of all its strength.

"Have you heard? Rusik-the-Nail was killed! It happened today," he rasped, barely audibly.

Angela froze for a second, thrown off balance by the topic. Then she licked her lips, leaned forward toward Murat, and nodded her head, which was still covered in her scarfs.

"Of course. I even saw the doctors come. They tried their best, but couldn't do anything. Rusik was always a little strange. And it was a strange way to die."

"He was murdered," Marat coughed, trying to clear his throat.

"What are you talking about, Marat? He fell flat on his skull on the concrete during a squabble with the guys. Always spoiling for a fight, that Rusik! Oof! What was that he had written on his placard?"

"'I am an agnostic.'"

Angela snorted:

"Ganostic? People sure like to use big words these days…Someone told me that the placard was against Allah…"

She fell silent and strained her ears: from the porch came the sound of bottles dropping and rolling across the ground, and a orange tomcat poked his lecherous muzzle into the room. Angela hissed and stamped her foot loudly. The cat recoiled and vanished.

"Why aren't you asking how things are with me, who my husband is?" she smiled sweetly again at Marat. He mumbled, glancing to one side, and rubbed his temple.

"I'm in shock about Rusik…First thing tomorrow I'm going

straight to the investigator's office in the city to ask him to consider the case without bias, without getting into any kind of 'us versus them.' Alishka is sure to be imprisoned, he's been on their books for a long time now, but this is something new, with all the religion thrown in."

"Marat, you're not looking at me," Angela sat beside him on the sofa and heaved a soulful sigh. "Want me to take off my scarf for you? No one is going to come in."

"Why do you wear it anyway? When did you start?" Marat reluctantly raised his head and looked her over.

"My husband told me to, so I covered," Angela brightened up and gave him a coy look. "He lives in Pyatigorsk, because it's dangerous for him here. He's an investigator on especially important cases, and they're all getting murdered. Khalilbek was behind one of them."

"Those are rumors. No one knows whether they're true or not," Marat turned away.

"Pooh-pooh," drawled Angela. "'No one knows!' He sent your own brother, no more than a child, to the next world, and here you are defending him. Mama saw Khalilbek in prison once when he was being led down the hall. She says he was haggard, his skin was all green and he had dark circles under his eyes. One glance and you could see his conscience was tormenting him."

"We were planning to go to the shore today," Marat said suddenly.

"What?"

"Rusik and I. I can only imagine what they did to him when he tried that infantile stunt with the placard! And right in the center of town where everyone could see him!"

"Want to see something?" Angela interrupted, lowering her voice and adjusting the scarf that had slipped down onto her eyebrows.

"But I forgot about it. How could I!" Marat wasn't listening. "Mama with her fortune-teller...And I could have prevented it."

"Marat..."

"Meanwhile, Shakh is pulling out all the stops to get his friend out of trouble."

"Marat! You're not listening to me!" Angela clutched him angrily by the shoulder.

"I'm sorry," Marat shook off her hand. "I'm bringing you down. I shouldn't have come. I'll be on my way."

And he stood up.

"Stop!" Angela snapped, springing up after him. "What, you're going to get up and leave, just like that?"

She was panting, and her brows trembled, as though they didn't know whether to come together and form a single line, or to rise up under the scarf, or to relax in sweet languor. Marat tugged at the tip of his nose, still looking past Angela and trying to come up with an excuse.

"Your husband will show up. He'll see us and get the wrong idea."

"I told you," she beamed again, "my husband lives in Pyatigorsk, he has another family there. And I'm here. He only comes once every ten days and the rest of the time I'm so lonesome here all by myself!"

"'So lonesome,'" Marat interrupted the temptress, "so give Shakh a call. Or some other guys. What do you need me for? Especially at a time like this. Rusik just died..."

"You're really getting on my nerves with this Rusik of yours!" Angela gave him a shove. "You and I haven't seen each other for such a long time, and look at you! Have you forgotten how you chased after me when you were a snot-nosed kid? You even wanted to marry me!"

"I'm not a snot-nosed kid any more, you can see that yourself." Marat calmly and firmly eased her away from him. "And I don't spend my time entertaining repentant sinners."

Angela wrinkled her lips and punched him in the chest with her fist:

"Oh, so now you're teaching me morals? Bringing up my past? I'm a decent woman now. A legally wedded wife, got it?"

"A second wife. A kept woman. Does the first wife even know about you? I bet she doesn't."

He went to the door, and she followed, beating him on the back and shouting:

"So what if I am a second wife? So what! It's in the Prophet's *sunnah*! It's completely legal!"

When he reached the porch, she sprang to him, seized the collar of his shirt, and ran her hands across his body like an animal.

"You know you want to! You want to, but you're afraid. Don't be afraid..."

Marat tore himself away, and a button detached from his shirt and bounced down the wooden porch stairs. Angela darkened, and launched into a string of staccato curses:

"Ah, you... You reptile, so you've found some new girl? So you think you're going to get married? Think again: may you be cursed, may the earth swallow you up on the very day of your wedding!"

Marat crossed the yard to the gate, and before he could get it open, one of the glass bottles that the cat had tipped over crashed and shattered against the iron gate.

9. AT ZAREMA'S

In the morning, we were expecting guests. I was scared it would be the Magomedovs: the chubby chatterbox, the mute veterinarian with the long nose, and the widowed mother. But I was lucky: the visitors were some of Mama's distant relatives from the village. The mystery novels were stashed in a neat stack under the bed. a pot of sun-dried meat bubbled on the stove all morning. Mama stirred it with a huge ladle, occasionally interrupting her work to rush from room to room, issuing commands:

"Patya, polish the electrical outlets!"

"Patya, clean the tiles! Use only dry cleanser, and be sure not to leave any smears!"

"Patya, you lazybones! You didn't clean the silver! Do it now! Make it snappy!"

Granny got her best fringed scarf out of the trunk. Papa washed the car and drove off to the city to pick up the visitors.

Aida dropped in, and naturally came up with all kinds of theories: "Just wait, they're bringing you a bridegroom."

I brushed her off. "That's the last thing I need!"

Finally they arrived, lugging heavy duffle bags. One of them was full of mulberries and apricots; the mulberries stained everything violet, and the apricots were a special aboriginal variety called *khonobakh*, "pull-eggs," in Avar—tiny, orange, heart-shaped fruits with fine, shiny skin, pungent, fruity-smelling pulp, and pits that rolled out like tiny eggs. The second duffle bag contained jars of *urbech*, an ancient local delicacy: a paste made out of stone-ground roasted sunflower seeds, nuts, black flax, sunflower, apricot, and dark, brown hemp. The third bag held bottles of sweet and sour whey, fermented colostrum, packages of *tvorog*, and a bag of barley powder for brewing "beer kasha"—a delicacy just for women. In the fourth...but before I could scope out the fourth bag, Mama's usual hostess panic set in—from the kitchen came a great racket: stampeding footsteps, shrill squeals, and the metallic clatter of spoons.

We gathered around the table, which was laden with corn *khinkal* and meat, along with bowls of bouillon, *adjika* sauce, *urbech*, and sour-cream garlic sauce. Simplicity and restraint: natural flavor, honest calories. My uncle and Papa immediately lit into the cognac. The two aunties settled down next to Granny, one on each side. Mama occupied one end of the table and I was seated opposite the singularly unimpressive-looking distant cousin they had brought along. I thought that he would blush and remain reserved in the presence of our family, as the village customs prescribed, but that was not at all the case. Without the slightest inhibition, he addressed me directly and struck up a conversation:

"I've been in Moscow myself. I did my military service there at the Kursk Station. I caught thieves there a couple of times. One time I found a bomb."

"What, a real one?"

"It was a dummy. They were testing our vigilance. I liked it there. Helped establish discipline, worked to prevent bullying. I got promoted to sergeant early, and they recommended me for a military career, offered me a contract. I thought, that's all well and good, but what's the point? This is no career for a guy who likes his freedom.

We worked in the metro too."

"Those grim-looking soldiers who patrol in groups with dogs?"

"They look grim because they're sleep-deprived. You never get enough sleep... Where do you live in Moscow?"

Mama caught the edge of the conversation and intervened sternly.

"Not 'lives,' but 'used to live.' She's sponged off her brother long enough. Time for her to settle down back here with us."

The cousin nodded imperceptibly in her direction and winked a mirthful eye at me.

"Tough on you, eh? As for me, I'm planning to move to the city. In the village I taught in a sports club: free-style wrestling and taekwondo. Within a year I had three southern district champions. They went on to nationals. Now I want to start coaching in the city."

"Do you go to Moscow often?"

"Not really. I went once after I got out of the military, but didn't see much—didn't even go to the Lenin Mausoleum."

"Why would you go there anyway?"

"You know, just to check it out. I'd stop in, pay the guy a visit, ask, 'Is that really you lying there, man?' Think I should, Patya?"

I giggled. I pictured this cousin of mine barging into the stifling, dead interior of the mausoleum, taking off his hat... Though what kind of hat would he even be wearing?

Meanwhile, Mama was talking about yesterday's incident with Rusik.

"Imagine, he went out there with a placard saying 'There is no Allah.' Some of the young guys saw it, and naturally they got upset."

"And right then and there he was struck down by lightning," Granny declared, flaring her wide nostrils with authority.

"Come on, Mama, what do you mean, lightning?" Papa frowned

irritably. "A Wahhabi from Mukhtar's family, Alishka the roughneck, knocked Rusik down. That's all there is to your lightning."

"No, it was lightning," Granny insisted, talking in our native language. "From on high. And without a drop of rain, too."

"People are saying he just fell but I don't believe a word of it. The neighbors saw it. They say there was a brawl," Mama reported, piling more and more *khinkal* onto the plates of the protesting aunties. "What's worse, they've gone out and rounded up a bunch of young people in connection with case. Not just that damned Wahhabi—they arrested the Abdullaev boy too. Abdullaev is one of Khalilbek's associates, by the way. Small peanuts, of course, but, still, he has his own company in town. They are very well respected around here..."

"Their son's engagement was broken off recently. And now he's under suspicion of murdering that clown Rusik," Papa added. "One misfortune after another."

The tragic tale caused a great stir among the guests. The aunties ooh-ed and aah-ed, the uncle kept asking for more details, and the cousin nodded knowingly, tapping his index finger on the table, as though none of this was news to him.

"It's the curse!" Granny announced. "At the engagement party that woman cursed the Abdullaev boy—said that he would rot behind bars. And, sure enough, here he is in prison."

"What are you talking about, Mama! They'll let the kid out," Papa countered, chewing his meat. "Our young lawyer from town, Shakh, is a close friend of his. He's already on the case."

"'Kid!' Did you hear that? 'Kid!'" Mama exclaimed scornfully. "This 'kid' of yours is prowling the city knocking up college girls."

The cousin laughed again, silently, with his sparkling eyes.

The uncle proposed a toast: "May all these misfortunes pass us by!"

Glasses were again raised high and drained dry.

After lunch, the women closed themselves in with Mama to sort through some cloth. I could have joined them, but a wave of restless longing had came over me. Books tumbled from my hands. Under normal circumstances I would have tried to get in touch with Marina, but she had troubles of her own. In Bulgaria she had met a married man and had gotten tangled up in a vacation romance. They had agreed to continue the affair in Moscow. But what had started out so easy and carefree had turned into a whole drama, complete with damp, salty pillowcases and torrents of black jealousy directed at the lover's lucky wife. Marina had drained every possible expression of pity, sympathy, encouragement, and consolation out of me, then had vanished from the scene—undoubtedly to cry it out on someone's chest—a real, live, flesh-and-blood person, not some distant phantom like myself.

The uncle had gone off somewhere with Papa, and the cousin went into the city on some business of his own. The aunties tried all kinds of tactics to get me to go with him, hinting that surely I need someone to take me to the city. But I begged off. The moment the cousin set forth, though, I immediately put on my skirt and blouse and decided to go out for some air alone, with no entourage. My fear of Timur had subsided; he seemed to have abandoned his pursuit. After the incident with Rusik he had stopped barraging me with phone calls and text messages sprinkled with spelling errors. According to the neighbor woman with the silver tooth, Timur had also been mixed up somehow in yesterday's accident (or murder, even); if he hadn't actually shoved the disgraced atheist physically, at the very least he had shouted louder than the others, "Serves him right!"

I slipped out the gate and started walking slowly down the Avenue past the deaf-mute Gagarins' house. Suddenly, a man rounded a corner and stopped, facing me. Marat! The man who had been on my mind constantly since the moment we'd met. Khadizha and Aselder's son. Moscow lawyer. Shakh's friend. His face profoundly familiar and dear. As though it were myself standing there, though a man.

He stopped short, hesitated, and his motionless black eyes stared into me. My heart gurgled and swelled to bursting inside me, my fingers trembled, and drops of perspiration dewed my upper lip.

"Hi, Patya," Marat finally uttered with a warm smile. "Where have you been? Going far?"

"I'm just out for a walk."

"Why don't you answer the phone?"

"What, have you called me?" I exhaled.

"I called and called. You didn't answer and you didn't call back."

"I didn't see your calls, honest!" I exclaimed, terrified and, at the same time, dizzy with joy. "Wait, I remember. Someone called, but the caller ID was blocked. I thought it was someone else."

I meant Timur. My face flushed red.

"You're a clever one, now, aren't you?" Marat laughed. "You clever thing, you…"

We continued down the Avenue. My body followed its own laws, unsubmissive to my will. I marveled that my legs knew which way to bend, that they did not snap in two.

"Did you hear about Rusik?" he asked, darkening.

"Of course. It's terrible. I didn't know him very well, I can't understand why he did that. Why would he write on a placard that there's no God?"

Marat stopped short.

"That's not what he wrote. People keep lying and getting it mixed up! I saw the placard. It said "I am agnostic."

"Really? But that's completely different!"

"Of course it is," Marat confirmed, relieved. "Of course, he shouldn't have gone out there waving that statement around, but remember what Mashidat Zalova taught us in literature class—he was a victim of his environment. There you have it! The environment chewed him up and swallowed him."

Against my will I broke into a grim laugh. I camouflaged it with a fake cough and said, just to say something, anything:

"Take my parents: they thought he was some kind of clown."

"What, you think mine didn't?" Marat shrugged. "Patya, if we're being completely honest, his own parents thought the same way. And they disparaged him. He told me about it."

"What, you were friends?" I was surprised. "I didn't think that Rusik had any friends."

"Well, not friends, exactly, we spent time together. From the time we were kids. Did you know that at today's sermon the mullah called Rusik crazy and said he had been demon-possessed?"

"He just said that straight out?"

"Yes, can you imagine?" Marat nodded trustfully, intimately, like a close friend.

As we walked along, I occasionally caught passers-by eyeing us, burning with curiosity. Their glances snagged us like fish on a hook, and released us only when we passed beyond their field of vision. But I did not care. I was proud to be walking with Marat. Before we knew it, we were at the railroad embankment.

A freight train loaded with crushed stone lumbered past along the tracks dividing our suburb from what was beyond. The air smelled of diesel fuel, the pebbles on the embankment, and the sorrow of others. We stopped by a small adobe building that housed a café called At Zarema's. Zarema, the proprietor, was an eternally ailing old-looking woman with such a massive jaw that it seemed that the only thing holding it together was the tied-together ends of her scarf. The establishment's patrons were primarily locals, with an occasional mix of passengers from trains passing through. In the morning they were served by Zarema's nimble daughters-in-law, and, in the evening, by the proprietress herself, rheumatic and bundled in shawls.

"Shall we sit here awhile?" Marat suggested. "There's nowhere else to go in town. And it's a long way to the city."

I immediately agreed—though not without some apprehension that we might run into Papa and the uncle inside. Fortunately there was nothing to worry about; the café only had six or seven small tables, and only one of them was occupied. Several locals were noisily playing dominoes and sipping strong black tea, some of them in light shirts and panama hats, others in T-shirts with tattoos peeping out from under the sleeves.

"Look at those tattoos. we're obviously near the prison," whispered Marat.

Zarema's daughter-in-law, who had been dozing in the corner, spotted us together and stirred. From her distant perch she scanned me from head to toe, then shuffled over with a menu and unceremoniously, though with undisguised respect, addressed Marat:

"Hi, Marat, so glad you stopped in. You with your girl?"

"As you see," Marat smiled, and asked me: "What will you have, Patya?"

We ordered tea and baklava. The waitress shuffled behind a partition, and a few seconds later some scarfed female heads peeked out from there. They wanted to have a look at the girl Marat had brought.

"They know you so well," I said, not without irony.

"My mother is friends with Aunt Zarema," Marat explained guilelessly. "So they know me. But I wanted to tell you about Rusik. I went to see his family this morning with my father to give my condolences. It wasn't just us, half the town was there. It's a terrible loss, their only son, and in such a senseless way. We go there, cross the bridge to his house, and the gate is locked tight."

"Why?"

"People say that if the gate is closed and they are not accepting condolence visits, that means that the family is preparing a blood revenge."

"What a nightmare! But against whom?"

"That's the problem—essentially everyone is guilty. Alishka, for example, who pushed him. Or Abdullaev. But anyone else could have done it. Your Timur, for example."

And Marat looked straight into my eyes. That set me off. I flared up, waving my arms in the air:

"He's not 'my Timur'! I don't know how to get rid of him! He thinks that just because I exchanged some friendly messages with him—and, by the way, I had no idea he was such an idiot—that means I must like him."

"He's an enviable match: youth committee leader, always up onstage making speeches," Marat teased.

"Enough, please!" I moaned. "I already called Shakh to see if he could help me get rid of Timur. But Shakh refused to get involved. He says that Timur is serious about me. He says I should let him go ahead and propose, and then just turn him down."

"Shakh?" Marat turned serious again. "Better avoid him. He'll say anything. He even spread it around that you and Timur are engaged."

"That's not true!" I blushed furiously, yet again.

But Marat wasn't about to disagree or to doubt what I said. He just smiled and sat there with his hands calmly folded on his lap, observing me with a smile, as a man would watch his own child at play.

"What are you looking at?" I completely lost my bearings.

"I'm happy," he answered simply. "It makes me happy just to look at you."

His words went straight to my heart and gripped it with joy.

"So, why," I decided to return to our earlier topic, in the hopes of concealing my emotional state, "why were the gates locked?" But my voice trembled, betrayed me.

"Rusik's parents probably suspect and blame everyone. A lot of people, anyway. And they don't want to see anyone."

"Or maybe," I conjectured, "they're simply ashamed. Maybe they are so opposed to their late son's views that his act and his death are a source of shame to them and their whole family."

"Now that's interesting." Marat's eyebrows rose in surprise, even admiration.

We fell silent, first stealing glances at each other, and then, gradually, boldly looking straight into each other's eyes.

"Patya, what are you most afraid of?" Marat asked suddenly.

I thought. Scorpions? Creepy crawlies? My parents' deaths? Some hideous disfiguring disease? These were all old fears from childhood that I had suppressed long ago. I blurted out the first thing that came into my head:

"To be stuck in a sealed stone well, somewhere deep underground. Also, pain. Physical pain—that really scares me. What about you?"

"Recently I've started to be afraid of my own arms."

"What do you mean?"

"Sometimes I wake up at night, with my arms like this," he began quietly, crossing his arms across his chest, "and they are really heavy. You know, like steel. And I feel that I can't lift them and that they are crushing me.

I stared dumbly at his arms, not knowing what to say. He laughed:

"Did I scare you? Don't take it too seriously. It's just that I'm not getting enough sleep. It's not a good time for me to be on leave, I'm working on a really hot case right now in Moscow. A human rights worker, a woman, was murdered. The higher-ups are poking sticks in the spokes, trying to get an innocent man convicted. It's a contract job, and they're protecting the guy responsible."

"Do you know who ordered the murder?" I whispered.

"Yes. I'll tell you later," Marat leaned over to me, and his tea-colored eyes shone close to mine.

I felt my cheeks flare up again.

Zarema's daughter-in-law suddenly appeared beside us, set a porcelain teapot down on the table with a gentle clink, and transferred the baklava and cups from the tray to the table. She asked me:

"Whose daughter are you?"

I told her, after a brief internal struggle. My instinct was to snarl and send the inquisitive barbarian flying back to the kitchen behind the screen. After getting the answer, she lingered for a while longer by the table, holding the empty tray and surveying the café from there. The tattooed men sat over their game, laughing uproariously.

"Bring the check now, please. That's all, we don't need anything else," Marat ordered, casting a disapproving look at the shameless girl's fat hips.

She roused herself and sauntered off. Meanwhile, a bearded young man in a skullcap and a long, tightly buttoned-up white shirt entered the café from outside, ducking through the door with a stack of pamphlets under his arm. He noted with disappointment the scarcity of clientele, and scowled in the direction of the guffawing men at the domino table. His glance lingered briefly on Marat, and he made his way hesitantly toward the partition:

"*As-salam, as-salam, as-salam...*"

En masse, Zarema's daughters-in-law and daughters, a good half of them veiled, sprang to their feet. Showing due respect to the visitor in his role as guardian of morality, they led him to the nearest table. He handed each one of them a pamphlet, settled down comfortably, and babbling something incomprehensible, again surveyed the room.

"He's annoyed that there are so few people in here. And none of them suit his needs," explained Marat, smirking.

"What needs?"

"Propaganda. He's from the mosque on the Avenue. He comes here often, hangs around and hands out religious pamphlets. Announcements. Zarema, harbors him, so to speak, here."

The pamphlet guy had indeed made himself at home. Our fat-hipped waitress brought him a small, steaming cup of Turkish coffee and hovered over him in an expectant, reverential pose.

"A *djinn* had taken root in him," the pamphlet guy mumbled, reclining sideways on his chair so we could hear. "If his parents had brought this lost lamb to us in time, everything, *subkhanalla*, would have been fine. Here, read this: it's today's sermon. Our mullah explains everything here."

Marat pricked up his ears and stealthily seized the handle of the teaspoon I was holding, as if to say, "Shhh, quiet, just listen." His index finger brushed mine. Something deep inside me rumbled, like barbells along a wooden floor. And we sat and listened.

The pamphlet guy sipped his coffee, the men clattered the dominoes—white with black dots—on the rough surface of their table and wiped their mouths with crumpled napkins, and Zarema's entire female suite read the pamphlets aloud, tripping over the words:

"The folly of vice...unbelief...trampling of faith in the Almighty... the Prophet, *salalau alaikhi vassalam*...retribution from on high..."

The pamphlet guy finished his coffee and used his spoon to scrape into his mouth the grounds of coffee that had adhered to the bottom of the cup. Munching on the grounds with his bad teeth, he stood up, grabbed the remaining pamphlets, and headed over to our table.

"*Assalamu alaikum va rakhmatulai va barakatu.*" He extended his hand to Marat.

Marat greeted him reluctantly and cast an inquisitive look at the unshaven visitor.

"Take it, brother. Read this, brother," jabbered the guy indistinctly, handing him a pamphlet.

"Read what?"

"About that man who had gone astray, the one possessed by *djinn*s. The *iblis* whispered in his ear, tempting him to renounce the Lord of the Worlds, and the Lord of the Worlds wreaked justice on him that very day."

"Is this about Rusik?" Marat looked the man up and down.

"Yes, about that scumbag who denied Allah," blinked the bearded guy.

"Do you even know the first thing about him?" Marat rose from his seat.

I cringed. Don't get in a fight, please...don't start a scandal. In terror, I pictured it all: the pamphlet guy yelling for help, a gang of thugs in skullcaps rushing over from the Avenue, invading the café; a horde of bearded men without mustaches in short trousers—Wahhabis, in other words—joining them from the other side, crossing the bridge from "across the tracks." They surround Marat, and he falls dead to the floor, just like Rusik-the-Nail.

But nothing happened. The guy took a half step back and jabbered in a loud, though now much thinner, voice:

"Who the hell do you think you are?"

Zarema's entourage huddled together and whined:

"Marat! *Vai*, Marat!"

"First, tell you me who you think you are. And what gives you the right to peddle false rumors about Rusik?" Marat was just getting started. "You get the hell out of here and let people drink their tea in peace!"

The men abandoned their dominoes and strained their ears, trying to decide whose side they were on, and who needed to be thrown out onto the street.

"He'll leave, Marat, he's on his way out, calm down," the fat-thighed waitress rushed over to our table.

"Maybe I will," said the bearded guy, clutching his pamphlets to his chest and retreating toward the door, "but I will let them know in the mosque that an *iblis* has taken root in you, brother. It must be driven out! *Inshallah*, we will drive it out!"

One of the dominoes players, a gray-haired muscle-head, stamped his foot menacingly at the guy:

"Look, I've had just about enough of you! You're the one who has to be driven out! Scram!"

The guy flushed scarlet and made his exit. The fat-thighed waitress rushed out after him with her fists pressed to her chest, apologizing profusely. The veiled daughters-in-law by the partition gaped malevolently at me and Marat.

"Marat, let's get out of here." I poked him gently.

"All right," he agreed, calming down and tossing a banknote on the table.

We left, abandoning the uneaten baklava to a fat green fly that had been eyeing it. In the doorway, we crossed paths with the waitress as she came back in, wagging her head mournfully, then we set off down the dusty road toward home.

We parted at my gate. The early southern evening had already tinted the world black and white. And as I hastened through the yard to Papa, Mama, Granny, Uncle, the aunties, and my cousin, I knew that Marat's eyes were following me.

10. A PATCH OF GREEN

Marat was in the city at his father's office at the Institute. A meeting was in progress. They were talking, as usual, about Khalilbek.

"All right, explain to us, Aselder Khanych, how we're supposed to plan for dissertation defenses now," nervously asked a thin dry woman in a sheer blue blouse and gaudy filigree bangles. "I mean, people are writing dissertations about the activities of a convict!"

"That's exactly what I'm talking about, Irina Nikolaevna..." mumbled Marat's father.

Marat had been lured here on an absurd pretext—to help move some boxes—but in fact (and Marat was fully aware of this) his mother was trying to get him together with the latest on the list of potential brides. Namely the young secretary.

There she sat in a white business suit. An expensive pendant plunged into the alluring neckline of her jacket; she had legs like sturdy columns, curled, fragrant, oiled, and sprayed platinum hair, and full lips on a coarse, crafty face. Looking at this stranger, Marat recalled his walk yesterday along the edge of the steppe, yellow from the sun, with tiny white snails clinging to the bushes like barnacles. Patya's sincere, bell-like laughter, her slender waist under her belt; the way she had bent over to peel a snail away from the surface of a leaf, and said that it smelled like dried glue... Then she lifted it to Marat's nose, and he had sensed a subtle, transparent joy and the faint tangy fragrance of a woman's palms.

"They haven't sentenced him yet. We need to wait for the sentence, and then we can decide," mumbled Aselder.

"But we can't wait!" exclaimed Irina Nikolaevna, lifting her bangled red arms. "That could take a month, or a year or even two. And then what? Maybe we can advise the doctoral candidates to change their topics?"

"Oh no, that would mean they'd have to rewrite everything; who would do that?" A man in the corner with dandruff-dusted shoulders who seemed to be made out of chewing gum waved his hand. And sneezed with evident enjoyment into a checkered handkerchief, eliciting a chorus of subdued "bless you's" from the women sitting nearby.

"Aselder," said a dark-complexioned woman of forty, well preserved, with brightly painted lips, "could you use your connections to learn what's going on? None of it makes sense; one day we're preparing a publication to celebrate our benefactor's return; the next, we're cringing and hiding. How long can it go on?"

"The other departments are laughing at us..." the rubbery man added petulantly.

"Maybe your son could help!" Irina Nikolaevna nodded in Marat's direction.

Marat woke from his trance. "No point in trying. There are lawyers swarming the investigators' office night and day. They have more rights than I do here, but they can't get any information either. It's a dark case... And what, are all your students working on Khalilbek? Isn't there anything else for them to study?"

Silence. Then Aselder spoke, wiping his warty face as he did when he got nervous.

"You know what kind of a man he was, Marat. Like an encyclopedia. He was involved in literally everything..."

"Why do you say 'was'?" Irina Nikolaevna jingled her bangles. "Is. And will be. We must not be pessimistic. You saw the demonstration they had for him. And the concerts! Even out in the suburb."

"The stories people tell about him!" exclaimed the secretary, out of nowhere.

Having contributed to the discussion, she exerted some effort and crossed her legs. The precious locket quivered and tapped against her soft bosom.

"Let them talk. The main thing is that you refrain from recording them in our minutes," Marat's father grimaced at her.

"They say, for example, that's he's immortal. That he's some kind of Khidr."

"Cut it out with your Khidr!" The rubbery man frowned and sneezed again into his handkerchief.

"But hold on, it's an interesting topic," objected the dark-complexioned woman. "Mythologization of living contemporaries. Well worth studying. Do the rumors go into any detail?"

"All I know is that he can show up in any form. Like a bug, for example, so long as it's green."

"Why green?" smirked Marat.

The secretary smiled at him and tipped her head back triumphantly.

"That's what the legend says. Khidr helps people, but they usually don't appreciate it. They think he's crazy."

"But how does that make him like Khalilbek?" Irina Nikolaevna gave a hollow laugh. "No one ever thought Khalilbek was crazy; I sure didn't!"

Everyone started talking at once about the good deeds, fine mind, and general grandeur of Khalilbek. His generous donations, useful initiatives, his vision, full of love for the people…

"He helped children, too! Children!"

But amidst the general tumult there again came the sound of a nasal sneeze, and the rubbery man shouted indignantly:

"You could at least hold your tongues around Aselder!"

The women fell silent and exchanged embarrassed glances. Of course they knew that Khalilbek had been involved in Adik's death, the boy who had been their Aselder's illegitimate son. But in the heat of the conversation they had completely forgotten that fact.

"Khalilbek is not a saint, and we all know this. He has human blood on his hands," added the rubbery man amid the general silence. "And I'm not only talking about Adik."

Marat's father lowered his eyes and nodded. Marat felt awkward; why even bring up this private family topic?

"Who is this Adik, anyway?" asked the secretary tactlessly, but no one answered.

Instead, the people sitting in the office began whispering among themselves. Rumors began to make their way around the room, phrases spoken in hushed undertones:

"That special investigator…"

"And the director of the meatpacking plant…"

"And the Information Minister…"

"And that wise mufti, and the chief of the investment foundation…"

As Khalilbek's presumed victims were enumerated, they multiplied and came to life. If all these people were to be lined up in ranks, they would have made up an imposing, variegated, mournful-looking regiment of wealthy men, politicians, and deputies enrobed in all the trappings of power. Awkward, modest little Adik would have brought up the rear, Marat's neighbor Adik, who had met his end under the wheels of the ill-fated jeep.

Marat stood up and headed through the din to the rubbery man, to shake his hand and say goodbye, then to his father; with a nod, he paid his respects to the women, and finally flung open the door to leave. But there in the doorway stood a large mongrel dog, quietly wagging his matted gray tail. The dog's broad shaggy nose featured a roundish emerald-colored patch in the shape of the Australian continent.

"A-a-a-h!" squealed the secretary, leaping to her bulky feet and trying to duck under the table. "It's Khalilbek! Khalilbek! He's been listening in! He's keeping track of us!"

"Marat, don't go any closer, he'll bite you!" shouted the dark-complexioned woman with the bright lipstick.

"Don't touch him, Marat," his father's alarmed voice echoed hers.

Everyone panicked and stared bug-eyed at the monster.

"Don't be afraid! It's just disinfectant! Someone poured it onto his nose!" explained Marat, bending over the dog, who kept on calmly wagging his tail.

"Who let him in here?" said Irina Nikoaevna, jangling her bracelets. She had calmed down slightly.

"Damned if I know," spat the dandruffy man.

The secretary abandoned her efforts to crawl under the table, anxiously sidled up to Marat, and stared intently at the dog with her round eyes, encircled by black mascara lashes. Marat did not want to stand next to her. There was a danger that if he let down his guard, he might fall into his mother's trap. Marat picked up a piece of sausage wrapped in paper that was lying on Irina Nikolaevna's table and used it to lure the dog down the hall and then outside. The dog sauntered good-naturedly along after him, though without any particular enthusiasm. In the Institute's courtyard, Marat tossed the sausage on the ground and the dog immediately poked his green bristly nose into it.

Meanwhile Patya texted Marat that she had gone with her pack of mountain relatives into the city to "make the rounds of the *tukhum*" and wouldn't get back until late that evening. Who knows, she could be right here next to him, breathing somewhere just around the corner, in someone's cramped apartment, or driving at this moment past the Institute in the back seat of her father's car, squeezed in between a couple of lively aunties. Marat heaved a sigh and was overcome with a sudden feeling of despondency. Then he recalled Rusik again, who used to ride his bike from the settlement to the city, even in the fall, when the mud made the road nearly impassible. He might have even ridden along this street. He had worked near here.

While Marat was crossing a busy street, his phone rang unexpectedly. It was a colleague calling from Moscow with bad news. There had been a raid on their law office by people who, some sources said, were tight with the police. They had burst in and changed the locks. Undoubtedly they would dig around in their papers, looking for any evidence they had against the higher-up who had ordered the murder. It was a catastrophe. Marat had to drop everything fly to Moscow immediately, to help try to salvage any documents they still had.

"Did you provide an official written statement to the police?" Marat questioned his colleague.

"Yes, but the boss says that if we make a fuss, then they might shut us down completely, and could even come up with something to arrest us for.

After their conversation, Marat spent some time wandering the busy streets and cracked sidewalks, trying to gather his thoughts. He came upon a cacophonous wedding cortege, emerging from around a corner in a long procession of cars. Laughing young people leaned out the gaily beribboned windows.

Finally he flagged down a private car to take him back home. He rolled his window all the way down and opened his mouth wide to breathe in the dry, pungent wind blowing from ahead. The car passed charcoal braziers and refrigerators that people had taken out to the roadside to sell, gas stations with prayer rooms and tire-repair shops.

At home Marat went online and changed his ticket to Moscow to the next available flight. He scrolled through the news reports to see if the raid had been mentioned, but there were no details, just some basic facts: "cordoned off," "occupied," and "refused to comment." He texted Patya about it, and spent the next few minutes in suspense. No answer. He dialed Shakh. Shakh answered in a distant, altered voice that he was in the middle of trying to get Abdullaev released and couldn't talk.

Marat rattled around the house for a while, then went outside. He decided to stop by Angela's, to apologize for his rudeness the other day. He had been unkind to her after the incident with Rusik. The cause of it all was the whistling kettle that would not boil. But Angela's gate was closed, and his frantic knocking was to no avail. An old woman, a local, shot a sly, inquisitive look in his direction as she passed by, then darted to the other side of the street.

When Marat got home, his mother was already back, clattering dishes and silverware in the kitchen.

"How were things at the Institute?" she asked anxiously.

"Nothing special..." mumbled Marat darkly.

"Did something happen?"

His mother tossed a pile of washed forks to one side, strode over and stood right in front of Marat.

"Nothing at all, Mama, calm down. There are problems at work, I had to change my ticket."

"When are you going back?"

"Friday."

His mother gulped and resumed her work with the forks.

"So that's how it is, off you go, anything to get away. And your father and I are knocking ourselves out trying to arrange things for you."

"Mama!"

"You didn't tell me how you liked the girl."

"What girl?"

"Marat! At your father's office! The beautiful energetic one."

"Enough, already, with that girl of yours. I've got a full-on crisis in Moscow and here you are meddling…"

"Me, meddling?" Marat's mother huffed, and turned angrily to leave. But she reconsidered and went on the attack with renewed energy:

"Don't even think. I know all about yesterday. You are playing a dangerous game."

"What are you talking about?"

"Zarema told me all about it. You really scared her daughters-in-law. Showed up in their café with some girl, attacked a cleric from the mosque."

"Don't make me laugh! 'Scared them,'" groaned Marat.

"Do you understand what you've done? There are going to be rumors about you now, like there were about crazy Rusik! Just you wait, they'll tie you up and drag you off to drive out the *djinns*."

"'Drag me off!' A lawyer! Just let them try," Marat snapped.

"Not only will they try, but they will catch you and drag you off, and I won't be able to do a thing. Because you're acting like a maniac. And who was that babe you were with in the cafe?" his mother bombarded him with words.

"Don't call her a 'babe,' Mama. And if you go into hysterics, I'll leave."

Marat collapsed onto the sofa and stared up at the whitewashed ceiling. His mother poured herself a glass of water, sprinkled in some valerian concentrate and downed it in one gulp. Then she sat down on a chair next to Marat and inspected his high, faintly wrinkled forehead.

"All I want is to help you get set up in life, Marat. Go to Moscow, work things out there, and come back. We have the banquet hall reserved for the thirteenth... You know, Luiza is driving me crazy. She goes, 'You promised my niece a fiancé. So where is he?' Her niece is on pins and needles. She likes you."

"Yes, I'll go to Moscow and then I'll come back," stated Marat, without listening. "And you'll have your wedding on the thirteenth, just as you planned. So don't worry."

His mother warily twisted a thick knot of hair from one side to the other:

"What? Marat... I'm so glad! So you like the girl?"

"Yes, but not the one from Papa's office. And not Luiza's niece either."

"Who, then?" His mother dug her fists into her knees.

"The one who was with me in the café yesterday."

"A-a-a-h," she darkened. "I found out about her. Zarema filled me in —who she is, where's she's from. Her father is a simple worker. And he worked for Khalilbek as a mechanic. Remember the police investigation of Alik's death?"

"I do. And?"

"Well, your lovely girlfriend's father protected Khalilbek. Said that Adik himself had run into the street. Helped hush everything up. So there's no way you can marry her," concluded his mother, folding her hands together tightly.

"So we're going to cancel the banquet hall reservation?" Marat got up from the sofa.

His mother's chin trembled, and she burst out sobbing. Great round transparent drops spilled down her cheeks. She drew a handkerchief out of her robe pocket and blew her nose into it noisily.

"Adik! *Vai*, Adik! *Vai*, Adik…"

Hysterics, then. Marat went out onto the porch, put on his shoes and headed onto the street. And there he beheld that same Colonel Gaziev. As before, the colonel was in civilian clothes and had bent over to inspect the bottom of Adik's former car, which he had bought on the cheap along with the house.

"*Assalamu alaikum*!" he straightened up and greeted Marat. "Here you have it, just another day at work for the defenders of the fatherland. I'm checking to see whether there are any wires, or whether there aren't any wires…"

"What, are there always wires?" asked Marat, realizing that he was talking about explosives.

"Depends. But this looks clean, it can be started up."

There was so much Marat wanted to ask. Where to begin? Adik? Rusik? Khalilbek? The war between the mosques? He hesitated a moment, then asked:

"What about Rusik's parents? Do you know where they are?"
"They left with their daughters. Immediately after the funeral.

They decided not to stay here."

"So there won't be any blood revenge?"

"Against whom? Abdullaev's son is in jail. The other one, the extremist..."

"Alishka?"

"Yes. He's been arrested too. They can't take revenge against the whole settlement, can they?"

"But they're raising money for Abdullaev," Marat mumbled, as if to himself, without looking at the colonel.

"So you're worried? You want him to be thrown in prison? What, were you friends with the victim?" the colonel asked in his peculiar accent.

"We did spend time together," said Marat, fending off the question as usual, but then added: "Or, well, you could say that we were friends. Rusik was completely honest with me. It was hard for him across the tracks."

"He should have come to see me, should have written an official statement, with details, like, who, what, where: 'they're trying to recruit me into an illegal, armed organization.' And name names. How about you—can you give me some?"

"No," Marat interrupted him. "I don't know any names; you know far more than I do about all this. No one was trying to get Rusik to go into the woods and join the partisans. They just talked about religion."

"That's where it all starts!"

"And? In the other mosque, on the Avenue, it's just the same. People going around with pamphlets. Miracles, *djinns*. How is that any better?"

"The ones from the Avenue are normal. Their Islam is traditional, what do you need me to explain to you? They don't want to kill anyone, that's obvious. And so far, no one has incurred any serious problems from *djinns*," noted the colonel, getting into the car and shaking Marat's hand.

The colonel drove off, sending back brown clouds of dust. Marat headed towards Patya's house. She was still "making the rounds of the *tukhum*," that was clear, but near the house where this girl, so dear to him, spent the night, he felt himself stronger, and more secure. As though in answer to these thoughts, her answer finally came: "I just read your message, I'm sorry. So you have to leave? For a long time????!" Four question marks and one exclamation point. Patya did care.

Marat overtook a child on a tricycle. The mud on the road, which had dried in rough waves, made for rough going, so the child was pushing himself along using his feet, shod in rubber flip-flops, a few sizes too big. Marat recognized him: it was the boy from the psychic Elmiuraz's house. He called out to him:

"*Le*, where are you headed?" But the child did not heed him, just rounded the corner and disappeared, as if he had never existed.

Then the streetlight, which usually was dark, flickered and illuminated the dusk. In response to the light—new, artificial—the crickets filled the air with sound.

11. HAND AND HEART

No sooner had I met my prince than he had to leave me. Off to Moscow, where urgent business awaited him, great feats, while I was to remain confined in the clutches of the dragon. My woes multiplied when Mama summoned me into her bedroom, conspiratorially blocked the door, and announced, with poorly concealed joy:

"You have a suitor."

"Who?" I froze.

"Timur, from the youth committee—his father came over to talk with Papa. He said that the two of you have been in love for a long time. Why didn't you say anything?"

"They made it all up! We are not in love!" I snapped.

Mama flashed me a contemptuous look:

"Here you are, practically an old woman, but you have the brains of a five-year-old. He is a most worthy fiancé, and you led him on yourself. Now, don't try to weasel out of it, and don't try to deny it. Lyusya won't give your brother any children, you at least can give me some grandchildren."

"I am not having Timur's babies!" And I flew into a tantrum, just like a child. "No way!"

Mama took revenge by sending me out to the bathhouse with a scrub brush. The work was not only exhausting and boring, but disgusting too, because of the fat wood lice crawling all over the damp walls. I had to snag them with a stick, scoop them off the wall and flip them onto the floor, then drown them by spraying them with water from the hose, which I did with my eyes squeezed nearly completely shut. One of the aunties poked her head into the bathhouse, spotted me at this task, and clucked approvingly:

"Attagirl, nice work, doing what a good girl should."

And off she went, back to the house. I winced. How was it Auntie's business to decide what good girls should and shouldn't do? I tossed the hose aside and squatted down on my heels to have a good cry. But the tears wouldn't come, and that just made everything worse.

Then we had dinner, just us women, in the kitchen. The cousin had zoomed off again on some business of his own, Papa had been hired by someone to fix a lathe, and the uncle was out visiting friends. The aunties had completely taken over the house, and they babbled nonstop about yesterday's excursion to the relatives. Who had a baby, who the baby looked like, who died when and at what age. My throat went dry from the sheer abundance of names—all these cousins and second cousins, nieces and nephews, brothers-in-law and sisters-in-law on both sides, daughters-in-law, great-grandmothers and great-grandfathers, piling one on top of the other like the great Egyptian pyramids.

I finished my borscht and skulked off to my room, already missing Marat, who hadn't even left yet, upset that he wasn't writing me, and thinking that maybe I should write him myself. At that point Mama reappeared and dug her claws into me again.

"Patya, don't make a terrible mistake!" she started in. "You'll regret it your whole life. If only I had married Magomedov when I had the chance and not some hick!"

"Mama!"

"Look, Timur earns good money, he has an apartment in town. And he's building a house here in town, too."

"So?"

"He's got the gift of the gab, his bosses respect him, he's got a great career ahead of him! They say that Khalilbek himself..."

"This Khalilbek of yours is in prison! I'm sick of hearing about him!" I shrugged her off.

Having lost the second battle, Mama appealed to the aunties. She sent them to my room, where I was reading an old science fiction novel, having tucked my cell phone under my side in case Marat called.

"Patimat," the aunties started in our language. "You're not seventeen any more. Take pity on your parents. Just another couple years and you'll be a total old maid. Who will marry you then? Just some divorced guy with kids or an old widower, no one else. Look what happened to poor Khalisat..."

And the aunties launched into a mournful litany of all the overripe, over-the-hill, barren old maids in my mother's clan. All those girls had been haughty know-it-alls who had stuck up their noses at good, simple young men, and then withered up, went gray, and sunk so low that no one would have them.

"And this is just what awaits you!" admonished the aunties. "Look out, don't miss the last train."

"Aida is younger than you, and she is already pregnant with her fourth!" Mama just had to throw that in.

"What makes you think she's pregnant again?" I snapped.

"You think I can't tell? She was over here the other day, and I noticed her belly immediately."

"Aida has just put on weight." I refused to believe it.

"Your brother ought to fatten Lyusya up like that." Mama sighed cattily, "And if it doesn't work, then she should let him trade her in for someone who can."

"*Mashallah*, what will be will be," the aunties tried to comfort Mama, stroking her bony, tense shoulders with their big hands.

I felt like running out for the evening, but here, too, Mama contrived a way to torment me. She undertook an ambitious project to clean Papa's garage while he was out. The aunties were only too happy to join in, to drag things around, scour, pack, wash, scrub, scrape, clean. If our guests had harnessed themselves to this hard labor, then who was I to shirk my duty? So I joined them, choked on soot and crawled into inaccessible, distant corners with a soapy scrub brush.

Finally, we finished the garage, but then the aunties came up with another one of their ideas. They huddled in the corner with Mama, then announced:

"By the way, Patimat, your third cousin has really taken a shine to you."

The cousin! Great, just what I needed.

"He's younger than me!" I wailed.

"What difference does it make? My husband is also a year younger than me," confided one of the aunties.

Well, let's suppose that's true. But what did that have to do with me?

Mama also seized upon the idea. Of course, she preferred Timur as a man of substance with a bright future. But the cousin was also a fine catch. First of all, he was already in the family. Second, he was energetic and ambitious. Third...Mama didn't make it to "third;" I absolutely and categorically refused to listen to another word.

The phone rang, sending my heart into my throat, but it wasn't Marat, rather the loathsome, accursed Timur. As usual, I didn't answer, and sat down next to Granny, who was hemming the edge of some fine-patterned material.

"I know everything," Granny announced. "Someone proposed to you, and you turned him down."

"Yes, he's a horrible person, honestly," I frowned.

"Don't frown!" she took me down a peg. "Put a Band-Aid on the bridge of your nose so it won't get wrinkled.

I laughed. What else could I do?

"How can I convince my parents that those guys are wrong for me? You're smart, tell me." I went for flattery.

Granny said nothing at first, just pinched the dangling thread with the needle on the end in her colorless lips. Then she drew out the thread and started blubbering some gibberish in our native language:

"You've seen the sea, haven't you? You've seen it?"

"Yes. And?"

"Who are the ones who cling to dry land? Those who know the law. The *Ustazy*, wise teachers, say that such people are literalists. They know every tiny detail—how to do what when. But there are others who seek the truth. They go out into the sea and dive to the very bottom, seeking pearls. They are the voyagers. And there is a third type. They go out in boats, since that is safer. It's not my words: it's what the *Ustazy* say."

"So who are the people of this third type?"

"Those who have reached the end of their path…I can see that you want to set forth on your journey, to go out and dive for pearls, but your mother is back on the shore. It's your choice: stay or move."

"I don't understand…"

Granny has a way of muddling things up in my head. Why not just give a straight answer, without equivocating? She herself had probably never gone out on the water, though the sea is right here, right under her nose. All she has to do is to go toward town, then turn to the shore. It churns, it surges, it billows, it beckons.

A boy I used to be friends with when I was a child drowned one September in the Caspian at the beginning of the eighth grade. He had skipped school and gone to the shore. He hadn't gone too far out, but the treacherous current had swept him away toward the horizon. They say that the boy panicked and resisted, trying to fight the waves, but ultimately had became fatigued and sank below the foamy surface for all eternity. No one saw him; no one came to his aid. They figured out later what had happened when his trousers and sneakers were found on the beach. To hire divers, the boy's bereaved parents sold all their furniture and their TV set. The body was found far away, unrecognizable, beaten against sharp stones. They identified him by his swimsuit. When he was carried through the streets to the cemetery, the drowned boy filled the whole town with the smell of seaweed.

My brother, spooked by this sad story, had instructed me:

"If the current carries you out to sea, never try to swim against the current, never try to return to shore. Let yourself relax, don't panic, and the sea current will curve back around and carry you to dry land."

He had put it differently, of course, but what difference did it make? Fortunately, I never had occasion to need his advice.

I realized that I hadn't gone swimming in the sea since I got back from Moscow. Papa had offered to take me many times, but I hadn't been in the mood for splashing and collecting slippery shells. And now, suddenly, I had this urge to go. To the sea, the sea... It was all Granny and those divers of hers.

The telephone rang again. Marat!

"Patya, hi! Can you come in twenty minutes to the corner where the road turns off to the prison?"

"Yes!" I blurted out, though I had no idea of how I was going to slip away from Mama.

I combed my hair, powered my glistening nose, waited until Mama went out into the spotless, gleaming garage, and took off through the gate. Marat was waiting for me at the corner. There were practically no houses around: just a gatehouse, a couple of uninhabited private residences, and the elevated gas pipelines extending into the distance. The prison looked out at us from the other side of the field, not the slightest bit frightening, just an ordinary building.

"You know that I'm leaving soon, Patya," Marat began and then hesitated, seeking the right words.

Everything inside me burned. Something important was happening, but I didn't understand what exactly. Marat was tense, couldn't speak. I prompted him:

"Go ahead and tell me. I will understand."

He looked at me with joy in his eyes, and the words tumbled out:

"It's all so absurd—absurd that I have to rush off so soon, when we've just met. But I'm leaving, and I don't know if I'll be able to get back here in time. What I'm saying is probably going to scare you… "

"What words? What are you talking about? I promise you I won't be scared!" I reassured him.

The anxiety vanished from Marat's face and he laughed:

"You're so funny, Patya! How can you know?"

Then he turned sad again, and again hesitated. I perched on a gas pipe and gave him an encouraging smile. He continued:

"Don't be disturbed by what I'm about to say. My mother is a real scatterbrain. She persuaded my father to reserve a banquet hall for my wedding, and they spent a huge amount of money on it. It's on the outskirts of town. I don't recall the name of the place, you may know better than I do…"

"What, are you having a wedding?" I asked huskily. The sky plunged downward, as if it were about to shatter into pieces. If I hadn't been leaning on the pipe, I would probably have fallen backwards into a faint.

"No, no!" Marat hastily corrected himself. "I'm not! I mean, I am, but only if you agree."

He stopped short and stared at me expectantly. I couldn't understand any of it.

"What do you mean?"

"I want you to marry me. Not because the hall has been reserved. But because I feel that I've known you from the day I was born. And you are dear to me. Already. But I'm leaving, and the hall has been reserved."

"What hall?" I lurched sideways, like a blind woman.

My head was spinning with the happiness that had come over me, and also with my lingering bewilderment as to what Marat was trying to say.

He came over and took me by the hand, and brought his tea-colored eyes close to mine.

"Do you feel sick?"

"No, not at all, but I don't understand."

"It's my fault. I'm not making any sense," he sighed, still gripping my hand. "Patya, tell me, will you be my wife?"

And again a stifling, effervescent fog descended over me and adhered to my lips and nose. I drank in as much of the steppe air as I could, then exhaled, nearly whistling the word:

"Yes!"

"August thirteenth."

"Already? So soon?"

"The hall is already reserved."

"Strange, Marat, very strange…"

"I know but you see…I don't want to be trite, I don't want to. But it's as though we already know each other. It's meant to be."

"I think I understand. But we need more time. We have to check, to be sure."

"We will have time! Our whole entire life!" Marat exclaimed joyfully and embraced my trembling shoulders.

But a little knot of uncertainty still throbbed inside me. I pulled away and exclaimed:

"Maybe it doesn't matter to you who you marry? Slam, *bam*, anything, just get it done by the thirteenth!"

Marat too raised his voice: "Patya, this whole saga with the banquet hall is just a pretext. Don't take things literally." He opened his arms wide, to me and to the wind.

"Literalists 'cling to dry land.'" I repeated what Granny had said.

A sudden gust of wind hurled a cloud of steppe dust at us, along with shreds of cardboard boxes that looked like dry crackers, a faint, simple melody from a distant tape player, and the dreary sound of cows mooing.

My petty fears dispersed, and I threw myself onto Marat's chest, squeezing my eyes tight against the sand, the setting sun, the tears of joy that were bursting out of me, against conventions, and against the prison towers spying on us.

It was so hot, so hot, my head was spinning. It was time to say goodbye. We held each other's hands tight, talked, giggled, interrupted each other, and couldn't finish a single sentence.

Finally, Marat said that he would send his mother over to meet my mother and talk it over. Then, while he was in Moscow engaging in battle with the hellhounds of the justice system, they would work out the details. And then. And then…

"'Cat soup!' Don't put off till tomorrow…" I giggled.

He also bent double with irrepressible laughter, bracing himself with his hands against his knees. We couldn't stop.

When I arrived home, my whole body was still quivering from nerves, and the giggling fit had left a tingly sensation in my sides. I went into the room where Mama, the aunties and Granny were sitting in front of the television cracking walnuts with pliers. They must have sensed something; they turned away from the goings-on on the screen and stared at me expectantly.

"All right, I'm getting married after all," I announced triumphantly to the gathering like a royal herald with a message from the queen.

"Good for you!" buzzed the aunties. "You changed your mind! You've seen the light!"

"To Timur?" Mama beamed.

"To Marat, the lawyer, Aselder and Khadizha's son."

"Wh-a-a-at?" Mama sprang up, and her pliers clattered to the floor. "What do you mean, 'I'm getting married!' You'll get married if we give permission."

She didn't know how to react—to scold me or to rejoice—and she rushed over to the neighbors' to see what they knew about Marat. While I waited for her to come back, I paced the room in a daze like a lunatic. I sang under my breath a catchy, tiresome popular song; I trembled at my own thoughts, heaving audible sighs; I hopped around in one place, stumbling and jumping up again; I radiated a million smiles.

Mama returned stern, with pursed lips.

"So, you were out walking the streets with him arm in arm where the whole town could see you!"

"Not arm in arm!"

"And you were in that dive!"

"What dive?"

"At Zarema's, at the station! Not a single decent girl would let herself be seen there!"

"Mama, what do you mean, a dive? It's a café!"

"Right, a café! Has a single one of your friends ever been in that café? Take any one of the girls—Amishka, Mimishka—not a single one of them has fallen so low! At Zarema's! In the company of all kinds of rabble and lowlife trash!"

"There weren't any lowlifes there."

"Not another word out of you! The whole town knows about it already. Out alone with devil knows who and devil knows where! Look what Moscow has done to you. You've completely lost your conscience! You have brought shame upon me!"

Mama seethed. Shadows of neighbor women stirred in the corners of our house, burring their r's, jabbering, flapping their long tongues:

"Shame, shame, shame!"

One of them flitted behind the wooden tub in which Mama kneaded dough. Another flew like a night moth over a flickering light bulb that was swaying on a crooked cord; another flipped the curtain against the windows.

"Flap, flap, flap!"

The walls launched into motion, and the voices roared, flowing into one another, calling back and forth; reproaches flew through the air, chasing one another, catching me everywhere I sought refuge.

"Tramp, slut, good-for-nothing!"

Mama enumerated my sins until she gasped for breath: tablecloths I had scalded with the iron, overcooked soups, late nights out, bright-colored pants that were too revealing, hair cut short like a eunuch's.

"Don't you realize who this Marat is? And his father? Womanizers, both of them. The papa knocked up the girl next door, ruined her life. She had his baby, a boy, and was forced to wander, homeless, the length and breadth of Russia. And the son runs around with that slut Angela, a prison cleaning-woman's daughter. Just the other day he went knocking at her gate, the neighbors saw him over there!"

Knocked at her gate, the neighbors saw it…they are everywhere, eagle-eyed, ravenous. Their entire purpose in life is to notice things, to denounce, report what they say.

"And he's brought shame on you, too. There's no guarantee that he'll marry you. And if he does, you will spend your days counting his lovers, one after the other. The moment you turn your back, he'll be at Angela's gate."

I tried to evade them, to dodge the stones falling into my soul, even as it sang for joy.

"So what, it doesn't matter, so what…We'll go to Moscow, and who cares about some Angela?"

But deep in my chest a shaggy tarantula had made itself a nest: what if it were true? That Marat was a womanizer. Shameless women would besiege him, block him from me with their taut bodies, lead him off into the slough of degradation, vice, oblivion…

Dive for pearls, leave the shore behind. The main thing—no matter what—dive for pearls. What could it mean?

Granny whispered to me that she would talk with Papa and that everything would be fine. And that Mama's panic was meaningless. The aunties sat side by side in the kitchen, listening to the storm, all ears, chins protruding. Well, they sure got lucky: here they were in the thick middle of a juicy family scandal. Lick their chops, devour family gossip, be a part of the story.

"No, just look!" Mama would not be pacified. "Just listen who this tramp chose for herself! A friend of crazy Rusik, who was so stupid he brought on his own death!"

"Don't blab about things you don't understand," Granny clucked. "Patimat's fiancé can't be a friend of his."

"But that's exactly what they told me! He could be just the same as his dead friend—may his sins be washed away! Map collector! Disco dancer!"

"Tango, Mama, tango," for some reason I bothered to correct her, but my voice was drowned out in a hailstorm of fresh abuse:

"Friend of a complete wacko, son of a fornicator and money-grubber! His father, Aselder, warms a seat there in his Institute, makes himself out to be a learned man, worms his way into favor with the authorities. And his mother! That woman! Khadizha!"

"What?" the aunties chorused.

"His mother is a viper, all she can do is hiss at Khalilbek, even though he was their family's benefactor. Claiming that Khalilbek wouldn't let Aselder sell some stocks, that he supposedly killed feeble-minded Adik. Total malarkey. And not only that, she's friends with that corrupt woman, Zarema!"

"What Zarema?" the aunties asked.

"She runs a café at the station, where the riff-raff hang out. Men only! And my daughter right there in the middle of it! Would a decent guy have taken a girl to a place like that?"

"Ts-s-s-s-s," hissed the aunties. "It's terrible! Scandalous!"

Marat wrote: "I had to have a real battle with my mother, but tomorrow she'll come over. I embrace you, my soul."

"My soul." How strange to be his soul. And his mother would come over tomorrow. Terrifying. I'll have to tell them about the banquet hall. That the place is already reserved for the thirteenth. That will put Papa and Mama even more on their guard; they'll be suspicious. Why so soon? Why such haste? What, one of the old folks is dying, so you have get the wedding over with before everyone has to go into mourning? No. Can your bride be so past her shelf life that she'll say yes to anything? No, of course not, no. Doesn't her family have any pride at all? Why don't they make a fuss, try to hold off for another six months or so, for decency's sake? Why such haste?

All that would come down on me tomorrow, and the fuss and preparations would begin. And then Marat would leave, and we would be apart right up until the wedding. What if he met someone in Moscow? What if what I had seen in those tea-brown eyes were to fade away? Then Mama would make my life a complete misery, cut me to pieces. I pictured her with her teeth clenched, painstakingly working back and forth with a saw, chips flying every which way, with the aunties gawking and laughing.

Papa came home late. The cousin and uncle were long gone, they had returned to their mountain village before the aunties, who lingered behind.

After I went to bed, I could hear my parents talking on the other side of the wall. I snuck over to the door and strained my ears, but it only irritated me, intensified my agitation, and kept me awake.

Mysterious night sounds burst through the screened ventilation window. The chirring of a cricket, the solitary honking of a stray car passing by, the onslaught of the wind howling and somersaulting across the steppes to the sea, the drowsy barking of dogs, a cat's yowl rending my soul. Soul, soul... "My soul," he had written. If I had seen it somewhere else, I would have sneered, it was so trite. But now I melted at the mere recollection. I gazed with tear-blinded eyes into the letters gleaming on the telephone screen. "I embrace you, my soul."

I embrace you, embrace you... My heart moaned, sweetly, mournfully, like that of some pathetic lovesick fool.

12. CONVERSATION WITH A DRUNKARD

After leaving Patya, Marat lingered by the pipeline, rubbing his hands together absent-mindedly and smiling at the miracle that had taken place. The forlorn mansions, which had eavesdropped on their happiness, eyed him from the road, frowning with envy. A torn, black plastic bag flew past, borne by the wind, and disappeared. The steppe was devoid of people.

But when Marat turned toward the dark prison, he suddenly noticed a man walking briskly toward him through the salt marsh, breathing heavily. He looked to be around fifty and wore a dingy, pale-green, out-of-season raincoat.

"*Le*, hold up, wait!" the stranger wheezed. A tattered canvas bag dangled from his shoulder.

Marat figured the man was a vagrant or a homeless wino. The vagrant trotted up closer and clutched onto the gas pipe with his short fingers. Sure enough, he emitted a suffocating reek of home-brew.

"Had a few drinks, Father?" Marat asked the man with a smile.

The stranger raised his shrewd, penetrating eyes and opened his bag, revealing a large bottle with a gleaming neck. Marat shook his head.

The wino looked surprised. "What, not interested? Not even to celebrate Khalilbek's release?"

"They let him out?" Marat was stunned.

"Sure did! Today, on the quiet. Though tomorrow the entire district will be talking about it, you'll see. Here, let me pour you some. I even have glasses."

Marat took a closer look at the vagrant. Despite the way he was dressed, he didn't look at all like the usual fall-on-your-face boozer.

The happiness that filled Marat stirred and shone forth, filling the air:

"All right, there's a good reason. Pour me a little, Father."

The stranger reflected a moment, then extracted two glasses from his raincoat pocket, handed them to Marat and filled them from his big bottle.

"To Khalilbek!" he proclaimed, taking a seat on the pipe.

Marat drank from the glass, and felt the warmth flow through his veins.

"They keep on talking about Khalilbek, Khalilbek," he nodded to the stranger who was sitting next to him, blinking into the sunset. "But I can't make sense of it.

"Of what?"

"Of his logic. All right, I get murdering competitors, thievery on a massive scale, that kind of thing. But why all the petty stuff?"

"What petty stuff?" the drunk squinted.

"Well, for example, building a gambling house in town. It ruined the youth, and he didn't particularly profit from it. Just threw away money."

"I can explain it," announced the drunk, taking a sip. "Look. He built a casino, right?"

"Right"

"Then what?"

"What?"

"They closed down the casino, then gave the building to the children's arts center. If they hadn't built the building, there wouldn't have been an arts center. So everyone benefited, right?"

"So? How could Khalilbek have known that that would happen?"

"Well, he knew," the drunk giggled.

The plastic bag reappeared and soared past them in the opposite direction. Though who knows, it might have been a completely different one. Marat took another sip and continued:

"All right. Let's say that he knew everything in advance. So why didn't he let my father sell his stocks at the right time? He harangued him all night long, persuading him it wouldn't be profitable. And then it turned out he was wrong. My father lost out, and this other guy, Magomedov, who did sell, made so much money that he was able to build himself a house in the city."

"Then what?"

"What?"

"I know about this Magomedov. What happened to him?"

"He was murdered, I think."

"There you have it. Murdered because of his wealth. And if your father had also sold his stocks, then he would have been murdered, too. So Khalilbek actually saved your father!" The drunk shook his index finger in the air.

"Ah, so that's it." Marat took another swig of wine. This was getting interesting. "Benefactor of children, savior of fathers... But what about Adik? Why did he run over Adik? Pure chance?"

"Not at all," replied the drunk thoughtfully. "On purpose. Ran over him intentionally."

"What?!" Marat sputtered.

"Here's what: that boy was destined to be a terrible villain as an adult."

Marat stared at the drunkard. What did it mean? But the man didn't look at Marat, just sipped his wine. His dingy green raincoat radiated iridescent reflections of the sunbeams. His canvas bag lay in the dry, prickly grass by his feet, surrendering to the power of the gray grasshoppers.

"Can I hear a little more about Adik the villain?" Marat probed cautiously, as though afraid he might frighten the drunk from his perch.

"Well, it's all very simple. Adik had been recruited by the guys in the forest. Terrorists, basically. It was for them that he built that guest-house in the yard."

"I remember some kind of construction project."

"Well, he was building them a hideout. He provided them with food. And they gave him money. The boy bought himself a Lada Priora. He felt needed, like a hero."

"What are you talking about! Adik didn't even pray! How could he get involved with the militants in the forest?"

"They didn't need his prayers. What they cared about was how he could be of practical use to them. Shelter them, aid and abet. They were planning a big action in town, and were going to rope Adik into it. Cannon fodder. And Adik's involvement would have led to the deaths of a large number of people. So what Khalilbek did was remove him from the path in time."

"Do the police know about it? Do they know that Adik was involved with the militants?" Marat pressed the stranger.

"Of course they do," the drunk shrugged lazily. "And your father even bribed them to keep their mouths shut and not ruin your family's reputation. And Adik's wife, have you asked yourself why she ran away to the *kutan*? Because she was all mixed up in it, too. And the police got Adik's house and his car, basically, for free."

"Colonel Gaziev."

"Yes, that's him. He told your father Aselder: 'If you want things hushed up, then keep your distance, and I will take the criminal's house for myself.'"

"So Adik was a criminal. And my father knows and hasn't said a word about it."

"That's right. And he thanks Khalilbek, too. If Adik hadn't died and the militants had succeeded in their plan, your family would have been branded as the family of a terrorist. Everyone knows that Adik is your father's son. And they've known it for a long time. You're the only one who didn't know."

Marat was silent. He stared at the quiet guardhouse on the roadside, and beyond it at the horizon shimmering in the blinding light of the setting sun. Then he turned to the drunk and asked:

"How do you know all of this?"

The drunk laughed, fussed over the bottle, splashed some of the dark pink liquid into his glass and wheezed:

"Because I drink wine. *In vino veritas*. So what shall we toast to?"

"To my wedding!" Marat suggested, returning to life.

"*Vakh*, so you're getting married? Soon?"

"August thirteenth."

They clinked their glasses and raised them to their lips.

"You know," Marat opened his heart, "even before I found my bride, I knew that my wedding—if there was going to be one—would be on the thirteenth."

"And now?"

"Now I know for sure that there will be a wedding. I'm marrying for love. I met her myself. Here in town. I've only seen her three or four times, but it feels as though I've known her for a long time."

The drunk drained his glass and tossed it into his bag, got up from the gas pipe, stretched, wheezed, and scratched his sparse, reddish-gray hair. Grasshoppers scattered, bending their strong legs and leaping through the air.

"You can't know anything for sure," he suddenly said, in a sober voice.

"Meaning?" Marat glanced at the stranger.

"There might not be a wedding. It depends on predestination."

Something rustled in Marat's memory, and he suddenly recalled sitting with Rusik-the-Nail in the cheap seats on the train, traveling through wasteland, clinking their metal tea-glass holders. That conversation had been about predestination too. Marat couldn't remember what had started it.

"What comes to pass was not destined to pass you by. What passes you by was not destined to come to pass," the stranger intoned, scratching his head again and picking up his bag.

"What about man's free will?" asked Marat.

"Free will and freedom of choice remain."

"So how does this freedom mesh with predestination?" Marat smirked and downed the rest of his wine, then slipped the empty glass back into the drunkard's bag.

"It's forbidden to probe into the question of predestination. Abstain from such conversations." The drunkard frowned.

"Sure. So if we can't explain something, we just put it out of our minds," laughed Marat, getting up from the gas pipe and extending his hand to the stranger. "All right, Father. Wishing you all the best."

"You too," the drunkard said, gruffly. He suddenly seemed to shrink and fade.

Marat left him at the gas pipe, turned his back to it all—the prison, the field, the stranger—and started off for home. The wine lingered in his stomach, evaporating and sending its fumes upward into his lungs, filling his vessels with life. In one of the alleys, Marat noted Shakh's car passing by. He waved, but it didn't stop, just rushed past. Shakh probably hadn't seen him.

Along the way, he recalled all the weddings he had ever attended. Hundreds of guests, deafening music, the tossing of the grooms up in the air. At one of them the groomsmen had lifted an entire table onto their shoulders, with the groom dancing on top of it. It had been terrifying just to watch. The groom had twirled and jumped on the table, waving his fists and kicking his legs out to the side, while below his friends had kicked up the toes of their polished shoes, holding the table by its wooden legs. No one had fallen or gotten hurt.

Another time a group of daredevils climbed up onto the bride and groom's platform, and did backflips onto the floor. They somersaulted the whole length of the hall, from one end the other—one flip, two, three, four.... And when the bride entered the circle, each dancer tried to outdo the others. The riskiest move was when the dancer clasped his hands behind her back without touching her waist. Rusik-the-Nail wouldn't participate in that kind of dance. He would lurk in the corner and then leave early. He probably would have done the same thing at Marat's wedding.

Marat pictured himself driving along the streets to Patya's house at the head of a long line of cars filled with his family and friends. Children would stretch a rope across the road to try to block the cortege from reaching the bride, and would extort sweets from the groom's party before they would let them pass. A man would get out of his car with a tray and toss pieces of chocolate to the children, like bread crumbs to pigeons.

And the path would clear. And Marat would follow the path. The main thing—he understood this now, after his conversation with the stranger—was to follow the path. Turning this thought over and over in his head, Marat felt his happiness grow. And the birds circling in the air over the town understood this too, and flapped their ragged wings overhead.

13. WEDDING

I awoke at dawn with a throbbing head. Everyone was up already, slamming doors, cooking *chak-chak*, setting up festive tables in the yard. On sleeping pads that had been laid out on the floor of my room, wedding guests were getting dressed, shivering in the chilly morning air.

I had managed to see Marat only once, in passing, after his trip to Moscow. He noted with some concern that I had lost weight and looked peaked. He comforted me, saying that it would soon all be over—all the anxiety, preparations, hassles, and waiting. The thirteenth would arrive, we would break away from the clamor, and would escape to a place where we would finally be alone, free of meddling and unwanted advice. And, finally, the day had come. Just one more day, the ordeal would be over and we would be free at last.

The days leading up to the wedding were excruciating. Initially, Papa and Mama put up a strong resistance, and would not yield to Marat's side. They asked us to delay the wedding. They felt that this haste was unseemly, that it cast a shadow on me: a good girl would not say "yes" until the matchmakers had completely worn out their shoes. All the squabbles and demands added to the stress, and of course it didn't help that Marat was away in Moscow the whole time. I recall how long it took his mama, Khadizha, to fasten a gold bracelet on my thin wrist. The clasp refused to work. Afterwards, Khadizha complained to her cronies that her son's bride had stood there like a dummy and hadn't deigned to help her. Whereas I had simply thought that it was not proper to help, that it would have seemed presumptuous or greedy to pounce on her gift like that.

Ultimately, my visit to At Zarema's with Marat turned out to be a real godsend. The shocking news had spread like wildfire through the suburb's drab neighborhoods. Gallivanting around the outskirts of town alone with some guy! Pigging out on baklava with him and a pack of ex-cons! Given the circumstances, Marat was simply obligated to marry me, and as quickly as possible, to put the story to rest.

On the eve of the wedding, Papa and Marat went with the witnesses to the mullah to complete the religious formalities. My Moscow friend Marina kept asking, "What's in the contract? What's written in there?" but I really didn't care. She bought tickets the moment she learned about the wedding, and flew down a few days before the ceremony. She just had to be a part of it all. She brought heaps of clothes in a leather suitcase and threw herself into the fray, rushing around the house with my relatives and friends, asking constantly about the wedding customs:

"Do they have to ransom the bride here? Will there be competitions? No? Why not? How is everything done?"

Every day Aida would come over lugging stacks of fresh glossy magazines and dress catalogues.

"You know, Patya, you should go for the 'Mermaid' silhouette, you have the perfect body for it."

"I don't want to!" I fended them off, exhausted from sleep deprivation, all the rushing about, and the vague fears that oppressed me.

Granny was afraid that I would choose a dress with a low-necked, strapless bodice. Marina insisted on a gold-trimmed one with lacing. Lyusya, who came with my brother for the wedding, advocated for a simple, satin, ivory-colored gown. The girls leafed eagerly through the colorful pages, marking their favorite photos with their fingernails—luxurious wide skirts, *fleurs d'orange*, a long, trailing bridal veil...

Every day we went into the city and rushed from one bridal salon to another. In a panic, impatient, we sorted through endless arrays of rhinestone-spangled diadems and barrettes. Mama was strained to the breaking point. Half-terrified, half-proud, she dashed around the house, assembling my trousseau. Granny languished over the fabrics in the iron-clad trunk. Papa kept out of my path and pretended to be nonchalant.

Ultimately, we decided to rent a straight-cut, embossed lace gown with no train. We engaged hair stylists and make-up artists to come to the house. I'd barely gotten up and washed before they arrived and sat me down at the mirrored dressing table just as I was, rumpled, with dark circles under my eyes. They rubbed toner on my skin, warming it with the pads of their fingers, and applied makeup using brushes, powder puffs, and their bare, dexterous hands. They shadowed my eyelids, brushed my cheeks with rouge until I looked like a wax doll, thickly penciled in my brows, and pasted on sparkly eyelashes.

"You should have ordered mink lashes," Aida whispered, awestruck, nodding her tall turban. "That would have been perfect."

Out of the mirror a marionette looked out at me, a carnival mask, not my own face. The lips were outlined with dark contour and painted cherry red; in the middle of each lip a drop of gloss had been applied to make them look plumper.

"Your hair! What about your hair?" fretted Marina, sorting through chignons—short, long, wavy, smooth, and plaited.

"We'll extend your hair, of course." The hairdresser from the city circled me thoughtfully. "You simply can't get married with such short hair."

"Do whatever you want," I thought, digging my manicured fingernails into my chair's armrests. "Just don't ask my opinion, and don't yank."

Finally a chignon with long curls was attached to the back of my head and pinned up at the sides. An organza scarf was fastened with ribbons to my head, and someone sprayed me with Chanel No. 5, filling the room with molecules of ylang-ylang, bergamot, and lemon.

The girls lined up to apply their makeup and fix their hair. Now the air smelled of pomade and hair mousse. Eye-shadow palettes—matte and glossy, powder and liquid—piled up on the dressing table. The room filled with sound: the rustling of dresses; the babble of negotiations over exchanging a skirt or borrowing a shiny ribbon. Aunties flocked in and out, kissed me, bestowed words of farewell, beslobbered my thickly powdered cheeks with their big lips, and blotched my delicate openwork lace sleeves with flour-powdered fingers.

Lyusya tried to force-feed me. She brought in a tray of boiled meat, salads, and flatbreads with sheep's-milk cheese, but the mere sight of food nauseated me. I waited, straining my ears for the sound of honking horns, for the cortege bringing Marat. He would come for me, would lead me to the festively-set tables, and would drive me to the banquet hall, thronged and thundering with a deafening din—but when, when... when?

The cortege did not arrive. Noon came and went, then one o'clock, then two, but there was still no news from Marat. I dialed him several times, but the party I was trying to reach was unavailable.

The celebratory mood began to dissipate. I sat in my lace gown on my bed's embroidered silk coverlet and waited. Dreadful thoughts besieged me. He had gotten cold feet and abandoned me. He had died in an accident. Been kidnapped by Timur. I could not dispel this last fear. The night before, Timur had sent a message: "No one has ever wiped their feet on me. I always get what I want." I had told Lyusya about it, and she had calmed me down, laughed it off. But now everything was turning out just the way I had feared. Timur had decided to take his revenge and to prevent our wedding. He had lurked in wait for Marat, apprehended him, and attacked him together with his posse, the thugs from the Youth Committee…

My brother dispatched one of the boys to find out what was going on at the groom's house. The boy came back with the news that the cars adorned with scarves and flowers were lined up in front of Aselder's house. Meaning the cortege hadn't started out yet.

Mama dropped into my room, and gloated quietly into my ear:

"If you had said 'yes' to Timur like a normal girl, nothing like this would have happened. Just wait, this Marat of yours will trample us in the mud."

Marina didn't know what to say; she just paced around the room making suggestions:

"You should just send someone over there to ask straight up: 'What's going on?' Maybe they're just exhausted, and have gotten off to a late start. Isn't there some easy way to find out? I mean, you live in the same town!"

Aida rocked her youngest in her arms and kept offering variations on the same theme:

"You'll see, Patya, Timur hasn't forgiven you. I thought so. I suspected that he wouldn't give you up that easily, that he could come straight to the wedding and kidnap you. Or do something to Marat. Anyway, I don't trust this Marat of yours. He's one of Shakh's buddies, and you can't expect anything good from Shakh."

How could it be, how could it be… My nose smarted with repressed tears. Marat wouldn't treat me that way. The more likely theory was that the stocky bruiser with the buzz cut had snuck up on him, taken him unawares, and slugged him. Blood poured from his nose and stained his snow-white shirt...That's the holdup, that's why they haven't come.

The lack of a groom did not put a damper on the frenzy of preparations. Women called back and forth to one another in the front room. A multitude of second and third cousins carried heavy platters of food out to tables that had been set up in the courtyard, which were besieged by a throng of disorderly, feasting neighbors. Even deaf-mute Gagarin and his wife had been invited.

Granny looked in now and then, asking sternly in our native language:

"So, where's the groom?"

What could I say? Nowhere. He was obviously nowhere to be found. Find Timur and scalp that disgusting buzz cut off his head. And what about my brother? Wasn't it his job to figure everything out, to ferret out the offender and give him a good thrashing?

Periodically, young neighbor girls came and knocked on the windows of my room, hoping to get a look at the bride. One of the aunties flung open the window and tossed out a handful of chocolates. The girls exulted, shouting and squealing as they gathered the candies up from off the ground:

"Bride, bride! Can we touch you?"

I got up from the bed, went over to the window, and stretched my hands out to the girls. They jumped up, dropping the chocolate from their palms, trying to touch me:

"So beautiful! Beautiful!"

Meanwhile, Aida came up from behind.

"Shakh is here!"

I cringed. What was he going to say? Of course, they didn't let him into my room. Shakh conferred with my brother in the front room. I dispatched spies to eavesdrop, and they returned with an announcement:

"The groom has gone missing!"

The walls heaved. Someone's hands supported me under my lace elbows, eased me onto the bed.

"Don't be afraid! Don't be afraid!" whispered Lyusya. "Your brother caught Timur. He has nothing to do with it."

"Then who does?" Marina anxiously twirled a lock of hair around her finger.

So it wasn't Timur. What, then? A little couplet came into my memory, who knows from where:

My love is off somewhere, he has no time for me.
Why would he care at all? He's got new girls to see…

Angela…No, that's ridiculous! I had barely managed to dispel those absurd thoughts when we heard a fresh rumor: Shakh suspected that Marat had been captured by people from the mosque on the Avenue. They hadn't been able to forgive him for that scene in At Zarema's, when Marat had driven away that guy with the pamphlets right in front of everyone.

What would they do to him? "A violent exorcism"—that's how Shakh put it. Marina kept dashing out to listen in and bring back reports. What he said was shocking. A completely inappropriate, unwelcome fantasy came to mind: Marina and Shakh fall in love: a wedding, a little cradle, a baby carriage…In moments of trouble you think of the most ridiculous nonsense. How easy it is to get distracted! So that's what had happened—Marat had gotten distracted. But what if Shakh was right? What if at this very moment he was at the mosque in the clutches of exorcists? What if they had already dosed him with some disgusting potion, had laid him down on their rugs and begun driving out the *djinns*? Marat lies there on the floor, writhing and twisting, struggling to break away, to withstand the toxin. A fog of resin-tar incense fills the room, they beat the "sick man" mercilessly, intoning spells in some alien tongue:

> *Bismillai rakhmani rakhimi, al'khamdullilai rabbil' allamin, arrakhmani rakhim, malikki-iaumiddin, iiakanabuduva, iakanastian...*

I had learned about such exorcisms from witnesses. A strange clotty lump runs through Marat's vein. It flows along the capillaries to his index finger, and from there it spurts out in a great splash of black liquid. The possessed man is delivered of the *djinn*. He rises, and there is a submissive, god-fearing look in his eyes. Never again will he dare to attack the pamphlet bearers. From this day forward he will go docilely to the mosque, will attend every sermon.

I recalled another story. A girl in our town had suffered terrible headaches. They were so bad that she couldn't work or look at people, and all she could do was groan and beat her head against the wall. They took her to a wise man at the mosque. And he asked:

"Are you a person or a *djinn*?"

And the girl answered in a man's voice:

"I am a *djinn*."

Then the learned man shouted:

"Come forth, enemy of Allah!"

But the *djinn* replied:

"I will not come forth, and I will forever wage war on Islam."

And then the learned man began reciting from the Qur'an. And he intoned the words, on and on, until the *djinn* burst into tears and wailed:

"I am coming out! I am coming out!"

And he came forth. The girl vomited him out and came to her senses, as if awakening from a dream, and left the mosque with a carefree spirit.

O God, o God, free me from these idiotic thoughts. I was so consumed with anxiety and exhaustion that my brain could only produce nonsense. And what if Shakh himself had abducted Marat? Marat had told me before the wedding that Shakh was upset with him and had at first even refused to be his best man. All because of Rusik-the-Nail. Abdullaev, who had been locked up for manslaughter, was the guy whose engagement had been broken off in such grotesque circumstances. When Shakh lost the case, he somehow blamed Marat for Abdullaev's arrest. As if, since Marat had been Rusik's friend, he must have had it in for his assailants. And, supposedly, he had talked Colonel Gaziev into influencing the judges to impose a tougher sentence.

Nonsense, complete nonsense, of course. Marat hadn't tried to influence anyone, but Shakh refused to believe it for a long time. And now he's making himself out to be his best friend. He's worried…I was so upset, I was about to rush out of my room and interrogate Shakh personally. But the aunties clucked and blocked the door. Mama ran in, waving her hands at me as though I were a cow trying to get out through the pasture gate.

"You get right back in there! You've completely lost your mind! When the groom comes for you, that's when you can go out to greet your guests. And if he doesn't, you can just sit right there in the corner. A jilted bride."

I'd barely made it back to my bed when the door burst open, letting in a clamor of shrieks, whispers, and suppressed gasps. In strode Angela. She was in a white hijab. Hands to her sides, elbows out, a gloating smile on her face, she cast a mocking look around the room, then exclaimed:

"So, Patechka, you're expecting your groom. Good for you, you just keep on waiting. I'm sure that he will arrive soon."

"What are you doing here?" I blurted, half-rising.

"I came to congratulate you. May I give you a kiss?"

And she took a step toward me. The women had had all crowded into the room, rushing to push her back to the door.

"Stop! Back off! Is this any way to greet your guests?" Angela shrieked. At the sound of her voice, more faces appeared in the doorway. All the women—neighbors and relatives—wanted to have a look at this harlot who had taken the veil.

"Leave her alone!" I snapped. "Let her say whatever she wants. She doesn't scare me."

They released Angela, who with disgust rubbed the places on her body where strangers' hands had touched her.

"You think I'm a prostitute. On the other hand, I am married. To a man who did not abandon me on my wedding day."

I winced from the pain. Taunted on my wedding day by a filthy street slut!

Suddenly Granny pounced on Angela from behind, violently tore off the scarf that Angela had fastened carefully with safety pins to conceal her hair and neck, and shoved her toward the door. Angela fell flat on the floor, hair bared, furious. She glared up at me, lurched to her feet, and fled the room.

It all happened so fast that the women could only gasp. But Granny yelled at the top of her voice:

"And who let her in, the scumbag? Let her get the hell out of here and slither back to the shit pile she came from!"

Papa appeared in the doorway, petrified, but the women shooed him away. The hands on the clock showed that it was already past three. By now Marat and I should have been sitting in that banquet hall, the one that had been reserved for our wedding before we even met. And the marriage registry officials ought to be there too. But where was he? Where was my groom?

I'd barely managed to recover from Angela's scandalous visitation when Lyusya, who had gone on a reconnaissance mission, came back with an update. It turned out that Angela, incensed at Marat's decision to marry, had called her husband at the police station the night before and had slipped him word that Marat was involved in the underground, with secret ties to the militants in the forest, just like his half-brother, Adik.

We had known absolutely nothing about Adik. Could it be true?

"Anything is possible!" Mama asserted, bursting into the room, instinctively adjusting the organza bows in my hair. "Your Marat could have concealed the fact that he's a Wahhabi. That slut couldn't have just made it up. Where there's smoke there's fire."

"She could have! She could have!" I refused to believe it.

But why had everything come crashing down so suddenly? Could a single phone call ruin a man? It could, it was that easy. Rat, snitch, inform. What right did she have? She was married—even a second wife is a wife, after all. So what did she need Marat for?

"My, oh my," Marina drawled. "Such drama! A regular soap opera."

Aida and her baby had vanished. The aunties and cousins ganged up on me:

"Eat something, have something to eat!"

As though their *chudu* would solve anything. I refused to eat and lay face down on the bed. Tears wouldn't come, no matter how I tried to force them. The fake lashes pricked my eyelids. I had to tear off all this unnecessary stuff, everything that prevented me from rushing out to find Marat.

Meanwhile, the men's voices in the front room got louder. There came the sound of ragged, anguished sobs, and in rushed Marat's mother Khadizha, dressed in her mother-of-the groom gown, draped in sparkling jewelry. She had obviously been crying, the blue arrows fringing her eyelids were smudged and blotchy.

"My boy, my boy! He's been kidnapped!" wailed my mother-in-law.

I sprang up from the bed, and she ran over to me, pressing me to her chest, and only then, at last, did my long-awaited tears burst forth.

"Oh, my little partridge!" Khadizha cooed, stroking my lacy shoulder blades. "May the heavens have mercy on us."

The women watching from the corners, touched, began to whimper.

"Who did it, who took him, Khadizha? Tell us!" Mama repeated over and over, as though unable to hear herself speak.

Marat's mother finally heard the question. She released me, myself now thoroughly tear-stained, from her embrace and took to dashing around the room.

"What do you mean, 'who?' Who? The police! Colonel Gaziev himself: it's no coincidence he ensconced himself right next door to us, in Adik's house. Grabbed it with his big, ugly meat hooks. And now he's started in on my son. Come on, tell me, how can you call Marat an extremist?"

"On what grounds?" I blurted.

"He was denounced! Some skunks framed him. Anything to add stripes to their uniform. They grabbed the boy, and now, dead silence. Where did they take him? Why? Aselder is already in the city trying to learn something. They won't get away with this. I will not give up. I'll go and smear this colonel's gates with shit. Abduct a boy on his wedding day! For no reason whatsoever!"

"Did they search your house?" someone asked.

Khadizha twitched violently:

"Search? Just let them try! They'll be sure to plant something: books, drugs, weapons. They're capable of anything."

"You need to get Khalilbek involved," Mama remarked, as if to herself.

"Khalilbek?" Khadizha frowned. "No way! He's barely out of prison himself. My son won't have anything to do with that guy!"

My mother-in-law sighed and perched on the bed. One of the cousins brought her some cold water in a crystal wine glass. Draining the contents, she looked me over and ordered me to go clean myself up.

"Your mascara's smeared, your face is all black. When we get Marat out of the Sixth Department, he'll see you and won't recognize you. He'll say, 'Mama, that's not my bride, that's not Patya.'"

I smiled through my tears and went to the mirror to wipe my painted face.

"To ruin such beauty, what a waste," one of the girls whined under her breath, but I kept rubbing my face until I didn't recognize myself—haggard, red-eyed, suffering.

I undid my chignon, untied the ribbons, shook my short hair loose.

"Wait, wait, Patya," said Marina, contemplating with alarm the doll-like image that was disintegrating before her eyes. Hairpins scattered onto the carpet; the necklace clattered to the dressing table.

"I need to go to the bathroom," I bleated, starting off again toward the door.

"No, don't go outside!" cried everyone at once, again blocking my path.

"Girls, go get a chamber pot for the bride!" shouted Khadizha, loud enough for everyone in the house to hear. One of the girls ran out to the garage for the pot and brought it back in—an enameled vessel with a cute picture of a flower on its rust-spotted side.

"Just go out, please, I can't in front of everyone," I asked quietly.

The women shifted grudgingly from one foot to the other, and then went out the door. Lyusya lingered, and offered:

"Let me hold your dress."

"I don't need your help!" I snapped. "I can do it myself!"

Left alone, I closed and latched the door and twisted the pot to and fro in my hands. And suddenly I realized what I had to do. I slipped off the wedding dress—which was surprisingly difficult—scratching my forearms in my haste. I stuffed it in the wardrobe and put on a robe of Granny's that I found folded on a shelf in there. I wrapped myself in a long chiffon scarf, pulled on a pair of rubber flip flops that were lying in the corner, and shoved my telephone and some money into the robe's pockets. Then I climbed onto the windowsill and sprang down into the garden. From there, hunching over and ducking, I ran to the chain-link fence, climbed over it, and dashed off through the back alleyways in the direction of the railroad station. My goal was to force my way onto a passing train and get out of town, to go back from where I had come, to go away, anywhere. I knew that my disappearance would only complicate things even more but I couldn't bear to stay in that room a second more. I gasped, struggling against my helplessness.

The wind rose and tore at my scarf. I had to retie it as I ran, knotting it clumsily around my neck. Past strangers' gates, garages, past towers under construction... dart unrecognized onto the platform, duck into a sun-warmed train car...

I reached the tracks, breathless, with a stitch in my side. This was about the time the train to the city usually arrived. And from the city I could go on foot straight to the shore. I'd plunge into the sea just the way I was, in my clothes, lifting the pockets so my bag and phone wouldn't get wet. Better yet, just leave everything on the sand. Jump in and start swimming. It was sure to bring relief—I would feel relief.

One of the proprietress's daughters-in-law sat on the porch of At Zarema's, gnawing sunflower seeds. She followed me with her eyes to the turn, but apparently didn't recognize me. My phone rang. Someone from home yelled:

"Where are you? Where?"

"Leave me alone for a while, I'm all right," I snapped and turned off the phone. The train was coming, right on cue. Perfect timing. I climbed up into the vestibule between the cars, which reeked of overheated metal. There I took refuge in a corner and waited, with my scarf covering me, for a little old woman to exit onto the platform. The door clattered shut, and finally the train lurched. Our town began to flow backwards. And the sea grew closer and closer, closer and closer.

***

By the shore, in the Tavern, the regulars were making their usual racket. Khalilbek poured Marat some sweet wine, clumsily spilling some onto his camouflage T-shirt, and pointed to the great luminary sinking down beyond where the sea met the sky.

"What does that mean, Pupil?"

"That the day has ended?"

"That's part of it. More precisely?"

"That everything has converged into a single point?" Marat murmured lazily.

"You're right," nodded Khalilbek, gladdened by his drinking buddy's quickness of mind.

The sun indeed had become an orange point, flowing away into the inverted world on the other side of the Earth. The former prisoner reached for a new bottle, blocking the luminary with his head, and Marat's inebriated eyes blinked. Suddenly he saw before his eyes not the wild shoreline with whitecaps rolling in, but the cramped walls of the dark interrogation room closing in around him and the silhouette of the investigator blocking the lamp with his body. Up to now the electric light had blinded him, and now he felt some relief.

"Have the militants from the forest been hiding in Adik's bunker for a long time?"

The investigator had a bass voice, just like Colonel Gaziev's.

"I don't know about any bunker." Marat could barely speak; his lips had stuck together and it took him an eternity to open them.

"Then you're going to get the shit beaten out of you. How's that sound?!" The investigator was exhausted from all the beatings and profanity; he issued his threats without any particular fury, and even with a tinge of amusement. "You've signed everything. The witness has given her testimony. And if you put up a stink, that's the last anyone will see of you!"

With a suppressed groan, Marat shifted his swollen, deadened leg in his ripped trousers. The dark walls of the interrogation room wavered, smearing Marat's vision, black streamlets trickling onto the floor. The silhouette trembled and lurched in its nimbus of prickly light.

"Speak, swine! Or we'll pin something on you that will make your own family disown you!"

A chorus of voices thundered from all sides, as though an invisible throng of interrogators were lurking in the cupboards:

"We'll pin it on you, we'll pin... we'll bind you!"

Marat somehow managed to shift his deadened leg.

"You are pinned, everyone is pinned down, attached to something," Khalilbek continued, leaning back in his chair and uncorking the bottle. "The main thing is to detach yourself from everything. And, also, if you look at the sun, and then at yourself, you will become the sun..."

The soles of his feet burned and stung. Marat's numb leg lay stretched out before him under the rays. The drunken vision passed. In the distance, parallel to the shore, a female figure glided slowly, knee-deep through the sea, with the hem of her shapeless dress trailing in the water. An old boat bobbed and swayed by the wharf, restless seagulls complained noisily at the oncoming night, and the sound of the surf drowned the voices of the regulars in the café. Yet again something was ending, so as to begin anew in the morning. It dwindled and closed in on itself and converged, and finally, quietly, without a sound, it came to an end. Only the sea remained. And the splashing of the oncoming waters, and the gurgling of the wine. So good, so fine: nothing, nowhere better than here and now. Just this one point, the end.

AFTERWORD

Dear reader,

Thank you for picking up this book and for reading it to the end. I hope that you found it interesting, funny, sad, and at times a little scary. But I will not go into extensive commentaries. The goal of this afterword is to address a quiet but very important subtext of the novel that has to do with Sufism, an esoteric Muslim teaching.

To distill its essence to an extremely simplified formula, Sufis seek Truth—a quest that allies them with philosophers from every tradition and school of thought throughout history. Truth is the Absolute—that is, God, Allah—that is distributed throughout everything that is. The Sufi's task, through a long path of self-discovery, asceticism, and absolute obedience to his teacher, is ultimately to arrive at a merging with God. Along the way, for complete knowledge of being, one must renounce all rationality and logic, and be ruled exclusively by one's heart. There are many psycho-mystical and trance-inducing practices associated with "*zikr*," collective invocations of God, that support this path. These invocations in part resemble mantras; they include long repetitions of the same verses from the Qur'an, accompanied by rhythmic swaying of the body, twirling in a circle, and other dances. Indeed, in some ways Sufism resembles Buddhism, in others early Christianity, and yet in others, Kabbalah, or pantheism. Sufism is a tremendously multifaceted belief system, open to the most varied cultural and religious influences.

The Naqshbandiyah, one of the Sufi's main brotherhoods, has, since the Middle Ages, had a strong presence in Dagestan, where *Bride and Groom* takes place. This is one of the only Sufi schools whose followers can participate actively in politics and engage in contact with political authorities. One contemporary Dagestani Sufi teacher was for many years a prominent spiritual teacher and counselor for the scores of pilgrims who would come to him in his remote native village to listen to parables and seek enlightenment. The respect he attained among the people was viewed as a challenge by local politicians and representatives of alternative Islamic groups. A few years ago, this Sufi teacher was assassinated by a female suicide bomber who came to him disguised as a pilgrim. The bomber was a member of the ultra-conservative salafis, a group who loathe Sufism and are opposed to mysticism, allegorical readings of the Qur'an, and the practice of revering teachers, holy places, and so forth. Dagestan, it must be noted, is just one of hundreds of places in the world where these two divergent worldviews have engaged in bloody clashes.

But to return to the novel: I wanted to structure my heroes' story not only as a movement of two hearts toward each other, but also as the path of a Sufi to the Absolute. Of course, the parallels here are very free, and I employ a considerable amount of creative license, but the attentive reader who knows Sufi poetry (you may be familiar with Sufi poets such as Rumi and Omar Khayyam), will find here a number of symbols and references. For example, one symbol that recurs throughout the novel is wine. Forbidden to most Muslims, wine signifies Truth to Sufis, and the state of intoxication provides a closeness to God. Accordingly, a drunkard becomes an ecstatic Sufi (recall Marat's encounter with the drunkard), and the wine seller in the first chapter serves as a spiritual advisor. In Sufism, the sea, to which the heroes arrive at the novel's finale, signifies Divine Unity. And in order to arrive at this Unity, one must free oneself from anything individualistic, from all attachments, and from one's own self. When the Sufi poets spoke of hair, they were speaking of the multitude, which covers the face of Unity (this is what Rinat is referring to in the scene with Patya in Chapter 1). And the point, or dot, another important Sufi symbol that recurs in the novel, refers to the point of origin for the Universe, to which, sooner or later, all shall return. The point signifies Inner Knowledge, and it is also a reference to the Arabic letter *ba*, which resembles a boat with a point below it (with one exception, all the Suras in the Qur'an begin with this letter). Recall the phrase Khalilbek is quoted using in Chapter 4 when speaking to Shakhov: "It all comes down to a point, comrade Shakhov."

Khalilbek is a complex figure representing several aspects of Sufism in the many rumors about him that circulate throughout the novel. People associate him with Khidr, or the Green Man, the teacher of the prophet Musa, or Moses (the Green Man is an ancient mythological figure who also appears in many other world cultures, from Europe to the Middle East and India). It is said that he is immortal and can arrive in any form. He is primarily known for three deeds, which at first glance appear evil or senseless, and for which Moses hastened to condemn him in the legend: the destruction of a boat; the murder of a small boy; and unpaid work fortifying a wall in the city where cruel and dishonorable people lived. Later, he justifies his actions to Moses: he disabled the boat, which belonged to poor people, so that the king, who was appropriating all vessels for himself, would not confiscate it; he murdered the boy, because in the future he would have grown into a fearsome tyrant and sadist; and he worked on the wall because there was a treasure buried underneath that, if the wall had collapsed, would have been taken by the dishonorable people of the city. Thus the parallels of Khidr's actions to Khalilbek's actions throughout the novel become apparent.

This character of Khalilbek/Khidr is extremely ambiguous, but the fluid nature of good and evil, the way one flows into the other, is what attracted me to this story. And I was drawn to teachings of Sufis and other orders that the world is an illusion. Things and people are not what they seem. What we consider to be characteristics of our true Self are only labels and conceptions that we apply to ourselves. There is a Sufi parable about a wandering Sufi who brazenly strode into the Khan's palace and settled down on his cushions to rest. The Khan naturally flew into a rage: "What are you doing in my palace?!" The Sufi answered, "You think that you are the Khan, and that this is your palace. But your ancestors came and went from this place. And you came, and you, too, shall leave. So this is not a palace, but a caravan-serai."

In place of a conclusion, I would like to quote from a letter sent to me by one of the novel's Russian readers, Yana Kunitskaya, a graduate student and specialist in Eastern cultures:

> *The Sufi path is a very transparent allegory for the method of knowing God in earthly life: by specific exercises, actions, and his way of life as a whole, the Sufi moves toward God, achieving particular higher levels— "stops"—along the way* (makam). *The ultimate stop, as a rule, entails dissolving into the substance of the divine—this is what Khalilbek is talking about at the end of the novel. Every Sufi strives for this, believing that the human soul, which initially was part of divine substance, became separated from it, and now must again cleanse itself from everything terrestrial, in order to reunite with it after death. Certain Sufi brotherhoods hold the opinion that this reunion can be attained even during earthly life; hence Granny says "die before your death" and Rinat tells the well-known proverb about the poet who said "I am God." This reunification and the striving for it are symbolized*

by such paired images in the novel as the "drop" and the "sea," and the "luminary" and the "light." So at the end of the novel, Marat parts with earthy decay in order to reunite with Truth.

But all of this is incorporated organically into Dagestani reality as it is created in the novel, interweaving so many different traditions together with elements from folklore.

I must confess that I was surprised to receive this letter, since I could not have counted on reaching a reader who would find all these meanings that I had concealed in the text. The novel is complete even without accounting for these allusions. But you might find it interesting to think back on what you have read from this new angle. The more angles, the better.

ALISA GANIEVA
Moscow, Russia
Summer 2017

ALISA GANIEVA grew up in Makhachkala, Dagestan and studied at the renowned Maxim Gorky Literature Institute in Moscow. After working as a literary critic, she published her fiction debut, the novella *Salam, Dalgat!*, under a male pseudonym. Upon receiving the prestigious Debut Prize in 2009, Ganieva finally revealed her true identity at the awards ceremony. In 2012, Ganieva participated in the International Writing Program's Fall Residency at the University of Iowa. Her debut novel, *The Mountain and the Wall*, was shortlisted for all of Russia's major literary awards and has been translated into seven languages, marking the first novel ever published in English by a Dagestani author. In June 2015, Ganieva was listed by *The Guardian* as one of the most influential young people living in Moscow. *Bride and Groom* is her second novel, and was shortlisted for the 2015 Russian Booker Prize upon its publication in Russia. Ganieva currently lives in Moscow, where she works as a journalist, critic, and teacher.

CAROL APOLLONIO is a literary translator and professor of the Practice of Slavic and Eurasian Studies at Duke University. Her most recent translations include German Sadulaev's *The Maya Pill* (Dalkey Archive, 2014) and Alisa Ganieva's debut *The Mountain and the Wall* (Deep Vellum, 2015). In addition to her work as an accomplished translator, Dr. Apollonio is also a scholar specializing in the works of Fyodor Dostoevsky and Chekhov and on problems of translation. She is the author of the monograph *Dostoevsky's Secrets* (2009), has edited volumes and published numerous articles on nineteenth century Russian literature, and has worked as an interpreter for the U.S. government. In 2011, Apollonio was awarded the Russian Ministry of Culture's Chekhov Medal. She currently serves as President of the North American Dostoevsky Society.

Thank you all
for your support.
We do this for you,
and could not do
it without you.

DEAR READERS,

Deep Vellum Publishing is a 501c3 nonprofit literary arts organization founded in 2013 with a threefold mission: to publish international literature in English translation; to foster the art and craft of translation; and to build a more vibrant book culture in Dallas and beyond. We are dedicated to broadening cultural connections across the English-reading world by connecting readers, in new and creative ways, with the work of international authors. We strive for diversity in publishing authors from various languages, viewpoints, genders, sexual orientations, countries, continents, and literary styles, whose works provide lasting cultural value and build bridges with foreign cultures while expanding our understanding of how the world thinks, feels, and experiences the human condition.

Operating as a nonprofit means that we rely on the generosity of tax-deductible donations from individual donors, cultural organizations, government institutions, and foundations. Your donations provide the basis of our operational budget as we seek out and publish exciting literary works from around the globe and build a vibrant and active literary arts community both locally and within the global society. Deep Vellum offers multiple donor levels, including LIGA DE ORO ($5,000+) and LIGA DEL SIGLO ($1,000+). Donors at various levels receive personalized benefits for their donations, including books and Deep Vellum merchandise, invitations to special events, and recognition in each book and on our website.

In addition to donations, we rely on subscriptions from readers like you to provide an invaluable ongoing investment in Deep Vellum that demonstrates a commitment to our editorial vision and mission. Subscribers are the bedrock of our support as we grow the readership for these amazing works of literature from every corner of the world. The investment our subscribers make allows us to demonstrate to potential donors and bookstores alike the support and demand for Deep Vellum's literature across a broad readership and gives us the ability to grow our mission in ever-new, ever-innovative ways.

In partnership with our sister company and bookstore, Deep Vellum Books, located in the historic cultural district of Deep Ellum in central Dallas, we organize and host literary programming such as author readings, translator workshops, creative writing classes, spoken word performances, and interdisciplinary arts events for writers, translators, and artists from across the globe. Our goal is to enrich and connect the world through the power of the written and spoken word, and we have been recognized for our efforts by being named one of the "Five Small Presses Changing the Face of the Industry" by *Flavorwire* and honored as Dallas's Best Publisher by *D Magazine.*

If you would like to get involved with Deep Vellum as a donor, subscriber, or volunteer, please contact us at deepvellum.org. We would love to hear from you.

Thank you all. Enjoy reading.
Will Evans, Founder & Publisher, Deep Vellum Publishing

PARTNERS

pixel texel

LIGA DE ORO ($5,000+)

Anonymous (2)

LIGA DEL SIGLO ($1,000+)

Allred Capital Management
Ben & Sharon Fountain
David Tomlinson & Kathryn Berry
Judy Pollock
Life in Deep Ellum
Loretta Siciliano
Lori Feathers
Mary Ann Thompson-Frenk & Joshua Frenk
Matthew Rittmayer
Meriwether Evans
Pixel and Texel
Nick Storch
Social Venture Partners Dallas
Stephen Bullock

DONORS

Adam Rekerdres
Alan Shockley
Amrit Dhir
Anonymous (4)
Andrew Yorke
Anthony Messenger
Bob Appel
Bob & Katherine Penn
Brandon Childress
Brandon Kennedy
Caitlin Baker
Caroline Casey
Charles Dee Mitchell
Charley Mitcherson
Chilton Thomson
Cheryl Thompson
Christie Tull
Cone Johnson
CS Maynard
Cullen Schaar
Daniel J. Hale
Dori Boone-Costantino
Ed Nawotka
Elizabeth Gillette
Rev. Elizabeth & Neil Moseley
Ester & Matt Harrison
Farley Houston
Garth Hallberg
Grace Kenney
Greg McConeghy
Jeff Waxman
JJ Italiano
Justin Childress
Kay Cattarulla
Kelly Falconer
Lea Courington
Leigh Ann Pike
Linda Nell Evans
Lissa Dunlay
Maaza Mengiste
Marian Schwartz & Reid Minot
Mark Haber
Marlo D. Cruz Pagan

Mary Cline
Maynard Thomson
Michael Reklis
Mike Kaminsky
Mokhtar Ramadan
Nikki & Dennis Gibson
Olga Kislova
Patrick Kukucka
Patrick Kutcher
Richard Meyer
Sherry Perry
Steve Bullock
Suejean Kim
Susan Carp
Susan Ernst
Stephen Harding
Symphonic Source
Theater Jones
Thomas DiPiero
Tim Perttula
Tony Thomson

SUBSCRIBERS

Ali Bolcakan
Andre Habet
Andrew Bowles
Anita Tarar
Anonymous
Ben Nichols
Ben Wilson
Blair Bullock
Brandye Brown
Caitlin Schmid
Caroline West
Charles Dee Mitchell
Chris McCann
Chris Sweet
Christie Tull
Courtney Sheedy
Daniel Galindo
David Tomlinson & Kathryn Berry
David Travis
Dawn Wilburn-Saboe
Elizabeth Johnson
Ellen Miller
Farley Houston
Geoffrey Young
Hannah McGinty
Holly LaFon
Jaimie Fritz
Jason Linden
Jeff Goldberg
Jill Kelly
Joe Maceda
John Schmerein
John Winkelman
Joshua Edwin
Kevin Winter
Lesley Conzelman
Lora Lafayette
Lytton Smith
M.J. Malooly
Martha Gifford
Mary Brockson
Matt Cheney
Michael Aguilar
Michael Elliott
Michael Filippone
Mies de Vries
Neal Chuang
Nicholas R. Theis
Patrick Shirak
Peter McCambridge
Reid Allison
Robert Keefe
Ronald Morton
Shelby Vincent
Stephanie Barr
Steve Jansen
Suzanne Fischer
Todd Jailer
Tracy Shapley
Wenyang Chen
Will Pepple
William Fletcher
William Pate

AVAILABLE NOW FROM DEEP VELLUM

MICHÈLE AUDIN · *One Hundred Twenty-One Days*
translated by Christiana Hills · FRANCE

CARMEN BOULLOSA · *Texas: The Great Theft* · *Before* · *Heavens on Earth*
translated by Samantha Schnee · Peter Bush · Shelby Vincent · MEXICO

LEILA S. CHUDORI · *Home*
translated by John H. McGlynn · INDONESIA

ANANDA DEVI · *Eve Out of Her Ruins*
translated by Jeffrey Zuckerman · MAURITIUS

ALISA GANIEVA · *The Mountain and the Wall*
translated by Carol Apollonio · RUSSIA

ANNE GARRÉTA · *Sphinx* · *Not One Day*
translated by Emma Ramadan · FRANCE

JÓN GNARR · *The Indian* · *The Pirate* · *The Outlaw*
translated by Lytton Smith· ICELAND

NOEMI JAFFE · *What are the Blind Men Dreaming?*
translated by Julia Sanches & Ellen Elias-Bursac · BRAZIL

CLAUDIA SALAZAR JIMÉNEZ · *Blood of the Dawn*
translated by Elizabeth Bryer · PERU

JOSEFINE KLOUGART · *Of Darkness*
translated by Martin Aitken · DENMARK

YANICK LAHENS · *Moonbath*
translated by Emily Gogolak · HAITI

JUNG YOUNG MOON · *Vaseline Buddha*
translated by Yewon Jung · SOUTH KOREA

FOUAD LAROUI · *The Curious Case of Dassoukine's Trousers*
translated by Emma Ramadan · MOROCCO

LINA MERUANE · *Seeing Red*
translated by Megan McDowell · CHILE

FISTON MWANZA MUJILA · *Tram 83*
translated by Roland Glasser · DEMOCRATIC REPUBLIC OF CONGO

ILJA LEONARD PFEIJFFER · *La Superba*
translated by Michele Hutchison · NETHERLANDS

FORTHCOMING FROM DEEP VELLUM

EDUARDO BERTI · *The Imagined Land*
translated by Charlotte Coombe · ARGENTINA

ALISA GANIEVA · *Bride & Groom*
translated by Carol Apollonio · RUSSIA

FOUAD LAROUI · *The Tribulations of the Last Sjilmassi*
translated by Emma Ramadan · MOROCCO

MARIA GABRIELA LLANSOL · *The Geography of Rebels Trilogy: The Book of Communities; The Remaining Life; In the House of July & August*
translated by Audrey Young · PORTUGAL

PABLO MARTÍN SÁNCHEZ · *The Anarchist Who Shared My Name*
translated by Jeff Diteman · SPAIN

BRICE MATTHIEUSSENT · *Revenge of the Translator*
translated by Emma Ramadan · FRANCE

SERGIO PITOL · *Mephisto's Waltz: Selected Short Stories*
translated by George Henson · MEXICO

SERGIO PITOL · *Carnival Triptych: The Love Parade; Taming the Divine Heron; Married Life*
translated by George Henson · MEXICO

ÓFEIGUR SIGURÐSSON · *Öræfi: The Wasteland*
translated by Lytton Smith · ICELAND